The Ten Count

Tom Schreck

ISBN: 1502837560
ISBN-13: 978-1502837561

For my best friends Sue and Annette

I'd like to say a special thanks to my agent, Barbara Poelle for believing in me, my good buddy Reed Farrel Coleman, to Ruth and Jon Jordan and the entire Crimespree family and everyone in the world of basset hound rescue.

I'd also like to thank Teresa Spadafora and Dush Pathmanandam for bidding on the character name auction to benefit Wildwood Programs.

And always a very, very special thank you to my wife for putting up with me.

Everybody has a plan until they get punched in the face.

Mike Tyson

Rhythm is everything in boxing. Every move you make starts with your heart, and that's in rhythm or you're in trouble.

Sugar Ray Robinson

My girlfriend boos when we make love because she knows it turns me on.

Hector Camacho

Chapter One

"I hate the fuckin' guy," Bobby Simon, my 3:15, said. "It's just him and the football team and everyone else is a piece of shit."

He didn't make eye contact, and his chin began to do that quiver that told me he was doing everything he could to keep from crying. I've been doing the counseling gig long enough to know that it wasn't cool for a sixteen-year-old to cry in front of a man.

"I'd like to fuckin' kill him. Just go up and slit his throat from ear to ear."

His chin stopped quivering, and now his fists were balled.

"Whoa, whoa, whoa, Bobby..."

I've never been a by-the-book human services guy, but he had drifted from ventilation into an unhealthy expression of what he was feeling. Maybe you could make an argument for the benefits of blowing off steam, but this just didn't seem right. I focused in on Bobby and paid close attention to not only what he was saying, but how he was saying it.

"I mean it, Duffy. I'd love to see that piece of shit bleeding like a stuck pig. Be even better if it was in Jefferson Park right after he got it on with some fag."

Part of Bobby's backstory involved being molested. Bobby's mom had died in a car accident when he was just a year old, and his father worked laying carpet during the day and driving a cab at night. The babysitter's loser boyfriend was the offender. A friend in Chicago, detective Jacqueline Daniels, had called me. She knew Bobby's dad, and when Bobby got in trouble, she thought I might be

5

a good fit or at least the best for him as a counselor.

I cut Bobby a little more slack when it came to expressing himself because of his history. And I knew sixteen-year-olds were all over the place when it came to emotions, but, even still, this was getting weird. It was time to put a halt to Bobby's rant.

"Alright, Bobby, slow down and listen to me for a while." I put my hands up in that 'take-it-easy' motion and raised my eyebrows. I didn't want it to seem like I was scolding him, but I did want it clear that there were limits to what you could say, even in therapy. Violence and homophobia weren't okay.

"First of all, you can't say you're gonna kill somebody in here. I have to call the cops and send you to the shrink and all that stuff. You've been around long enough to get that. We're talking violence here, not just anger. So, I'm gonna ask you very clearly—Do you intend on killing Coach Dennison?"

Bobby frowned. I let him keep some of his bravado by not questioning his ability to kill the muscle bound, über-macho coach and by showing concern for Dennison's safety.

"No. I'd like to if I knew I wouldn't get caught," Bobby said.

"And second, it's not cool with me to say homophobic stuff. What the hell is that all about?" I said.

Bobby frowned and rubbed the knuckles on his soft hands. I really wanted him to understand that it wasn't okay to be referring to gay people as "fags" or anything else like that. Bobby was a good kid; I liked him, and he should understand when his words were hurtful and wrong.

Coach Dennison had a rep for being the toughest coach in town, kind of like a high school Belichick. He was a disciplinarian and had been coaching there for a decade.

"I'm not gonna kill him." Bobby frowned. In some ways, it was a little comical. "And I'm sorry for saying the gay shit. I'm not like that. I've just heard the rumors—"

The phone rang and interrupted him. It was Trina, and she let me know Bobby's father was there to pick him up. Usually, we didn't allow phone calls to interrupt a session, but Mr. Simon worked two jobs, and he let it be known he couldn't afford to be late.

"Bobby—we've got to end for today. What rumors were you talking about?"

"I don't know. I've just heard stuff. I'll get into it next week." He had his knapsack over his shoulder, and he was standing, ready to go.

I looked him right in the eye. "Hey, man, it's okay to be pissed at someone, and I don't blame you, but it's important to know what's your responsibility and what's someone else's."

He gave me a noncommittal nod and left to catch up with his father.

Coach Dennison busted Bobby smoking a joint outside the cafeteria a month ago at Crawford Academy. That was why he got referred to our clinic for after-school sessions. Like most kids, he blamed the guy who caught him rather than accept the fact that he was doing something wrong. That is, if you consider getting high at lunchtime wrong.

I don't blame the coach. Hey, I'm not against getting high and if they want to legalize it and dispense free Cheetos to go with it, that's fine with me. But you can't rub it in the face of authority by firing up outside the cafeteria. It wouldn't matter what the rule was, if you broke it like that, a coach would have to bust you. If not, there's no structure. It was pretty clear to me that Bobby Simon knew what he was doing, at least on some level, and was looking to get in trouble to communicate something. I don't know who he was sending a message to, or if he even knew, but I believe Bobby wanted to tell someone or the world that he was rebelling. That's how it worked when you were sixteen.

I'm sure part of what was pissing Bobby off had to do with the fact that CA was in line for a football state championship and his little Rastafarian trip got him kicked off the squad. Bobby was a 160-pound, gangly benchwarmer who was on the second team for kickoffs, but, when you're sixteen, getting a state championship jacket ranks pretty high. Now, not only was he missing out on that, he also had to come see me, and I'm sure everyone at school knew it.

The state championship, known as the "Prep Super Bowl," was a huge thing in Crawford. It's all anyone was talking about, and it got on my nerves. Part of it bothered me because they beat my alma mater, Crawford High, in the semis on a last-second, bullshit call. I mean, I don't care about high school football, but the Crawford kids never win anything, and they had a Cinderella year.

I headed to the breakroom for a cup of the world's worst coffee. My fellow counselor, Monique, was there brewing a cup of what had to be some sort of holistic, organic tea.

"Hey, Duff," she said while bobbing that metal ball thingy that tea enthusiasts used. "How's Bobby?"

"Pissed," I said.

Monique strained the tea and didn't look up.

"Ever meet a sixteen-year-old that wasn't?" she said.

"No." It wasn't something I had to think much about, either.

"Especially with what that kid has had to deal with," Monique said and raised her eyebrows at me while she looked at her tea with some concern.

"Yeah, I know," I said.

Chapter Two

I went out to get Bobby's chart to do the notes from our session. I was doing my best to be on time with my paperwork lately because I've had a few issues over the years with getting it done. I had recently turned over a new leaf.

It had been the longest forty-eight-hour period of my life.

"Somebody named TJ called for you," Trina, the office manager, said. "Said she was from the suicide hotline." She hesitated for a second and made a face. "Did you get put on hold last night or something?"

Trina had on her 505s, an untucked men's white button-down shirt, and black cowboy boots. She was wearing her hair just a bit shorter since she started to date her latest beau—a guy who I guess was a lawyer.

"She say what it was about?" I felt a little something in my chest. I met TJ last year, and we kind of made a connection before she disappeared.

I may have read it wrong, but the playful twinkle in Trina's eye that came with the sarcasm seemed to fade a bit. Women have these antennae, or something, and they can pick up when a guy is interested in a woman. They can tell when you're interested in them, and they can tell when you're interested in someone else. Trina could've worked for counterintelligence if there were a need for discerning a man's love life.

"No, she just left the number."

I took the note, grabbed Bobby's chart, and headed back to my office. I could feel something in my chest, and a little bit of sweat formed under my shirt. TJ was a different kind of woman. She was an Iraq veteran, a workout nut, and a kick fighter. She volunteered on the suicide hotline. She had a body like one of those "after" testimonials you see for P90X. She was hard and soft at the same time.

She came to the gym, and we worked out together a couple times. It wasn't at all weird, and she could certainly hang in with my workouts and left me in the dust a couple times. We even got into the ring and sparred.

Nothing sexual or even romantic happened, or at least overtly happened, but you know that feeling you get—that little tingle of something that makes you feel crazy. The kind that leaves you wondering if the other person is experiencing what you're feeling? Well, I got a lot of that.

I punched the numbers into my cell and waited. I was uncomfortable with how nervous I was and how hard it was to breathe. I became acutely aware of how you can get embarrassed while being totally alone.

"Hello?" TJ said. There was an incredible amount of background noise. I could hear a really loud thumping and the muffled sound of someone yelling something in the background.

"TJ? It's Duffy."

"Hello?"

"TJ, it's Duffy. Can you hear me?"

"Hello?"

She hung up.

That was just great. I could feel the anxiety race through my body. I was no further along in understanding what TJ wanted, and that made me crazy. I'm not the most secure guy in the world when it comes to the opposite sex, and this kind of thing was enough to put me over the edge and get me institutionalized. And now I had just enough uncertainty to keep me second-guessing through an entire neurotic and sleepless night.

My phone vibrated and made that annoying jingle that let me know I had a text.

"Can't talk now—Call me later?"

I texted back that I would. My stomach did something. I sat and looked at the wall in front of me and didn't think. I just felt.

I went back out to the reception area and headed for the file cabinet with the charts. I pulled out the "S's" and couldn't find Bobby's file anywhere. I could sense Trina not looking at me.

"You seen Bobby's chart?" I asked her.

She just looked at me. She didn't smile. She continued to stare at me. The coyness was starting to piss me off.

"C'mon, have you?"

"You took it five minutes ago before your loud phone call with your friend, TJ," Trina said. She raised her eyebrows and gave me a smirk loaded with messages.

I headed back to my office and proceeded to not write in my chart.

Chapter Three

After work, the gym was busy—at least as busy as it ever got. The Golden Gloves were six weeks away, and there was still time for guys to start training for it. That was plenty of time for most of them to come up with excuses or injuries for withdrawing from the competition.

Boxing isn't for everyone, and for every fighter who actually gets in the ring and faces another boxer who throws real punches there are twenty wannabes. Oh, they'll talk about not being able to wait to get in there—they'll have strategies for opponents and they'll get new trunks and gear—but they'll never make it to the tournament. Along the way, they won't forget to get a t-shirt or jacket that says they were a "Golden Glover" or some shit. Most won't even have done a single round of sparring.

There's nothing wrong with being a wannabe boxer. Getting punched in the face for a hobby isn't the most rational thing. I used to shake my head at the wannabes when I was younger, but, as I've put years in the gym, I've come to accept them. People delude themselves into believing they are the image they want to be. Some out-and-out put up a front for the rest of the world, others convince themselves that the front is true. I often wondered just what a man who knows he's faking it feels like when he's alone with his thoughts. In pro wrestling, they call it "Living the Gimmick" and that's what this is like. You want an identity, so you adopt it without doing what would make up that identity.

If you base your ego on something that isn't real, where does that leave you? If your ego is tied up in being a fighter, and you have all the gear and the posturing, but you stop short of actually getting in the ring and facing another man, then what are you? Do men know when they are living the gimmick or is the self-delusion enough to hang their hats on? I have to believe that somewhere in there they know they are a fraud. That probably leads them down that rough road of overcompensation where a good part of the male population regularly travels.

I mostly go to the gym not to think, and this philosophical meandering was distracting. I decided to dispense with all the cognition and start hitting something. When I went through the doorway, I bumped into a guy at the top of the stairs heading out.

"Oh, sorry," the guy said. He was all duded up in a business suit.

"No sweat, buddy. I was in a world of my own there," I said.

He looked at me for a little while.

"You're Duffy, right? Dombrowzo."

"Yeah." I laughed a little. "But it's Dombrowski."

"Oh, sorry. I've seen you fight. You're pretty crafty with that left hand." He smiled. I don't get a lot of fan stuff, but I'd be lying if I said I didn't get a kick out of it.

"Well, thanks. There's plenty of pros out there who haven't found it crafty enough."

He chuckled. He was a big guy who had that look like maybe twenty years ago he played some football.

"In boxing, there's no shame in that. You gotta have some balls; I don't care what level you're at," he said. "I'm Rusty. I just left my kid off downstairs. Have you met Russ?"

"Sure," I said. "Big, strong kid. Getting ready for the title game, right?" Russ was a kid from Crawford Academy who played football. He was kind of a jerk, but I didn't need to tell his old man that.

"Yeah, he's all full of piss and vinegar." Rusty rolled his eyes. "Not always the sharpest knife in the drawer, but..." He didn't finish and just let the thought trail off. I got the impression that he was acknowledging in a dad's way that his son was a bit of a jerk. "Hey, I gotta get back to the office, nice meeting you."

"Likewise, man. Take care," I said and headed down the stairs to the gym.

Smitty, my trainer for the last fourteen years, was working with Raheen, a sixteen-year-old, lefty, 190-pounder with six fights. He had a decent shot in the novice division this year. He could really move, and I could tell his punches had that kind of snap to them that you either had or you didn't. You could improve a punch, but it was really hard to get that certain snap at the end of the punch that changed how the strike felt. It was the difference between getting hit with a bag of sand and being stabbed with a screwdriver—getting hit with the sand hurt, but the screwdriver was something else.

Billy was in and was banging away at the heavy bag and occasionally working in some elbows. We helped each other out a few years ago when he was a skinny, zit-faced nerd. Now he was about 195 lbs. of sinewy muscle and trained in MMA.

Russ was hitting the other heavy bag, and he hit hard—really hard—making it echo against the cement walls. He probably thought he was doing great and the fact was if he ever connected with a shot like that he'd really hurt someone. In reality, the punches were so wide that any boxer with any experience at all would be out of the way before the punches got close. Russ was supposedly in line for a Division I scholarship, and the boxing was supposed to augment his football training. The word was that his folks had kept him back in school so he could excel in sports. He was almost twenty, and I guess the plan worked if he was about to get a free ride to college. He worked out with Chico who was the local strength Svengali who I think had taken on Russ as a client.

Russ liked to talk, and he said he liked boxing so much that he was thinking about competing. For now, it was just talk. I knew of Chico from the gyms over the course of the years. He had an MMA background and was known on the street as the kind of guy who liked to let his hands go. He went away for a while and took the time to become an expert in kinesiology or some fancy physical therapy shit.

The bell rang ending the round, and the rhythmic thumping, skipping and grunting ceased all at once.

I was closing the Velcro on my faded yellow wrap when Russ came over.

"How's Bobby the pothead?" He said.

I pursed my lips and just gave him a look.

"C'mon Duff, everyone at CA knows you're his counselor," Russ said.

There was no question the kid had a build. At six foot three and about 220 lbs., his body was a tad bigger than mine, but not the 250+ that the big college football schools looked for. He had that annoying quality of a high school kid who was way too sure of himself in his big-man-on-campus way.

"Russ, why don't you stop being a dick and work on tightening up those lame body shots that even a fat, high school offensive lineman could get out of the way of?"

"Fuck you, Duff. You shouldn't be talkin' shit with your record," he said.

I've been fighting as a pro for a decade, and I have almost as many losses as wins. For those who know better, my time in the game, my wins, and the guys I've faced give me rank in the gym. Russ hadn't been around long enough to get that, and he probably wouldn't stay long enough to ever get it.

Raheen overheard the comment and stepped over.

"Who you talking shit to? Mr. 0-0-0 talking to a pro-fessional man, sh-it!" He strung out the shit into two syllables. "You fuckin' dumb as you look."

Raheen was forty pounds lighter than Russ and wiry, but he had five knockouts in his six fights and spoke with so much confidence that Russ froze. Raheen wasn't getting an athletic scholarship, nor were his successes ever in the sports page like Russ's were—but this wasn't about impressing a recruiter. Russ knew I wouldn't come up on him, but he couldn't be sure that Raheen wouldn't.

It's one thing to insult someone older than you with your piss bravado, but it's another thing when a peer confronts you. Raheen stood looking Russ dead in the eyes, no more than a foot from him. Russ's face flushed and he was clearly embarrassed. I looked over at Chico who paid attention to the situation but didn't intervene.

"Uh-huh, that's what I thought," Raheen said. He didn't look at me. It wasn't really about me. It was about Russ disrespecting the code.

I smiled to myself, realizing it was just another day in the psychic Petri dish known as the Crawford Y Boxing Gym, and headed to the ring to get warm. From the corner of my eye, I could see Russ head back over to the heavy bag while Raheen stood squared up where the two had been.

I began to shadowbox, and when the next break bell sounded, Smitty approached. Smitty was somewhere in his sixties and favored his faded green Dickies, white Chuck Taylors, and a plain V-neck undershirt for fashion. His curly, gray hair contrasted with his shiny, black bald spot.

"Hey, Duffy, some woman was in here looking for you," Smitty said. He said "woman" like someone else might say "alien." This had been Smitty's gym for thirty-two years, and a woman's presence was still unusual.

"She give you a name?"

"TJ."

Chapter Four

All right, so TJ was looking for me—really looking for me.

I finished up my workout—a day with shadowboxing, heavy bag work, three rounds of mitts, and these new plyometric things I've started doing that were supposed to make me explosive. I'm not sure what "explosive" actually meant, but I knew by the end of the day my thighs hurt so bad that it made me walk funny.

I told myself that if TJ was looking for me, it was no big deal. And it wasn't, really. Just a woman I got a few sparks from who probably didn't feel the same thing. Just a woman I got attracted to who then disappeared for a few months without any explanation. Just a woman who could look me straight in the eye and not back up.

Really, it wasn't a big deal. It wasn't. I knew that my mind would go into overdrive sometimes, and I need to ignore myself.

I tried calling her, and her cell went right to voice mail.

Great, more anxiety.

I had to do something other than sit and think. The day and the workout created an appetite and a thirst. Now, I probably should've gone for a recovery drink high in protein with low glycemic complex carbohydrates and combined that with a light snack of the same proportions that also had some fiber to fill me up.

That's what I should've done.

There wasn't much chance of that happening though. I was headed to AJ's for a half-pound grease-burger and a Schlitz or four. AJ's was about twelve blocks from the gym and sort of on the way home. Like some guys' La-Z-Boy recliner, it was where I went when I wanted to get away from the day and unwind. The counseling gig often left me with the need for mental floss, and boxing, especially these new plyometrics, could leave my body a little jangling. The Schlitz, the occasional bourbon, and the company soothed what ailed me.

When I got there, the boys were in and had already established some momentum.

"He took the propane," Rocco said. "That's what killed him." Rocco was a strong, stocky, older guy, perpetually in a state of annoyance, who liked scotch.

"I dunno. I don't think Michael Jackson was much of a camper," Jerry Number One said. The Jerrys were numbered at AJ's. This Jerry was short and pudgy, middle-aged, and otherwise, uh, not very complex.

"He took the propane by injection. It ain't cooking propane. It's the surgical kind," Rocco said.

"What about his nose?" TC asked. TC was a skinny, retired state worker who drank B&B and had a lot of opinions.

The Foursome stopped. They remained quiet for what, to them, was a long time. It's what happened when someone didn't have an immediate answer to a discussion point.

"His nose caught fire and fell off during that Pepsi commercial, didn't it? Or did his pet monkey attack him?" TC said.

I took my usual seat to the left of the guys, and AJ slid a bottle of Schlitz in front of me. He didn't make eye contact, and he had the look of someone who may have just eaten a bad egg. Being locked in a room all day with the Foursome could do that to a man.

"Do you gotta get a special monkey license?" Jerry Number Two asked. This Jerry preferred Cosmopolitans and had long, reddish-blond hair. He looked like he just got back from Woodstock and didn't have time to wash the tie-dye.

"At the DMV?" TC said.

"There is no Department of Monkey Vehicles," Rocco said.

It had gotten dark outside which warmed the ambience of AJ's up. It was fall in Crawford, and it wouldn't be long before the long winter would start. Despite the ambience, AJ's stilled reeked of 100 years of stale, spilled beer, and the dust on the fifty-year-old brewery signs would keep the manufacturers of Zyrtec rolling in dough—but there was something to the joint that couldn't be recreated by the design crew at TGI Fridays.

"Duffy's a drug counselor, ask him," Jerry Number One said.

"Duff—did Jackson die from taking that propane injection or not?" Rocco asked.

"I think it was Propofol. It's some sort of surgical anesthetic," I said.

"See, I told you," Rocco said and took a celebratory swig of his scotch.

The point somehow punctuated that segment of the evening, but it wouldn't be long before the boys began on other important issues. Tonight could be something entirely new, or it could be a redux of one of their greatest hits. Maybe the Wizard of Oz and Judy Garland's Ace bandage, perhaps things Rod Stewart may or may not have not ingested, or maybe even the use of toilet paper in Arab countries.

Right now, though, the local news was beginning, and, other than a Yankees' game, nothing was held in the same reverence at AJ's. The overdramatic lead-in music built to a crescendo, and then Scott Pratt, the light-skinned black guy or non-threatening Latin guy—it was hard to tell which—began.

"Our lead story... Crawford Academy beloved football coach is found dead in Jefferson Park with his throat slit just days before the state championship game..."

That was all I heard. My mouth went dry even as I sipped my beer. The hair on my neck stood up, and I felt a chill. I thought of Bobby. The CA coach was dead with a slit throat exactly like Bobby had raged about.

Holy shit.

Chapter Five

"With just days until the state championship game, beloved CA coach, Stanley Dennison, was found dead tonight next to the Peace Bridge in Jefferson Park. Police are not releasing any other details at this time. The body was found around 10 p.m.," Pratt said.

The Foursome went silent, and my gut continued to flip. It was only hours ago that Bobby had said what he said, and I knew I needed to talk to him ASAP. I fished my cell out of my pocket and Googled his father's name. He wasn't listed. I hit 411 to get information and waited. I listened as the robotic voice asked me the city and state, and then, the name.

"Crawford, New York. Simon, please," I said, and I waited.

"At the request of the subscriber, that number is unlisted," the robot said.

I exhaled hard and did my best to think.

"You gonna put a nipple on that tonight?" I looked up at an annoyed AJ who looked at my full Schlitz and then back at me.

"Nah, I just got distracted," I said and took a hit off the beer. AJ's was one of the few places where adults could still be peer-pressured into drinking faster and more than is recommended by most physicians, social workers, and addiction counselors.

I called my cop friend, Kelley, and his cell immediately went to messaging. That left me with the choice of going to the police department with my suspicions about Bobby, or waking up my boss, Claudia Michelin, and telling her what happened. Calling the police meant breaking confidentiality, but I thought there was justifiable cause in this case. Calling Claudia would mean an unjustifiable pain in my ass and little chance of actually resolving anything. Claudia had a way of not doing anything and doing it so officiously that it created a ton of work.

It was after eleven, and I could pretend I didn't see the news or that Bobby never said anything to me about slicing the coach's throat.

It didn't feel right. It felt way wrong, but the alternatives seemed worse. My stomach could no longer take the grease-burger, but I finished the Schlitz, said my goodbyes to AJ and the Foursome, and made an early departure. My mind raced during the short ride home, and I had trouble focusing on a point. There was no way Bobby could have done this, right?

My place was quiet when I came through the door, and I didn't waste any time getting to bed. I live in a converted Airstream trailer called the "Moody Blue" after my favorite Elvis song. When you live in a trailer, it doesn't take long to meander through your domicile before you find the bedroom. The butler permanently had the night off at the Blue, but, as the cliché goes, it was home.

In bed, I just looked at the ceiling—not sleeping and trying to make things fit in the right order in my head. I kept coming back to the one of the many, many rules in the human services business and maybe the only one that truly is very important. It goes like this:

"If any person becomes an imminent physical danger to themselves or another human being, that information MUST be turned over to law enforcement."

This is a have-to, do-not-pass go, ironclad rule. I worked with really dysfunctional and poor people. The clinic was on the tip of the ghetto, and the city of Crawford was riddled with crime. The people who grew up or gravitated to the Crawford ghetto, known simply as "The Hill," were generally rough around the edges. It wasn't unusual for me to hear threats or accounts of violence.

Bobby was a suburban kid who came to us because of a contract we had with the local school districts for early drug intervention. He didn't fit the usual clinic profile. Despite the rule, if every time I heard something threatening in a session I called the police, they could open a precinct at Jewish Unified Services. Going by the book, in my line of work, just wasn't a practical course of action. At least that's what I told myself.

But even I couldn't be flip about this. A man was dead.

This is the sort of stuff that ran through my consciousness instead of sleep. Somewhere after four, I faded into some light sleep that didn't last. It almost never did at my place. Around six, I got up to make coffee and read the paper.

"Errrrrr..." I heard the familiar, low-level, not-quite-growl come from my bedroom while I put the filter in the Mr. Coffee. It was Al, my roommate, the eighty-five pound basset hound. He was now on the bed. Last night he had slept on the floor through my entrance, which he did from time to time. He didn't sleep through breakfast.

Ever.

"Errrrr..."

I counted to three in my head.

"Grrrbbllle, Grrrblle, Grrrrblle... snort."

Right on schedule.

I counted off two.

I heard the weighty flop of Al hitting the floor.

I counted to three. I heard the subtle, chingy sound of his ID tag as he waddled to the doorway. I waited.

"Raaw, Raaw, Raaw!...Ruff, Ruff...Raaw, Raaw, Raaw!...Ruff, Ruff."

Same pattern, same cadence, every morning.

"Just a minute, fatso," I said.

"Raaw, Raaw, Raaw!...Ruff, Ruff...Raaw, Raaw, Raaw!...Ruff, Ruff." Al repeated his greatest hit.

"Easy…" I warned.

"Raaw, Raaw, Raaw!...Ruff, Ruff...Raaw, Raaw, Raaw!...Ruff, Ruff."

I moved through the kitchen and scooped two cups of hound food out of the bag and into his Elvis dog bowl. The instant he heard the scoop sound, he stopped the noise and waddled into the kitchen. He looked at me intently as I filled the bowl and with a somewhat suspicious glare that suggested I was shorting him on the deal. When I finished and backed off, he began the half inhale, half attack on the dish. This was the daily Al feeding frenzy.

There was no "Thanks, Duff." No wink. No tacit nod of grateful acknowledgment. There was, instead, a sense of dismissal, letting me know that I could go and that I would not be needed. Shortly after dining, Al would retire to the living room where he would sleep in front of the TV and watch the History Channel all day. He perked up only when Chumlee, from *Pawn Stars*, appeared, and he slept through *American Pickers*, *Swamp People*, and *Ice Road Truckers*.

I heard the newspaper smack against my front door. Al didn't stir from his meal, but it startled me. *The Union-Times* had more detail than last night's news. It described the wound as "...fiercely deep" and made with a "...serrated-edged knife consistent with the type used for gutting and dressing game..." It also reported, as the TV news did, that Coach Dennison was found in the Peace Bridge area of the park.

If you grew up in Crawford, you knew what the Peace Bridge area was known for. It was an area known for furtive, anonymous homosexual activity. Since the 60's or earlier, it was where men rendezvoused for sex. It was where ignorant thugs went to "roll fags" for no good reason, especially in the early 70's. In the 80's, during the AIDS outbreak, activity slowed, but in the last ten years, the bridge area had a resurgence.

I've learned quite a bit about it from one of my on-again, off-again clients. Froggy was a flamboyant man, quite comfortable in his sexuality, with a host of other demons, and who freely shared himself in the park. The news reporting the whereabouts of Dennison's body was surely not an accidental suggestion about the coach's last moments alive.

If I played this by the book, I'd have to call Claudia—a woman who lived for regulations. I mean really lived for it. They were her erotica. To me, more often than not, regulations were a pain in the ass, and, in this case, they would make life miserable for everyone involved. The chances of a teenager like Bobby slipping into Jefferson Park and killing a burly guy like Dennison just didn't seem to be a realistic thing, so why go through all the red-tape bullshit? It wouldn't solve anything; it would get Bobby in trouble for blowing off steam, and, perhaps most of all, it would really suck for me.

Could I wind up in trouble? Of course, I could. With Claudia, any deviation from a regulation was an opportunity for her to exert power. It kept life black and white for her, which was safe, consistent, and predictable. The problem, in my eyes, was that life was greyer. People tried all sorts of things—religion, laws, and rules and regulations to make life seem like it made sense. Life just didn't, and part of being human was dealing with the anxiety caused by life's uncertainty. Besides, I decided a long time ago that there was more to life than staying out of trouble.

On the other hand, Dennison died from a slit throat in a matter of hours after Bobby said he would like to do exactly that. It was not an insignificant point, and, at the very least, a weird coincidence.

Chapter Six

Thursday Morning

On the way to work, I tried Kelley again. It was a little after eight. He picked up before the end of the first ring.

"Yeah?" Kelley said.

"Man, you gotta work on the warmth, Kell," I said.

"Look, shithead, I'm in the nineteenth...no twentieth hour of this shift, and I'm not feeling all that touchy-feely."

"Dennison?"

"Of course, Dennison. The mayor went to Christian, and three-quarters of the successful businessmen in Crawford went there. With this bullshit Super Bowl coming up, the whole thing is a damn circus."

"Do they have any ideas?"

"Probably one of the park regulars in a hookup gone bad or maybe some sort of random murder, but we're also trying to pretend like the ol' ball coach wasn't a regular himself."

I paused. I probably paused a little too long.

"Hey asshole, you called me—what did you call me for?" Kelley said.

"Just thinking. I had no idea about the coach. Did you know about him going to the park?"

"Just rumors. Fifteen years as a cop—nothin' surprises me."

"So, which way are they leaning?"

"Look, Duff, not now will ya? I know your life is *Law and Order: Criminal Intent*, but I got nothing right now, and I'm really fuckin' tired."

I knew when to back off of Kelley. It didn't mean I always did, but this was the time. Besides, I was pulling into the clinic lot, and I had to go to work in the business of saving lives. I signed off with Kelley, knowing I'd catch up with him soon enough.

Trina was in first and already had a cup of coffee—I could smell the caramel flavoring in it. Today was a khaki cargo pants day, with a plain black t-shirt, and a pair of really white Nike running shoes with lots of fancy looking air shocks on the soles. She got up to file a chart, and I noticed the cargo pants hung low on her hips and that the soft faded fabric found its way between her cheeks. My trained eye let me know exactly the style of undergarment Trina favored. Of course, some life experience also helped form that opinion.

"You gonna take a picture?" Trina said.

"What?" I said, mustering as much indignation as I could.

She frowned and rolled her eyes at me. I don't know if I was imagining things, but there didn't seem to be the usual playfulness in the repartee.

"Do you know where Bobby's chart is?" I said.

"Uh, like, maybe, uh, in the file cabinet?" She tilted her head, bucked out her teeth, and crossed her eyes at me.

"That's pretty inappropriate," I said.

"I'll get it for you, Mr. Useless, but Claudia wants to see you in her office. Go do that first."

In my entire career at Jewish Unified Services, the sentence "Claudia would like to see you in her office," never came with any good news. It, usually, meant a double-secret probation, a suspension, or even, on a couple of occasions, an attempted firing. It was never an Anthony Robbins empowerment-type moment, and, considering last night's events, I braced myself emotionally.

"Hey, Claudia. You were looking for me?" I said in the threshold of her office. She had one of those sickening scented plug-ins in the room, ostensibly to give a welcoming air to visitors. I threw up a little in my mouth.

"Yes, Duffy." The Michelin Woman's black, curly, almost Afro was a little asymmetrical this morning. It veered to her right and kind of made it look like a gigantic magnet was pulling her. I gave her the private nickname that played off her surname because of her build. She was almost my height, and she gravitated toward a lot of flowing polyester for fashion.

"I'm sending you over to Crawford Academy to do grief counseling. You've heard about the coach?"

"Yes."

"Your assignment is just to listen and let the students grieve. You'll have an office in the administrative suite, and all visits are confidential. Do you understand?"

"Sure." I thought about it for a second or two. "We've never done this thing before, though, and it's not even a public school. Why are we doing it?"

She sat back in her chair and frowned, letting me know just how tedious my company was.

"We're doing it as a community service." She was short with

her answer and didn't make eye contact. That's when it dawned on me.

"Ohhh, and we got three guys on the board who went to CA who donate a lot." The board composition had slipped my mind during this. Sucking up to them with this grief counseling was the predictable move for Claudia.

"Duffy, part of our mission is community service. This has nothing to do with that. Now, I want you over there by ten." As usual, she didn't look me in the eye after I rudely suggested how self-serving and transparent her motives were. That was Claudia, and that's what she was about and why she would reign as a human services despot for as long as she wanted to.

She went on to finish the rest of my directions for the next few days. CA would be my work home until further notice. I would be given a space there to meet with students who asked to talk to someone. I didn't need to record names or take notes, just keep the number of visits recorded. There would be another counselor from another agency at some point to help out because they felt that the coach's death would hit the students hard.

It was a good assignment for a few reasons. It kept me out of the office and away from Claudia. I wouldn't be able to do paperwork while I was there, and it would be a change of scenery. It was also perfect for me because I'd get to check in with Bobby.

All in all, not a bad deal and it would be nice to be out of the office. I headed across town to my new, temporary digs and a trip down the memory lane that was adolescence and high school.

Chapter Seven

Elvis played in the El Dorado on the way over. I was listening to a collection of the best movie soundtracks—not the King's most critically acclaimed stuff but music I loved nonetheless. I rarely agreed with what the music geniuses had to say and just played what appealed to me. Coincidentally, the third cut on the short drive was "Poison Ivy League." It was a song Elvis did in *Roustabout* when he was singing at a spring break bar to a bunch of rich frat boys. "Poison Ivy league" made fun of the college experience and how cool frat boys thought they were. In the movie, when the frat boys got mad and confronted Elvis in the parking lot, he opened up a can of karate on their asses. It was, by the way, the first time that karate made it into a movie and was years before Bruce Lee.

Anyway, the song got me thinking about my destination, and I realized I had a little bit of a confession to make.

I always hated Crawford Academy.

I went to public school at Crawford High. It was a 1940's school, built with grey cinder block and had a badly faded paint job. It smelled like an old school, and, if you went to an old public high, you know exactly what I mean. It was a four-story cube with a small gym and a cafeteria with walls that held on to remnants of Salisbury steak, powdered scrambled eggs, and that weird spaghetti sauce that was more brown than tomato red.

Meanwhile, across town, the rich kids, whose fathers and grandfathers went to CA, liked to pretend they were better than everyone else. They dominated in most sports and certainly in football. Crawford High had a better hoop team but always had lousy coaching, and the best players were, usually, ineligible for the second semester of the season because of their grades. Crawford would kick CA's ass in a street game in the summer league, but official high school games had its rules, and the playgrounds had their rules.

In my day, CA was Wonder Bread white, and there was a not-so-subtle undertone of racism when they'd play us. Our football team wasn't very competitive, so it didn't matter there, but on the court, it was different. It was, usually, an all-white CA team against an all-black Crawford team. When they'd beat us with their passionless control game, there'd be a certain smugness and self-congratulatory air to their victory. In the summer leagues, most of the CA boys stayed home while Crawford beat up on all comers.

There was a much different dynamic going on today. The CA teams were at least half black. It certainly wasn't because the kids from the Hill section suddenly had parents working in the semiconductor business. It was because CA used their "mission" money—the money supposedly allocated to allow underprivileged kids to get a fine education—to give ghetto athletes a free ride. Well, maybe it sort of was still mission money—that is, if the kids could run a 4.1 forty or dunk a basketball after jumping over an SUV.

This year, Crawford High's football team was good but not great. They came on at the end of the year and got hot during the sectionals. They had CA beat, but there was a highly controversial, goal-line play, and the refs, like they always do, gave it to CA.

The CA alumni were a pain in the ass, too. They favored penny loafers with no socks and turned up alligator shirts. They golfed a lot and worked in financial services. Forty-year-olds still went to high school games even when they had no kids playing. I had a few friends and acquaintances from CA, and, don't get me wrong, they were ok guys—but as a group, they annoyed the piss out of me.

For Bobby's father, having his kid at the Academy was the best he could do for him. He went into hock for it, worked crazy hours, and devoted himself to paying the tuition. I often thought that if Bobby went to public school, and his father was home to spend time with him, they both might be better off. Men knew how to work and sacrifice their hard-earned money as a testament to their love. It was tangible, easier, and a hell of a lot more comfortable than demonstrating love—whatever that was. Jack had told me that Bobby's old man was a good guy who had gotten into some trouble for burglary, but he was one of the very few who was actually stealing to support a young family. He came east to start over with Bobby after the incident.

As soon as I checked in and did whatever I was supposed to do, I was going to find Bobby and have a talk about the coach. I was 99% sure he wasn't responsible, but I felt like I had to confirm it, or I wouldn't feel right. Part of that had to do with breaking all sorts of regulations, but it also had something to do with just doing the right thing.

Claudia's instructions were to go to the administrative wing and ask for Headmaster Spadafora. I wasn't comfortable with the term "headmaster" on about fourteen different levels. Have you ever seen a headmaster in any movie, TV show, or book depicted in a favorable light? It's like when they posted the job, the requirements would read: *Must be a tight-assed, unreasonable stickler for trivial rules. Unresolved anger and hatred for school-age children a must.*

A professional looking woman I guessed to be in her late forties greeted me at the counter.

"May I help you?" She asked.

"I'm Duffy Dombrowski. I'm here as a counselor for the kids."

"Oh." She frowned and looked down like she was reminded that something bad happened. "I am Penny Halle, the vice principal. Thank you for coming. I'll get the headmaster."

Maybe this will reveal what I spend my time doing on the Internet, but the line "I'll get the headmaster" sounded a little too S&Mish to me.

She had blonde hair, was slightly tan, and looked like a confident, forty-something catalog model. She wore a taupe suit with pumps, and everything fit a bit snug. I'm not sure if there's a fashion category known as "business-sexy," but, if there was, this was it.

She stepped toward the office, but, at that same moment, the fire alarms went off. They weren't the fire alarms I remember. These were piercing electronic sounds that hurt the eardrum, and came with flashing, white emergency lights.

A man I assumed was Spadafora emerged from his office.

"There's a brawl in the cafeteria. Let's go."

Chapter Eight

We were in a full sprint down the shiny, waxed corridors. The handful of staff—three women and another guy from the office—fell in behind us. We headed down the staircase and made a sharp right turn into the cafeteria.

In front of us, about twenty teenagers were fighting. There were torn shirts, blood, yelling, and bodies, both vertical and horizontal, in different positions all over the room.

This type of scene causes you just to react. You may turn and run, you may yell for help, or you may head straight into it. I'm not sure if the heading straight into it is a purely "let's look out for everyone's safety" move. There's also an animalistic thing— something that says I'm a male, and I need to be involved here.

It was chaos, and, as I moved, I tried to assess where my energy should be focused. I passed kids who were yelling and cursing awful things, but not physically hurting each other. There were pushing and shoving matches with a lot of posturing that my experience told me weren't going to evolve into anything. I also saw a few kids down on the floor wrestling which might be uncomfortable, but would ultimately wind up being a dance of dominance and submission.

In the center, I saw Russ—the kid from the gym. He was straddling a kid smaller than him and throwing punches with both hands. The other kid's face was obscured with blood, and Russ showed no letup. This needed to be addressed immediately.

I lunged at Russ with a shoulder block and knocked him off his victim. Russ was all muscle, and, though I was the battering ram, I felt the impact run through me. He tumbled and then rolled awkwardly away from the other kid who remained motionless.

"Fuckin' asshole!" Russ yelled at me and bounded to his feet. He was up a bit faster than I was, and he was out of his mind with rage.

He actually growled, lowered his head, and lunged toward me. He threw two of those gigantic hooks that he worked on in the gym. Just like before, they were way too wide, and I stepped in on him and simultaneously threw a short, compact, straight left hand into his solar plexus.

I felt him freeze for a split second, then collapse.

Russ doubled over on his knees, moaning, and then he

flipped to his side in agony. Tears formed in his eyes, and, in between his moans, he began to whimper. The pain would stop in about ninety seconds—but for these next few moments, he would think his life was over.

I backed up, and, like it always does when you come out of a fight, my vision returned to normal. The intense focus on what was right in front of me in the moment, actually the second, gave way to seeing the entire room. The fighting had mostly stopped, and Russ and I were in the center. Me, standing; Russ on his side, crying.

The room hushed. Every eye in the room was focused on Russ, curled up in the fetal position, crying.

I got the impression that Russ's badass status was lying on the floor next to him.

He was a strong kid, and the hooks that had grazed my back still hurt a little. If you had no experience, they could've really hurt—but they were so fundamentally off that they were easy to counter.

Suddenly, the attention went to the kid Russ was beating. Spadafora was over him, wiping the blood from his face. I saw him lower his ear to the boy's mouth, and then, without hesitation, he began chest compressions.

The rest of the room began to gather around, and I moved to push them back. Spadafora had a panicked look on his face, but he focused his concentration on the student. He was desperate.

I glanced down, and a chill went through me.

It was Bobby.

Chapter Nine

"Call an ambulance," Spadafora said over his shoulder while he did compressions.

I got out my cell phone, hit 911, and did as instructed.

The room got quiet, like there was a sudden realization that seemed to run through everyone in the room—that what they were all doing had turned into something other than just teenage testosterone letting. It had gone too far, and there was a tragedy.

Bobby's bloodied face was lifeless as Spadafora pushed down on his chest. The headmaster didn't utter any of the clichés like "C'mon, breathe!' or "Live," but he had the look of desperation on his face. This was ugly stuff.

Bobby's face coughed, then he squinted, and then he tried to clear his throat. It went from what looked like an involuntary reaction to a purposeful one. The coughing increased, and he tilted his head up.

"Clear the room," Spadafora said. He half rolled to his side, and I could see perspiration covering his face and seeping through his dress shirt. He looked right at me, and I knew he was in charge—this was a crisis and not a time for power struggles. I turned and started giving orders to the teachers in the room I didn't know.

"Get them back to their classrooms," I said like I knew what I was doing.

"Teachers, record all names," Spadafora said without looking up from Bobby. The simplicity of his words chilled the cafeteria. These kids were in trouble.

Bobby vomited hard, but he was on his back, and he began to choke. Spadafora rolled him to his side, dug two fingers into his mouth, and cleared his breathing passage. Bobby's chest went up and down, but he wasn't speaking or reacting to anything. Spadafora looked at me, and I looked back. Neither of us said anything.

The paramedics came in. They wiped the blood from Bobby's face, checked his blood pressure, then got him all blanketed up on the gurney before taking him out. He took a hell of a beating. We watched as he was wheeled out of the cafeteria.

One of the paramedics spoke to us.

"His blood pressure and heart rate are stable. He's moving a bit, and I think he might have responded to our instructions. We're going to Crawford Med." He was efficient and without emotion.

We remained silent until Spadafora broke it.

"Should I come?" Spadafora said.

"No, not now. This is an emergency. Call his parents and wait to hear," the paramedic said while he loaded Bobby into the ambulance.

Spadafora stood and watched them wheel Bobby out. He pursed his lips, exhaled, and muttered under his breath. He took another deep breath and seemed to come back to the room. He looked at me.

"You're the counselor, huh?" He said.

We watched the ambulance pull away. We stayed quiet for a long moment until Spadafora spoke.

"Thanks for the help," he paused. "I saw what you did to Russ. That's a really strong kid."

"Is that going to be a problem?" I said. "Knocking a high school kid out goes against some sort of code of ethics, doesn't it?"

"This is a private school. I run it. There won't be any issues," Spadafora said. "Besides, that 'kid' is almost twenty and is built like an NFL linebacker."

"What about the police? Won't the paramedics file some sort of report that the cops will pick up on?"

"I don't want any police in my school. I can make a phone call to take care of that. We handle things internally here."

"I'm not so sure that'll be the case when it comes to what Russ did," I said.

"Yeah..." Spadafora acted as if that thought had just dawned on him. "What a week to have to deal with this shit."

CA had a lot of connections, and I believed a couple of well-placed messages in "the best interest of the school" would be received and adhered to. It's how things were normally done, but this wasn't a couple of kids spraying graffiti on the opposing team's building before homecoming. I wasn't sure that even the Super Bowl could make this get swept under the rug.

I had another question for the headmaster.

"You think this is going to interfere with my role as a grief counselor?" I wasn't trying to be a smart ass. I was trying to think of what I would have to tell the Michelin Woman if I was sent back to the clinic two hours into my special assignment.

"Oh, I think your grief counseling will remain largely unaffected," he said. I got the impression that maybe the headmaster wasn't a real believer in the benefits of counseling.

Spadafora looked at me for a moment like he was trying to think of something to say. Then he spoke.

"You want a cup of coffee?"

"Sure," I said.

"C'mon, let's go back to the office."

Chapter Ten

"You're the fighter, aren't you?" Spadafora asked. He was done calling Bobby's father and had slid me a cup of black coffee in a gold Crawford Academy mug.

"Yeah," I said. His office was exactly as you'd picture a headmaster's office to be. It could've been Dean Wormer's from *Animal House*.

"How does social work and counseling fit with that?" he asked. It wasn't sarcastic so much as it was a question from someone who didn't put a lot of stock in touchy-feely stuff.

"I try to hit them where it doesn't show."

He leaned back in his chair and crossed his legs, resting his ankle on his knee. He smiled and raised his eyebrows as if to say "touché." There was a little posturing go on.

When other men hear that you box, they tend to do a couple of things. Some look at you as a barbarian and others as a freak. Then there are the alpha males—or at least those who perceive themselves as alpha men. They tend to try compensating for the fact that you box and they don't, so they try to show their machismo in exaggerated ways. Spadafora leaning back in his big headmaster chair and his unimpressed smirking sent me that message.

"What happened to your football coach?" I said.

"God, how awful. I don't know much more than what I heard on the news. I just hope there isn't a serial killer on the loose." He paused for a moment. "And right before the state championship."

"Was the coach gay or secretly gay?" I asked. It was direct, probably too direct, but the fact that Spadafora and I just were involved in the same fight kind of had me feeling like we could be direct.

"What the hell kind of question is that?"

"He was found by the Peace Bridge."

He gave me a blank look. "So."

I tilted my head.It was now my turn to smirk.

"You've lived in Crawford how long?"

"Seven years." He uncrossed his legs and folded his hands in his lap. I noticed the game ball from the Crawford game was in a glass case behind his desk.

"You've never heard about the Peace Bridge?" I asked.

"Look, Duffy, stop being coy. What's the significance of the

Peace Bridge?"

"It's famous for being an area where men go to have sex with each other. Has been for decades."

He furrowed his brow, sat up and looked at me seemingly confused.

"Huh?" He said.

"You're kidding, right?"

"Well, first of all, I'm not the kind of man who looks into such things. Second of all, I don't get involved in gossip." I couldn't tell if he wasn't being truthful, or if he was one of those guys who remained naïve to the real world around him.

"I didn't pass judgment on anything. I also am not making anything up. It's been something that has gone on in Crawford for a long time. I suspect every city has a section in town where stuff like that occurs." I was getting a little annoyed and felt like I was being played.

He didn't respond, and there was an odd silence. I got the impression that he was strategizing the conversation and letting things hang. I didn't really care about digging up information, but I don't like being manipulated. I decided to move on.

"So, is there anything you're looking for in the crisis counseling for the students?" I asked.

He leaned back and put his hands behind his head, interlocking his fingers.

"Well, I don't know. Please don't let them manipulate you, I guess," he said.

"I'm not sure I understand."

"I just don't want kids getting out of class for no good reason," he said.

Chapter Eleven

"I take it you're not much on the therapy thing," I said. Spadafora's secretary, er, I mean, administrative assistant, had brought me a second cup of coffee.

"I sometimes think it is used way too much in our culture as an excuse." He took a sip from his mug. "Honestly, what do you think of it? You seem like a mostly normal guy."

It was a fair question and one I felt the need to answer directly.

"I think a lot of it is bullshit."

He smiled as if he had just won something even if he was the only one competing.

"Well, then—"

I cut him off.

"And other times, I believe it is a matter of life or death, or, maybe with a little less drama, the difference between living and living a miserable life."

He seemed just a tad less pleased with himself.

"How do you tell when it's bullshit and when it's life or death?"

"A lot of the time, you can't," I said.

"Well, when these students of mine come to you, how are you going to be able to tell if they're manipulating you to get out of Mrs. Pierce's algebra class or whether they're thinking of killing themselves?"

"I talk to them."

He shook his head. I could tell he was about to make a counterpoint, but the knock on the door distracted him.

"C'mon in," he called. Penny Halle, the vice principal I had just met, opened the door.

"What's up, Penny?" Spadafora asked.

"I told you yesterday about the State Ed. Curriculum reports. I was checking to see if you had completed them." There was firmness in her tone.

"I have not," Spadafora said. "I was orienting Mr. Dombrowski."

She quickly glanced at me and then back to Spadafora.

"The report is due by the end of the week, and I would like to review it before it is submitted."

Spadafora puffed his cheeks and then forced air out of his mouth through pursed lips.

"Okay," he said, "Not sure if you noticed, but it has been kind of an eventful day." He waited a beat and then asked her a question. "What time are the recruiters coming in?"

"Right after dismissal." Halle nodded back and turned to me.

"It was nice to meet you, Mr. Dombrowski. If I can help you with any of the students, please don't hesitate to ask." She smiled at me. It may have been me, but it seemed like she lingered just a second or two more than usual.

She closed the door behind her.

Spadafora shook his head in frustration. His face scrunched up in serious pissed-offedness.

"That's your *vice* principal?" I said.

He rolled his eyes and shook his head. He looked like he had just sipped some sour milk.

"Penny is very professional and thorough. She likes all of our I's dotted and our T's crossed. Sometimes she misses the big picture. She also seems to be a tad ambitious and would like to move up some day."

He was choosing his words carefully.

"That doesn't seem to make your day any easier," I said to be saying something.

He snickered. It was a laugh with no joy.

"She does everything she does perfectly. Everything you could measure, she does on time, completely, neatly, and thoroughly. There is not a single negative thing I could document about her."

"Sounds like you long for the days of *Mad Men*," I said.

"Well, I don't know if I'd go that far. But there is something charming about the notion of having underlings who cared about pleasing you rather than taking pleasure in getting under your skin," he said.

I didn't pursue it any further. It didn't seem to be a happy topic, nor one that knowing about would help in any way. I switched subjects.

"By the way, how's this brawl going to affect the football game?" I asked.

"I don't follow," Spadafora said with a blank look on his face.

"There was at least one football player in it. The kid I punched in the stomach."

"The brawl was a school thing. Football is something

different. That kid is ready to play in the state championship and sign a D1 Scholarship."

"Really? Is that what the recruiters are about?" I said.

"Yeah, nice group of guys from Florida. They're really high on five of our football players." Spadafora seemed pleased.

"Five, at a D1 powerhouse? Whew!" I said.

"Yeah, that's pretty amazing and great for the school."

"Kids get a free education; that's a pretty big deal with the cost of college."

Spadafora seemed a little caught off guard. Then he seemed to realize what I was saying and quickly adjusted.

"Absolutely, that's what I mean."

I thought to myself that what he really meant was that nothing was more important than football at CA. That's how it had always been.

Another knock came to the door, and Ms. Halle stuck in her head.

"Mr. Dombrowski, there's a student who would like to see you."

Chapter Twelve

"Before you go in with the student, could we chat for just a second?" Vice Principal Halle said.

"Uh, sure, I just don't want to make the kid wait too long," I said.

"It'll be just for a second," she said and motioned me to her office. I followed her in and took a chair when she invited me to. Her office was half the size of Spadafora's without any of the pretension.

"I'm really, really pleased you're here." She exhaled. "I don't want to be unprofessional, but the headmaster doesn't really believe in counseling."

"I got that impression," I said. She looked at me without smiling but with a sort of warmth in her eyes. She looked genuine.

"I think what you're doing is vitally important, and it is something that I don't think anyone on staff here could do. I want so much for you to know that and to know that what you're doing is appreciated."

I wasn't sure, but I think she started to well up a bit on those last few words.

""I'll do my best," I said and met her eyes. She extended her hand, and we shook. She looked at me and nodded.

"Thank you," she said warmly. "The student will be in your office."

I noted the somewhat schizophrenic way of the place. The administration certainly wasn't on the same page, but I knew it didn't really affect anything I was about to do. I just needed to listen to the kids and do what I could to help. When I opened my office door, the student was there.

"So, like, anything I talk about here, doesn't like, go in my file or anything like that, right?" The teenager in front of me said. He was gangly thin with faded acne that gave the look that whatever pharmacological treatment his parents paid for was starting to work.

"You don't even have to tell me your name if you don't want," I said. His hair was tussled, but not in that designer mess way you pay for.

"Really? You could find out easy enough cause Halle saw me come in here," he said. I figured him to be fifteen, maybe sixteen.

"Yeah, I suppose it wouldn't be too hard. I guess when it comes down to it you're gonna have to trust me a little bit."

He seemed to think about that for a little while, scratching at a small scab on his forearm.

"My name is Aidan."

"I'm Duffy." He didn't acknowledge our formal introduction.

"I think what happened to the coach was fucked up." He didn't look up.

I waited.

He didn't make eye contact.

Over the years of counseling, I've learned that keeping my mouth shut was about as therapeutic as any technique in my toolbox. That and I had no idea what to say a good deal of the time when someone in front of me was in pain.

"He was a good guy, you know. Not just if you played football."

"You're not on the team?" I said.

"Ha—I'm not exactly built like a linebacker, am I?" He made brief eye contact—not because I made some sort of connection, but because he didn't like being patronized.

"You were close with the coach?" I asked.

"Not that close, but he talked to me once. He came up to me and just asked how I was doing. Nobody around here does that."

I thought for a second about Bobby and his hate for the coach. His view of the coach was as the tight-ass, drill sergeant type. Aidan's coach was clearly different from Bobby's. People are rarely one thing, especially in the eyes of a group of adolescents.

"I thought I heard the coach was kind of a hard-ass?" I asked.

"He could be, especially if you broke rules, and he really got pissed if you were disrespectful to anyone." Aidan scratched his arm again.

"What did you guys talk about?" I asked.

He shrugged and stayed silent for a moment before he responded.

"Just stuff. Just stuff about being my age and getting by and feeling like a loser."

"Do you feel like a loser, Aidan?"

He shrugged. I waited for him to expound. He didn't.

"What makes you a loser?"

"Aw come on, man. I have no friends here. I don't fit in, and I feel like a piece of shit."

I let that hang for just a moment.

"And the coach understood that," I said.

He stayed motionless, but his eyes welled. Tears ran down his face, and he ignored them. When his nose started to run, he had to wipe it and sniff.

"It hurts to feel alone," I said.

He nodded and cried a little harder. Sometimes, just acknowledging what someone is feeling is enough to get them to go a bit deeper. It did this time.

"It hurts when you lose someone who understands," I said.

He put his elbows on his knees, held his head in his hands, and cried. He cried hard but tried to remain silent. When he had to breathe, it came out in a gasp. His face was red, and his nose ran along with the tears.

"I gotta go," he said and went for the door.

I got up and put my hand on the door to keep him from leaving. He didn't challenge me. He hung his head and wiped his nose with the back of his hand.

"Losing someone who supported you is heartbreaking. You don't have to be okay with it. Intense feeling can be really scary. If you want to come see me or someone else just to be around someone when you feel like this, you can. That's what this is for."

He nodded and sniffed without looking at me.

"You wanna talk some more?" I said.

He shook his head.

"You sure?"

He shook his head again.

"C'mon back and talk to me any time if it helps, okay?" I stuck my hand out just under his face. He noticed it and gave me a passive handshake. Just before he opened the office door, he looked up at me and nodded.

Aidan's view of the coach and Bobby's didn't match up. Sounds like the same by-the-book coach that busted Bobby found it in his heart to lend an ear to one of the academy's lost children. This kid wasn't a baller, wasn't ever going to be, and didn't fit the jock profile in any way.

The late coach was already looking a bit more complex than your average high school Lombardi type.

Chapter Thirteen

I went back to my desk and sat down. This business frustrated the hell out of me. A kid comes in to see me, ostensibly to feel better. He talks to me. He leaves with his pain amplified.

The bullshit about experiencing your pain and "sitting with your feelings" was never quite all right with me. It seemed like a cop-out for being in an ineffectual line of work. It probably contributed to why I love boxing so much. Boxing has little of the vagaries of therapy. You get hit if you don't keep your guard up, and if your opponent hits harder and more often, you get beat up. If your opponent hits you hard enough, you lose consciousness. Simple.

My fascination with my thoughts was interrupted when a light knock came to my door. It was Vice Principal Halle. She poked her head in without fully entering.

"How'd it go with Aidan?" She said. She leaned against the doorjamb and folded her arms.

"Fine," I said. I didn't want to say much more than that.

"He's a troubled kid."

I nodded.

"Did he get into the stuff that bothers him?" she asked.

"That's why people, usually, come to talk to someone like me."

She smiled and nodded.

"I don't want to be evasive but, you know, confidentiality," I said, trying not to sound judgmental.

"Well, thanks for being here. It means a lot to us." She smiled and turned toward the door. There was something to her turn—it wasn't quite flamboyant, but her jacket lightly opened as she spun, and it let me see a firm waistline with a nicely proportioned bust. Her tailored pants and pumps gave her noticeable form. I got the sense she was aware of all of this.

Her questions were her subtle way of prying without crossing the blatant line of asking me to break confidentiality. I've learned over the years to answer questions like this by giving authority figures a few obtuse responses and by employing silence. It becomes apparent to them pretty clearly that I know what they're trying to do, and I'm not going to allow it.

I've also learned that I can avoid any direct confrontation by using these techniques. I wasn't quite sure what Crawford Academy was all about, what it meant to my job, or what VP Halle was all about. I didn't want to get into battles until I knew the stakes involved.

She was getting ready to say something else when I heard Spadafora's door open, followed by voices and laughter.

"Oh, the boys are here again!" Halle said, turning from our conversation. Through the door crack, I could see what was going on.

Four guys, each wearing the same multi-colored golf shirts emblazoned with their college logo, stood just outside the headmaster's office. Each gave Halle cheek kisses and hugs. I noticed the guy kissing Halle had the college logo on his left bicep, and I knew from Sports Center that it was the logo that appeared on their helmet and at midfield of their stadium. I got up from my desk to get a better look, and I saw all four had the tattoo. Geez, I guess that's commitment.

"You like our chances in the big game?" she asked. She had become almost girlish.

"Yes ma'am," a forty something guy with a high and tight crew cut said. "I like CA's chances quite a bit." He had that affected good ol' boy lilt to what he said. He was a big guy, like maybe fifteen or twenty years ago, he played linebacker.

These guys rubbed me the same way that car salesmen do. Even when they're just making small talk, I found it laced with manipulation and a lack of authenticity. If you spend your life trying to get people to think a certain way, it can't not get into your skin. For some, it's about Hondas being the best vehicle, and, for others, it's about a certain southern university being the best choice for a muscular adolescent and his parents.

I heard another voice come from behind the college guys.

"Who wants brownies!" Right behind the recruiters was a smiling woman with a bobbed haircut and big, blue eyes. He skin was perfect, and her teeth were straight and white.

"Mrs. Redmond, now you know the brownies are so good I bet the NCAA wants to outlaw us receiving them," the oldest of the flattops said. "But there's no way it's gonna stop me!"

This had the depth and nuance of a Brittney Spears video.

"Please, Chuck, it's Anne Marie—dig in!" Mrs. Redmond said, holding the platter for Chuck to grab a brownie with a meaty paw. She was about five foot four and didn't have the look of a high-powered attorney's wife. I would've expected more of a Real Housewives of Crawford look. Instead, she looked like the model a few years removed from being on a Catholic girl's college catalog. Her red sweater sported the AMR monogram.

I really didn't want to be part of this saccharin-laced conversation. I thought about getting more coffee, mostly so I'd have something to do, and I went hunting some out. Before I got to the door, I saw a hand come up, and I heard a knock. I backed up behind my desk so I wouldn't startle my visitor by being at the door too suddenly.

"C'mon in," I said in a voice just a little louder than a conversational tone.

In walked a big kid, probably six foot two inches with a football player's build. His hair had that greased flip in the front, and his tie was askew. He had Mediterranean features: thick eyebrows and a long, thin nose. He sat without being invited.

"Are you the guy we can just go talk to?" he said.

"Yeah, I'm Duffy Dombrowski."

He smiled like he was suppressing a snicker.

I sat without saying anything, doing my best to create the active listener image. He didn't say anything.

After a long, pregnant pause, I decided to start us off.

"What would you like to talk about?"

He sat forward and rested his elbows on his knees without making eye contact. He turned his head to the side.

"I think I might be gay," he said. Then, he tried to hide a laugh.

Okay, so I got my first practical joker looking to get out of chemistry class or something.

I let it stay quiet.

"I mean, I think about boys all the time," he said.

I'm sure he thought this was going to be really, really funny when he went back and told the defensive line how he put me on. I guess I kind of expected some of this when I got this assignment, but, coming right on the heels of working with Aidan, I got distracted.

"Every time I'm in the shower after practice I worry about getting a boner." Again, he snorted, unable to contain just how funny he thought he was.

I didn't say anything.

And I waited.

He looked up at me. He saw that I was staring at him without smiling. He cleared his throat.

I didn't say anything. I waited. It was probably no more than twenty seconds, but silence felt much longer.

"Uh, aren't you going to say anything?"

In the fight business, I was used to staredowns. I did it at weigh-ins. I did it at the opening bell, and sometimes I did it when the round ended. I did it at the handful of press conferences I've been to in my boxing career. I could do it for hours.

I just looked at him.

He started to shift his position. He ran a hand through his hair, sat up, and then leaned forward again.

I didn't move.

He looked up, but this time he made eye contact for an even shorter period.

I hadn't moved or changed expression at all. I didn't make an angry face or scowl. I just looked at him. He put his head down, I heard him let out an exhale, and he wiped his hands on his pants.

"Uh, I'm gonna go back to class now," he said without looking up at me.

I didn't say anything and I didn't move.

I watched him leave.

Chapter Fourteen

I waited until 3:30 before leaving the office. Dismissal was at 2:30, so that gave any student time to come see me for a little while after classes were over. I had that weird feeling you get when you're out of your element and away from the structure that keeps you centered. Throw in the huge cafeteria fight, some serious injury, and a troubled kid, and you had enough for a mini PTSD episode.

I was worried about Bobby. Word had come from the hospital that he was stable and that he would be moved out of the emergency area at around four. They requested only family for visitors, but I'd go check on him in some way as soon as I got out of here.

Trauma is a curious thing. When something different and disturbing happens in front of us, or to us, it short-circuits our brains. Things aren't trusted, predictability is questioned, and life's uncertainties become enlarged. Then, you retreat a little, keep your guard up a bit more, and you go into yourself. The self you go into is shaken, and the perception of what's happening around you and your emotions are off-kilter. Those variables play off themselves and synergize and, left unchecked, get worse.

The same thing happens when you get hurt in the ring. When you get your bell rung, you go on the defensive, you keep your hands higher, you stop being aggressive, and you become hesitant to do what you've planned. You think too much and become over cautious. If you don't snap out of it in the ring, you get knocked out.

In life, you just go into a defensive shell, and the world beats the shit out of you a little every day.

I have a little experience with trauma. Some of it as a counselor, but more of it from living. It has changed how I perceive my clients. Reading and studying about mental health is one thing, but knowing a bit about what troubles people because it troubles you is something else entirely. It makes the process, on both ends, more genuine.

I had a half hour to kill before I could go to the hospital, so I walked the CA halls. I went past the big trophy case with the decades of awards and statues. It held the brass basketball championship trophies, aged with patina and covered with the grayed nets, the deflated footballs with the carefully painted scores, and the plaques honoring heroes. The newer awards were closer to the glass and stood in the foreground, marking on one hand how times had changed, and on the other, how it stayed the same.

"Years of tradition," the female voice came from behind me. It was Halle.

I turned, and she smiled at me.

"It's tough not to get nostalgic when you look at these things," I said. I hadn't realized how tall she was back in the office. With her slingback heels, she was almost my height.

"I meant it when I thanked you for helping us out today. I also wanted to let you know that Bobby Simon has been moved out of the emergency department. We don't know a lot, but they've suggested that he not have visitors, at least tonight." She folded her arms and leaned against the wall. The stretchy material in the suit did what it was supposed to and formed to her where it should. It was a professional look for a woman who cared about the image she gave off.

"Well, thanks," I said. "It doesn't sound terrible, I guess."

"You're a professional boxer?" She did that subtle thing where she looked me up and down while asking.

"Yeah."

She didn't say anything. She half smiled, tilted her head, and half opened her mouth.

"What?" I asked.

"Nothing. You don't meet a lot of pro boxers; that's all." She had switched her stance and was now leaning with her shoulders against the wall, her hands behind her. She was smiling.

There's a feeling I get when I'm not sure if a woman is flirting with me. This was a weird enough day to begin with, but now, with this very professional, sharply dressed woman doing the head tilt, coy smile thing, it was getting stranger.

"Can I ask you something?" she said. She tapped her foot and, ever so slightly, moved her head.

"Sure."

She scrunched her forehead, and her eyes looked up like she was thinking.

"Yes?" I said.

"Do you... I mean..."

I waited.

"Never mind." She smiled and kind of laughed at herself. "I've got to go. Got a yoga class." Her face flushed just a bit. "I'll see you tomorrow?"

"Sure," I said and watched her walk back toward her office. There was no question she was put together.

Was I mistaken, or did the vice principal just hit on me? She was older than I was, but so were Salma Hayek and Halle Berry. I noticed my mouth was a bit dry, and my palms were just a tad damp.

High school work was definitely different. Definitely not what I was expecting.

The tri-tone blip that let me know I had a text sounded. I looked down and saw that it was TJ.

It said, "Got time for coffee?"

Chapter Fifteen

I let her know I'd be there in an hour after I checked on Bobby. I know Halle said that they didn't want visitors, but I felt like I needed to know more and see if there was anything I could do. Crawford Med was on the way to the coffee shop, and, after I had negotiated their pain-in-the-ass parking garage, I went to the front desk.

"I'd like to see a student of mine who was checked in this afternoon," I said to the receptionist. She wore a phone headset and looked vaguely angry.

"Are you immediate family?" She said without making eye contact.

"No, but—"

"Due to HIPPA regulations, I cannot disclose who is in the care of Crawford Medical Center." No smile, no eye contact, and no interest in bending any rules at all. I should have known this was how it would go. The HIPPA regulations govern everything, including my job at the clinic. I'm just used to circumventing them in lieu of common sense. Getting by this lady was going to take a little more planning. I'd do better tomorrow.

I headed over to Jitters Coffee Sanctuary, in Crawford's college ghetto. The ghetto was a once-decent, blue-collar neighborhood but had become an eye sore filled with rental properties and populated with downstate kids. The landlord strategy was to stuff as many underclassmen in a flat as possible, let them destroy it, and collect two grand a month from each of their parents. Nice for the property owners, but it kind of sucked if you lived in Crawford your whole life.

The coffee shop was next to the old Jefferson Theater. It had been a big screen place with 1,000 seats where, once a year, they'd take our school to see the Sound of Music, the Wizard of Oz, or Gone with the Wind. Now it was a multiplex with eight little rooms showing films on a screen you could get at Best Buy. Jitters had exposed brick, old couches, and a collection of mismatched, beat-up, old tables. The clientele tended to be U of C students with that perfectly honed slacker look, $75 ripped jeans, and tattered, $120 Ugg boots.

I didn't see TJ when I scanned the room. I headed to the counter and asked the guy with the three rings in his lower lip for a cup of coffee—extra light and extra sweet. He kind of snorted, and I assumed that my order was not consistent with how he believed their exquisite Arabica concoction was to be consumed. Of course, I didn't really feel pressured to impress a guy pouring coffee for a living who looked like he fell down a flight of stairs carrying a tackle box.

I sat in an orange, molded plastic desk chair from the seventies and thumbed through a leftover copy of the *New York Post*. The legs were uneven, and the chair did that annoying wobble. The headline of *the Post* was something about a pit bull attacking an eighty-three-year-old Brooklyn woman. I flipped to the sports section and read an article about Crawford's state championship game against a team from Staten Island. There was a photo of the team captains—Russ and the kid who came to see me at the end of the day, goofing off about being gay. The article talked about their D1 scholarship offers.

I was far more apprehensive about TJ than I really wanted to admit. I did that thing you do when you're trying to talk yourself out of an emotion that you're experiencing. I reasoned that TJ and I had been just friends. We worked out together, sparred together, and had a couple of beers. She looked really good in an absolutely no frills way. She was hard, and she seemed authentic.

We didn't go on a date. We didn't have sex—shit, we never kissed. I thought there might be something there, but who knows what she experienced. Actually, the fact that she disappeared for a couple months after we met may tell me all I need to know. She either didn't feel anything worthy of hanging around for, or she, like everyone woman I've ever dated, was nuts and felt the need to weird out after meeting me.

Yet, again, she contacted me. She reached out to get ahold of me.

Maybe it had more to do with my state of mind. It had been a long time since I had made a connection. TJ was definitely different. She didn't go to the tanning hut, and she didn't do jewelry—she just seemed to be real. Of course, I only saw her a handful of times, and, when that happens, I think your mind creates a false reality. You romanticize the person; you give her qualities that you want. You idealize the dream of what she could be.

If I had been getting laid on a more steady basis at the time, I may have seen her more as she really was. Or maybe she was all those things. I just know it had been and, I guess, still was, a pretty dry spell for me when it came to women.

Sure, Trina and I were still intermittently hooking up—but now she had a steady, and until that blew up, we would pretend nothing was happening, or, for that matter, had ever happened between us. Then, if I were involved with someone, Trina would respect that and stay away from me. It was kind of cool in the sense that we both silently respected each other's attempt to find the right one.

Trina and I were about comfort and release. Comfort, in the sense that we found each other at times when we both needed each other. We were also a reminder to each other that we were both adults with needs that were more than physical. Yeah, Trina and I were pretty compatible when it came to sex, but it wasn't ever that simple. It wasn't a gymnastic event designed for each of us to have some sort of release. It was real, even if it wasn't forever, or love, or commitment.

None of this with Trina was ever spoken. It was understood. There were times when I wasn't there for her and times when she wasn't there for me because of others. That didn't cause resentment toward each other, though I remember being pretty pissed off at the cards life was sometimes dealing. There were lots of lonely times I really missed Trina.

I don't know what happens to relationships like Trina's and mine. Do they smolder on until they peter out, or do they abruptly stop when the right person comes along? Or do people eventually grow out of the experience of sharing one another? I didn't have any answers, and all of it was making me more nervous and confused.

My large—excuse me, my *Grande*—was down to one cold sip at the bottom of the paper cup. It had that yucky coolness, and the extra cream and sugar made it that much more difficult to swallow. The caffeine intensity wasn't helping my nerves, and, as I stood up, something else upped the voltage around my anxiety.

There was the piercing sound of a motorcycle engine—the high-revving, fast kind, not the big ol' Harley sound. I looked up and saw TJ parking her motorcycle in front of the coffee shop.

Chapter Sixteen

"Hey Duff, what's up?" TJ said. She ran her hand over her short, cropped, brown hair. She wore it spiked and tussled, so it was almost impossible to mess up.

"What's goin' on?" I said. It was one of those moments when you became entirely aware of yourself.

She smiled. I smiled. I felt awkward. She didn't look like she did.

"Let me get some coffee. You want a refill?"

"Sure." I had already had way too much coffee today, and jet fueling my awkward insecurity didn't seem advisable. Still, I didn't have the self-esteem to decline.

TJ headed to the counter, and I waited. I watched as she walked. She had taken off her Carhartt jacket, and, underneath, she had on a faded Notre Dame t-shirt, loose carpenter jeans, and light brown work boots.

"You look like you've been training," she said while she slid a black coffee in front of me. I didn't want to make the point that I took my coffee extra sweet and extra light.

"I don't have anything coming up in terms of fights, but I try to stay ready. There's good money in the short-notice shit."

"Short notice?"

"Yeah, someone pulls out of a fight with a week to go, and promoters scramble to find a warm body. Most guys won't take a fight like that, but, because the promoters are desperate, they'll pay good money for someone willing to do it."

"And you're willing."

"It pays three times what I usually get."

"Are they tough fights?"

"They are almost always situations in which I get sent in to lose. It's usually some up-and-comer the promoters are high on." I felt like I was talking a lot.

I tried not to.

She sipped her coffee and looked out at her bike, then down at the table.

"How's Al?" She asked.

"Obstinate, disobedient, and consistently flatulent." That got a giggle out of her. I thought it was cool how she could, for an instant, become girlish. It wasn't contrived, and it faded quickly, but it was authentic.

"He's his own man," she said.

"You got a dog? Er, excuse me. What's the politically correct way of saying that? Do you have a canine companion?" I affected a high society accent.

"No. I did some work in the service with the canines. Had a bloodhound named Agnes assigned to me. We'd go after bad guys together."

"Agnes got promoted, and you didn't, so you took the discharge?" I was doing my best to be clever.

She smiled and looked at her coffee.

"God, I miss her," she said.

"What happened?" I asked.

"Military crap. They're not always big on feelings." She made a face, and I got the impression she wanted to change the subject. I made a note about her love for Agnes, though.

"Look, Duff, I'm sorry I just split six months ago," she said. She took a sip and looked out at her bike.

"No sweat. Shit happens." I said, doing my best dashingly-cool. I was afraid I answered too quickly and was pushing the nonchalance.

There was a moment of awkward silence, but, before I could panic, TJ spoke.

"Well, I guess you'll be getting enough of me for a while, anyway. I'm going over to Crawford Academy to help with the trauma counseling."

"Really? How'd that come about?" I said. I was glad the conversation moved away from the apologies. That was too close.

"I'm one of the more experienced volunteers at the suicide hotline, so they asked me."

"But, I don't understand. Dennison didn't kill himself."

She sipped her coffee and looked at me.

"We're cross-trained for critical incident stuff. Part of the community service stuff."

Critical incident counseling was a specific, situation-based, brief type of counseling. It was used when a trauma occurred, and it involved a very specific style. It was all about listening, encouraging the client to emote, and reinforcing that nothing that happened in the trauma was their fault or responsibility. In theory, if a client was able to do those things immediately, or as close to immediately as possible after the incident, they were less likely to have long-lasting psychological issues.

"Cool—when do you start?" I asked

"Tomorrow. That's kind of why I want to touch base with you. I had heard that JUS was working it, so I figured it'd be you. I wanted to get the lay of the land, so to speak."

I felt a bit of a twinge. TJ wanted to find out about her assignment. That's why she wanted to see me. That was okay, I guess.

"I've only been there a day. It was an eventful day, though, to say the least."

I went on to tell her about the brawl, Bobby, and Russ. Her jaw went a little slack as I explained.

"All that on the first day, and at a hoity-toity school?" She asked. "Is the kid going to be all right?"

"I don't know. They wouldn't let me see him at the hospital."

"HIPPA, right? That's so screwed up." She sipped her coffee and shook her head.

"The administrative dynamics is another study in dysfunction. The headmaster kept referring to counseling as bullshit. The vice principal, who, by the way, is a woman, seems to have the headmaster by the short hairs and bullies him around. He sees her as a real bitch. And it seemed like some people loved the coach, and some hated him."

She glared at me.

"And why shouldn't the female VP boss around the headmaster? If she were a man, you wouldn't call her a bitch. You'd call her a real go-getter. Martha Stewart's a bitch and Donald Trump is a success story," She had a real angry tone to her.

I didn't know what to say. Clearly, I said the wrong thing. "I..."

She continued to glare at me. Finally, she broke the silence.

"C'mon Duff, I'm bustin' your balls! Geez, I had you goin' there for a while."

We both laughed hard, and I felt some tension release inside of me.

"Fuck you," I said.

Chapter Seventeen

TJ drove the thirty or so miles back to Albany, saying she had to be somewhere that night and had to get ready. Our interaction left me uneasy, and the fact that we'd be working together also felt strange. The uneasiness was undoubtedly fueled by the 10,000 milligrams of caffeine that buzzed through my veins.

I headed back to the Crawford Medical Center to check on Bobby. Along the way, I called my buddy, Shelly—the lady who helped me out a few years ago with the puppy mill situation. We chatted for a little bit, caught up, and I asked her a few things that she was going to check up on. I told her what I wanted to do, and she said she knew someone who did this kind of thing. She went on to say it wasn't easy and that it would take some time. I told her to go ahead with it, and get back to me when she could. By the time we were done chatting, I was pulling up to the hospital.

CMC is a very highly regarded hospital, despite the fact that it is in my somewhat dumpy hometown. It has had so many additions that trying to navigate the place is next to impossible. I paid to park in the lot and headed across a walking bridge to the main lobby to find out Bobby's room.

There was a different receptionist on; this time it was a guy, and it was time to try another strategy. I'd be confident and self-assured. I'd simply ask like I belonged here, and the guy would give me what I wanted.

"I'm looking for Bobby Simon's room," I said to him. He had on a headset and he, just like his co-worker, never stopped looking at the monitor in front of him.

"Are you family, sir?" he asked.

"No."

"Due to HIPPA laws, we don't acknowledge what patients are in our care. I'm sorry; it is a federal regulation," he said.

"How could I get permission to know about him or see him?"

"If he were, indeed, a patient, he or the family would have to sign a consent."

So much for my confidence and its ability to influence others into doing what I desire. I was going to have to review my Tony Robbins material a little more closely.

I thanked him and went to head out, or at least I faked heading out. Instead, I ducked into a stairwell, went up three floors, and randomly selected a door to go through.

I stopped the first nurse-looking person that went past me.

"Excuse me, they changed my brother's room on me, and I can't find him," I said.

The pretty, twenty-something brunette, who looked in a hurry, glanced at me, sighed, and went to the nurse's station a few feet away.

"Name?" she said without making eye contact.

"Robert Simon," I said.

"And you're his brother?"

"Uh-huh," I said, focusing on nonchalance.

"He's been moved back to intensive care." There was a somewhat solemn tone to her voice. "You can visit with the rest of the family for ten minutes on the hour."

"Oh…" I said, "Thank you."

The words "intensive care" stopped me in my tracks like a punch. Things didn't seem to be improving. I didn't want to intrude on what was clearly family time, but I wanted to find out Bobby's condition. I needed to know.

"Excuse me, nurse." I caught her just before she turned away. "What's my brother's condition?"

Her face went emotionless.

"He remains in a coma."

I felt nauseous. I wasn't expecting this and had kind of unconsciously made up my mind that things were going to be okay. I think your mind deals with things like that. You can't let yourself feel what's real, so your head turns it into something you hope it to be. I thought of his hard-working father, a man who already, tragically, lost a young wife, and I thought about Bobby being abused as a kid. The fucking world was nowhere near fair. How awful and frightening this must be for Mr. Simon. I was scared as hell for Bobby; he was a good kid just struggling through adolescence in his own way.

Things at CA were about to get crazier. Russ had gotten himself into some serious trouble. School fights were one thing, but beating a classmate into a coma was another. It was going to get ugly—probably pretty soon.

Chapter Eighteen

Bobby's situation and the visit to the hospital, combined with all of my caffeine intake, had me on a weird edge. Hospital visits, under any circumstances, brought on suppressed emotions in me. I knew as I walked through the halls that people were dying, and others were grieving. The pain of people suffering and the memories of every time I worried about someone or lost someone came back, in one way or another, when I walked through a hospital. I may not have always been able to identify and name the emotion, but I could feel it not too far below my surface, doing something.

Getting out of the hospital and getting some fresh air seemed important. I didn't like hospital air, and I didn't like how it seemed to stay in my lungs and all over me. I purposely drove with my windows down.

It dawned on me that I needed to give Jack Daniels a call. Bobby and his dad came to me because Jack trusted me, and I owed her an update. Sure, no official Release of Information Forms were signed for Jack and I to talk, but, honestly, I didn't give a shit. Some things—shit, a lot of things—transcended the rules. I dialed her cell.

"Daniels," She gave the typical cop phone greeting.

"For a woman who looks as good as you in Armani, you would think you'd have a gentler phone presence," I said.

"Duffy! How the hell are you?" I could hear a lightness come to her voice.

"I'm great, Jack, you?"

"Besides being basset hound sleep deprived and in a constant state of annoyance, I'm wonderful." I helped Jack adopt a basset hound awhile back. "What was I thinking?"

"I tried to warn you..." I said.

"You know how it goes—I bitch and moan about him getting me up, eating my Gucci loafers, and farting like a machine, but all I gotta do is look at that expression and my heart melts."

"Uh-huh, and would you be able to print the words you yell at him at three in the morning when he wakes you up?"

"Of course not," She said. "Hey, how's Bobby and his dad?"

I paused for a second and felt something in my stomach.

"That's why I'm calling, Jack. Bobby got beat up pretty bad at school. He's in a coma."

"Holy shit..."

"Yeah, Jack, there's something else." I wasn't sure I wanted to go where I was about to go. "Something weird, too. The day before, Bobby got all pissed off in a session about the coach who kicked him off the team. Bobby said he wanted to slit his throat and then said some homophobic shit."

"Geez, I told you the kid was angry. A lot of adolescent rage there, Duff."

"Uh, you ready for this, Jack? That night, the coach was found dead with his throat slit."

The other end went silent.

"Jack?" I said.

"There's no way, right, Duff?" She said with more than a hint of desperation.

"I don't think so, Jack. Just a weird and disturbing coincidence, I think."

"God..." she said. "Look, Duff, I've got a call. Keep me updated, would ya?"

I agreed to, and we signed off. I felt good that I called her. I felt shitty about just about everything else. I couldn't think of a better reason to go to AJ's. Perhaps a Schlitz and maybe something more would settle me down a bit. Maybe, maybe not, but it sounded like a good idea. I needed something to transition me away from the hospital experience.

Before heading there, I had to pick up Al, who had been in all day and would need a short walk and some social interaction. People think that bassets are content with lying around all day, but that's a myth. Al needed to be around people. He needed to force his will on the world around him, and he needed to express himself. He needed AJ's.

AJ was never really thrilled when Al came into the bar, but he didn't out-and-out ban him. Over the years, AJ had cause for annoyance. There was the thawing hamburger incident, numerous urination scandals, and the biting of a deliveryman who made the mistake of saying "Hey, why the long face?' to Al and then laughing. I don't want to go into the lurid details of what happened, but suffice to say that the guys back at the warehouse now call the deliveryman "Lefty."

"The Priapus plugs in," Rocco was saying when Al and I came through the door.

"Plugs in?" Jerry Number One asked.

"It's a hybridization. It goes both ways," Rocco said.

Al and I walked right around the conversation and took our seats. I lifted Al onto the bar stool to my left. AJ slid a Schlitz in front of me and a saucer of milk in front of my partner.

"Isn't a priapus what they warn you about with Viagra? Like if you take too much you might get a woodrow that lasts four or more hours," TC said.

"I keep waiting for that," Jerry Number One said.

Rocco was getting annoyed. Maybe I should've said more annoyed.

"The Priapus is that electric car that runs on gas," Rocco said. He was escalating a tad.

"Isn't a priapus that animal that's half duck and half walrus or something like that?" Jerry Number One said.

"Kook-ko-a choo," Jerry Number Two said. He had on his purple tie-dye. "John was the walrus."

"John who?" Rocco said.

"I have no idea who the duck was," Jerry Number Two said.

Rocco sighed loudly. As he did, Mike Kelley came through the door.

Rocco's reaction left a natural pause, and the Foursome gave Kelley the greeting I didn't get. He nodded, said "Hi," and took the spot left of Al, who was now lying half on the stool and half on the bar. It looked uncomfortable to the human eye, but Al was so relaxed that his nose whistled a little bit in that pre-snore way. AJ set up Kelley's beer.

"Don't get up, Al. What's up, Duff?" Kelley said.

"You missed Rocco talking about that electric car, the Priapus." I said with as much of a straight face as I could. Kelley snorted his first sip of Bud Light out his nose.

"Thanks, Duff. I needed a nasal rinse."

The snorting stirred Al, who hoisted his bottom half out of his stool and onto the bar. He waddled slowly down it and began to sip out of TC's B&B.

"Aw Al! Duff, he's doin' it again! Shoo Al, Shoo!" TC said.

Al paused momentarily. He licked around his lips, looked TC in the eyes, and then spun around twice and lay down in front of TC and next to his empty rocks glass.

"Sheez, dog can't hold his liquor," TC said.

"Or his licker for that matter. He got a loogie on you, TC," Jerry Number One said and pointed to TC's sleeve. A little slobber had made its way to TJ's cotton oxford.

"Yeah, I never get tired of this act," Kelley said. "They start talking about Judy Garland yet?"

"Nope," I said.

Kelley's attention went to the TV and Sports Center. There was talk about the Yankees off-season acquisitions and some big slugger who was a free agent.

"If they don't get someone to pitch the middle innings, they're screwed," Kelley said, mostly to himself.

He sipped his Coors Light and tuned the rest of the place out. He was a black belt in tuning the Foursome volume off. I wasn't going to let him zone out on me tonight, though.

I paused for a moment and then tried him for information.

"What's up with the case?" I asked.

Kelley exhaled, and his eyebrows went up. He tilted his head and made a face at me.

"Who are you—Lenny Briscoe?"

"Just curious," I said, trying not to be defensive. "I'm doing grief counseling at CA now."

That brought a smirk.

"Grief counseling? If the guys start talking about the Priapus, can I get some of that for my trauma?" He punctuated his comment with an eye roll.

I waited.

"C'mon, Kell."

Another exhale.

"They know that Dennison went to the park frequently, always at night, often at like two in the morning. That also happens to be the time that a lot of the anonymous homosexual activity goes on," He paused. "Which is kind of what everyone in Crawford's been talking about for forty-five years."

"Anybody have a motive?" I said.

"You really got to stop watching one episode of *Law and Order* after another."

I waited but kept looking at him.

"There's three schools of thought. One is that it was a guy who set out to kill the coach, and another is that the coach was simply in the wrong place at the wrong time."

"What's the other?" I asked.

"They're toying with the idea of students who might've been holding a grudge."

I felt my stomach sicken just a little bit.

Chapter Nineteen

On my way home, I took a trip through Jefferson Park. The same landscape guy that designed New York's Central Park and Albany's Washington Park designed it, and it was really beautiful. I ran through it often when I was doing roadwork.

Like Central Park, it divided Crawford in half, but in my hometown, it exactly split the city by socioeconomic lines. To the south were the ghetto and the semi-ghetto neighborhoods, and to the north were middle areas. The upper class had fled out of Crawford and to the burbs with a case of "white flight" a long time ago.

The park had basketball and tennis courts that lined Jefferson Ave, a walking path that snaked through the entire park and a small man-made lake in the center that was surrounded by the park's steepest hills. The south side of the park was more wooded, and it sloped up to Adams Street where it bordered the two-hundred-year-old brownstones. The lake rested in the bottom of the valley, and the Peace Bridge divided the park in half.

I took a slow drive along the perimeter of the lake. You had to be careful when you took a slow ride, or, for that matter, a slow walk, around the lake, especially at night. The men, who hung out there looking for anonymous sex, or looking to turn a trick, took it as a sign that you might be interested. It wasn't dangerous, at least not usually, but there was always something a little unnerving about being propositioned for sex from a stranger. I wasn't sure how I felt about all of this. I didn't like to admit it to myself, but there was a lot about sexuality that I just wasn't sure about, or, at least, I wasn't sure how I felt about it.

In the amber glow of the park's street lamps, I saw a couple walking ahead of me. My headlights joined the beam of the streetlight, and, as I approached, I saw a familiar face and a more familiar wardrobe. High, pink Chuck Taylors; gold glam bicycle pants; and a Hawaiian shirt replete with cockatoos of various sizes and colors. It was Froggy, and I rolled down the window.

"I was gonna ask if you were looking for a date, but there's only one big bruiser who rolls into the park in a 70's, orange Cadillac pimp cruiser," Froggy said in his unmistakable Caribbean accent.

"Love the shirt, Frog," I said. Froggy had been in and out of the clinic for the last decade, and we had done each other a few off-the-books favors—though not the sexual kind.

"You decidin' to come over to our side? You know you been all latented up for a long time, Mr. Duffy."

"Well, tonight isn't the night, Frog." He was leaning with both hands on my passenger-side window. The moonlight shone off his rich, dark skin. His friend stood a few feet back, ignored us, and looked bored.

"Then what you cruising so low through the park for?"

"You hear about the murder?"

"Mr. Duffy, this park is MY house. Of course, I heard about it. It's got us all terrified."

"I'm curious about the coach." I hesitated for just a second and then decided to ask. "Was he ever, uh, a friend of yours?"

"He wasn't a regular playa, Mr. Duffy. He came in here, though."

"I don't understand," I said.

"He'd come into the park, but he didn't join in no reindeer games, if you know what I mean."

"You mean he was in here, but it wasn't about sex?"

"I don't know if it was never, but it certainly was never with me. And believe me, Mr. Duffy, Frogilicious is popular at the bridge," Froggy said.

"So, what was the coach doing in here?"

"I don't know. I know he'd walk around and sometimes chat, but then he'd move on."

Froggy's companion said something I didn't understand.

"Mr. Duffy, Ms. Rhonda is getting impatient. I's got to go." He turned and glanced at Ms. Rhonda.

"Hi, Rhonda," I said. The guy in drag gave me a flip-of-the-wrist wave.

"Mr. Duffy, The Frogman is settling down. I do believe that Ms. Rhonda is the one." Froggy gave me a smile letting me know how pleased with himself he was.

"Rhonda, come meet Mr. Duffy." Rhonda didn't move. She turned toward the pond.

"Mr. Duffy, Rhonda is a bit shy. She used to sleep right under the bridge and made it her home. I took him away from all that," Froggy called to Ms. Rhonda again "Come meet Mr. Duffy, Rhonda," he said gently before turning back to me. "I'm trying to get her to come out of himself." The disagreement in pronouns made sense in this case.

"That's okay, Frog. You guys been together for a while?"

Froggy smiled, and I believe that if he weren't so dark, he would have blushed a bit.

"Why, yes Mr. D. I guess as I age being a player isn't so important to me." He was sincere and seemed just a little embarrassed to admit that maybe he had fallen in love.

"Froggy, you staying clean?" I asked.

"Mr. Duffy, you're off duty, are you not?" he feigned an angry glare.

"C'mon Frog…"

He gave me an overdramatic sigh.

"Ms. Rhonda doesn't approve. So, now I'm no longer the park playa, and I have no form of chemical escape." He sighed again.

"You keep an eye on him, Rhonda." I half shouted past Froggy. Rhonda returned a small smile.

"Mr. Duffy, we's got to go," Froggy said.

He smiled and put his arm around Rhonda and headed toward the bridge.

"Hey Froggy," I called to him, and he turned. "Congratulations."

He gave me that big, white, toothy smile and held Rhonda a little closer.

Chapter Twenty

Friday

I got to CA the next morning around nine o'clock. TJ wasn't there yet, and Spadafora's door was closed. I helped myself to coffee in the administrative breakroom, and I got comfortable in my borrowed office with the morning's *New York Post*.

The office staff wasn't up for any congeniality awards. They barely acknowledged me when I came in, and no one was going out of their way to see if I needed any donuts or anything. *The Post* did its job of keeping me mildly distracted, and I read almost all of an article about a problem with public urination in the subway system.

About ten minutes after ten, Spadafora poked his head in my office.

"You got a minute?" He then turned and walked to his office without waiting for my response. Yet another warm, interpersonal experience at the Crawford Academy.

When I got to his office, he was already sitting behind his desk with his feet up.

"Did you hear the news?" He asked.

"What news?" I said.

"Bobby Simon is in a coma."

"What?" I thought quick and realized I wasn't supposed to be poking around the hospital saying I was Bobby's brother. It probably wasn't a huge deal, but I didn't need extra trouble in my life. I let Spadafora break the news to me.

"He has some sort of hematoma bleeding on the brain and he fell into a coma."

"Holy shit," I said.

Spadafora looked more pissed off than concerned.

"The police are going to arrest Russell Redmond this morning. I have to call his old man now and let him know. This isn't going to be pretty—team captain gets arrested a few days before the Super Bowl." Yeah, it was pissed off, not concerned. Russ getting arrested was an annoyance, especially with his father. Bobby's coma was almost incidental.

"Didn't Russ's parents get called last night?"

"No, I was kind of waiting for the shake-out of things before I started that shit."

That just seemed like a strange response considering the nature of the brawl and Spadafora's controlling nature.

"This place has a lot of politics that have to be handled in just the right way." He said it and looked at his lap. It was a tell letting me know that he knew he was full of shit.

"Redmond's father is the attorney, isn't he?" I said. I remembered him introducing himself the other day at the gym.

"You got it. Class of '89 and CA's biggest benefactor, by far," Spadafora said it like that explained everything. "This is going to be a circus."

"The father of the kid I punched in the stomach."

"Yep."

"So, what do you want me to do when he comes in?" I said.

Spadafora looked at me and paused. He looked as if he hadn't gotten that far with his thought process. Before he could say anything, Halle appeared in the doorway. She wore a black business suit with a starched white shirt and a single strand of pearls. Three-inch patent leather pumps finished her ensemble. She was professionally dressed, but her sexuality smoldered under the surface of her professionalism.

"The police are here to arrest Russell. They are outside the suite. Did you call the Redmonds?" Halle said, looking at Spadafora.

"Not yet."

"You better," she said.

Spadafora picked up the phone and dialed. It sounded like he waited through the phone tree and then Redmond's secretary. The headmaster tapped his Cross pen and waited. He cleared his throat when Redmond came on.

"Yes, Rusty, it's John Spadafora at Crawford Academy," he paused and sort of winced. "Yes, sir I'm doing well. Yes, sir I like our chances on Sunday. Sir, I have some bad news. Russell is in trouble. There was a fight, and he hurt another boy." He spoke like he was trying really hard to be conversational despite the news.

There was a pause that interrupted Spadafora.

"I'm afraid it is a bit more serious than that, sir," Spadafora said.

"Well, sir. The boy Russ fought is in a coma."

Another interruption.

"Uh, well, Russ started the fight and had to be pulled off the other boy, sir."

Interruption.

"Yes, I believe the boy tried to fight back," Spadafora said. Another pause.

"Sir, the police are here to arrest him now."

As Spadafora spoke, I heard Redmond through the phone. He wasn't yelling or cursing. The voice sounded calm and measured.

"Yes, sir. I will hold them until you arrive. Yes, sir. Yes, sir." Spadafora hung up and shook his head.

"How are you going to hold the police?" Halle said from the doorway.

Spadafora exhaled hard and didn't look at her.

"Well?" she said.

"Penny, why don't you give me a goddamn break!" Spadafora snapped. His face reddened, and he looked like a man about to lose it.

Halle's eyebrows went up, but she didn't recoil in the least. She almost half smiled and left the office. The light fragrance of her perfume kicked up as she turned. It was nice—something subtle and expensive. She was a total bitch to Spadafora, but she was almost girlish in our hallway interaction the day before; the dichotomy puzzled me.

Spadafora made a few internal phone calls looking for Russ, but apparently, he wasn't in the classroom he was scheduled to be in. Spadafora asked the women in the office where he might be, and they all shrugged. He was on his way back into his office when his attention was broken with a disturbance.

"Don't put your fuckin' hands on me!" The yelling came from outside the administrative suite. "My old man will have your ass!"

It didn't take a clairvoyant to know that the young Mr. Redmond was outside the office. The three of us went out to assess the situation without saying a word. Two uniformed police officers were there with Russ. One was doing the official thing where they say you are under arrest and have the right to blah, blah, blah, and the other had his cuffs out and was letting Russ know it was required that he be handcuffed.

"Fuck that shit!" Russ said. His voice cracked just a little which let me know that he was stressing. Seeing me didn't help soothe him. "Fuck this asshole, too," he said when our eyes met.

The officer went to grab Russ's wrist to put behind his back, and Russ whipped his hand away. The rights reading officer had seen enough and pulled out his Taser. He flipped the switch, and I heard it hum while the light connecting the two electrodes flared.

"Fuck you!" Russ screamed at the Taser cop.

He sent the electrodes directly into Russ's chest.

"Awwwwwww!" Russ screamed, his body spasmed, and he went down hard. It was all a mess and a spectacle. He continued to yell in pain, but the cops turned him quickly and efficiently got him cuffed. Clearly, Russ had never been through such pain, and it was obvious that he was traumatized.

And it must've looked pretty bad to Rusty Redmond who came through the doors somewhere in the middle of this entire horror show.

"What the hell is going on!" The elder Redmond said as he broke into a trot coming down the hallway. Chico, Russ's workout partner, was right behind him, and Anne Marie, without a tray of brownies, was running behind both of them with tears streaking down her face.

Chapter Twenty-One

"Take the handcuffs off my son," Redmond said. The two cops responded. Chico stood behind Redmond, just off to the left. He showed no emotion, but I watched as his eyes went back and forth from the cops and Russ to his boss.

"Russell, oh my God, Russell," Anne Marie was near hysterical. Rusty remained focused on his son.

The cops looked at each other, unsure of their authority for the moment.

"I'm calling your chief," Redmond said. He had been a pretty good college tight end and still kept the frame. He was in his early forties and was about six foot four and 245.

"Oh, Russell..." Anne Marie continued to whimper.

Rusty seemed neither panicked, nor worried. He turned back to the police officers and held up his hand with his index finger extended like he had an afterthought for a waiter.

"Please do not leave," he said.

Chico looked me up and down without saying anything. In fact, he almost looked like he wasn't breathing—he was so still. He wore a yellow dress shirt and a pair of beige khakis that just looked a little strange on him, but they were probably what Redmond required. Whenever I saw him in the past, he had on a denim jacket with the sleeves cut off. Gone, too, were the piercings that filled his ear and sometimes his nose and cheek. The shirt only covered part of the tattoo sleeve on his right arm. A fire breathing dragon's tail still poked out.

Redmond waited calmly for his phone call to go through. His confidence was disarming and, right or wrong, he gave off an air of being in charge.

"Chief, this is Rusty," He paused. "Actually, not so well. Two policemen are at CA arresting Russell—something the school failed to tell me anything about. Apparently, there was some sort of pushing and shoving match. This seems like a bit of an overreaction." He paused again. ""Yes, certainly."

He handed the Blackberry over to one of the police officers.

"Your chief would like to speak with you," Redmond said. It wasn't dripping with sarcasm or self-important cynicism. He was too confident for that, and you didn't get the impression that this guy thought he was in a pressured situation. He was used to things going the way he dictated them.

"Yes, sir." the cop said. He looked like he was about twenty-five-years-old, and he shared none of Redmond's confidence. "Yes, sir. Yes, sir. We'll do that immediately, sir" Another pause. "Yes, sir, and we'll do that, too, sir."

He unlocked Russ's cuffs and looked up at his father.

"We're sorry for the misunderstanding, sir." the cop said. Redmond nodded.

"I think my son also deserves an apology," Redmond said. Russ smirked from ear to ear.

"Yes, sir. Sorry, Russell." the cop said. His face was now crimson, and his jaw muscles flexed.

It wasn't hard to see how Russ got to be Russ. His father wasn't smiling, but he also showed no sign of anger or distress. He also didn't look arrogantly pleased with himself. He looked like he looked when he came in—confident and focused.

"I think it would be best if Russ went home with me for the rest of the day. The chief is going to process this personally, and he assured me he would be released to me. Tomorrow, he meets with some important recruiters, and I want him at his best. Is that okay with you, Mr. Spadafora?" The tone of the question gave Spadafora the tacit respect of being asked without the legitimacy of it. It was clear what was going to happen.

"I think that's a good idea, Rusty," Spadafora said.

Redmond nodded at Spadafora and made eye contact with Russ, who now was not smirking. Redmond turned and headed to the exit with Chico and, without a word or hesitation, Russ and his mom fell in behind them as they headed out the CA's front door.

"You have always been so incredibly stupid and such an embarrassment," I hear Rusty say to his son, without any eye contact, as they went through the doors. Russ's nonverbals told me that was all that needed to be said for him to be put solidly in his place. They headed to the Mercedes parked in front of the school in between the two "No Parking Any Time" signs. Chico followed.

"Man, there's a whole lot of weird chlorine in that gene pool," I said.

"No shit," Spadafora said, shaking his head and walking back to his office.

I didn't feel the need to follow Spadafora into his office. It is a bit difficult to describe, but when a man in authority—or, shit, any man—gets dominated like that, it is tough on the psyche. I had already gotten to know that Spadafora saw himself as a man's man, and this was going to be tough for him to swallow. He was just forced to submit, and if this was an interaction between dogs, Spadafora was the dog on his back, offering his belly. It was also done in front of a student, which further added to his humiliation.

Living in the fight game, you are forced to think about this—or at least feel about this—all the time. There is a forever-silent dominance game going. Walk into a gym and you can pick out the dominant dogs. It isn't necessarily the biggest guy. I've been in gyms where the best fighter was 122 lbs., and the rest of the gym submits to him in one way or another. There are other gyms where the trainer, though old and physically weak, remains dominant, like the Dog Whisperer who knows how to control canines.

Every encounter in the ring is about dominance. It isn't always angry—in fact, it rarely is—but it is unmistakably about who is the top dog. An experienced boxer will spar with an inexperienced boxer without ego involved, but if the inexperienced fighter gets wild trying to prove something, the experienced fighter will throw a calmer downer: a shot with just enough steam to let the new guy know what he is really up against and what he needs to respect.

Nothing is said. Nothing needs to be said.

Dominance occurs, and it keeps order. When two alpha males square off, the issue needs to be settled to preserve the pack. When one pack goes against another and the alpha's authority comes into question, he will once again need to fight within the pack to keep his role.

"I can't believe he allowed that to happen," Halle said. I was lost in my thoughts and hadn't heard her come up behind me.

"Huh?" I said.

"He lets people with influence walk all over him. I wish he had some backbone."

I hesitated.

"I guess I shouldn't be airing the dirty laundry. I'm sorry." She frowned.

"Don't worry about it. It seems like everyone has been stressed lately."

She smiled at me.

"You are very intuitive to emotion, aren't you?" She looked me in the eye and held eye contact. She tilted her head and smiled.

Chapter Twenty-Two

By one o'clock, the day returned to its normal pace. I had settled into the boredom of sitting in the office and surfing the internet. I had visited every site I normally log-on to and checked out some that I occasionally visit. *The Archive of Misheard Lyrics* and *Disapproving Rabbits*, two of my favorites, killed forty minutes all by themselves.

I was typing 'AwkwardFamilyPhotos' into the search bar when she came in.

"Tough gig, Duff." It was TJ.

She startled me, and when it registered that she was in front of me, I got that twinge.

"Is that some sort of double-secret-Navy-Seal-ninja stealth move they teach you to use instead of knocking? Geez."

She smirked. Her mouth curved on one side of her face, and her eyes seemed to brighten.

"Navy? What are you trying to insult me?" She was wearing pressed, flat-front khakis; a V-neck, navy blue sweater; and brown penny loafers. "Army, buddy, army."

"Penny loafers? You really did go to Notre Dame, didn't you?" I said.

"Go Irish. They issue you khakis and penny loafers at freshman orientation."

Truth was, the khakis showed off the muscularity in her thighs and backside, and the V-neck with no blouse hugged her upper body ever-so-slightly. Every inch of her looked like it was economically built for efficiency. I had to make a point not to look.

"So, what's it been like here at Duffy's crisis counselin' center?"

I filled her in on the Rusty fiasco.

"Wow, this is quite the Peyton Place, isn't it?" She said.

"It's got its share of dysfunction, for sure," I said.

"Dysfunction. Listen to you. You really are a social worker, aren't you?" She smiled and made a face at me.

"I need you to be appropriate. Otherwise, you will face challenges in achieving your essential outcomes. Please make a good choice," I said with the best social-worky lilt I could put in my voice.

"God, that's scary," TJ said.

"Impressive, isn't it?"

"Not so sure." She shook her head. "How about the reason we're here—any students?"

"Been quiet. Haven't had a kid all day," I said.

"Are we really needed?" She frowned a little. I was trying to figure if she wore any makeup at all. If she did, she had mastered subtlety. "I mean, two counselors for what—two or three kids?"

"Yeah, I know what you mean. Sure, I've talked to a couple of kids, but I can never tell if this sort of thing helps or if it allows the school to brag that they're being sensitive and doing everything possible to blah, blah, blah, bullshit," I said.

TJ sat on the corner of my desk. She smelled nice—not like cologne, but something softer. I noticed a little glitter on the back of her hand. That seemed weird and just didn't fit with the rest of the ensemble.

"The glitter is a nice touch," I said to bust her chops, nodding toward her hand.

She jerked her hand up quickly, licked her index finger and rubbed at it hard. The smile left her face.

"Were you at a rave last night?" I said.

"I rave almost every night," she said. She bounced back quickly. For a second, I thought I had hurt her feelings. She stopped rubbing it and looked at it to make sure the glitter was gone.

"Hey, on the way in, I met Ms. Halle. She seemed pleasant," she changed topics abruptly and without explanation.

"Pleasant?" I said.

"Well, she was nice enough and professional. She showed me my office and gave me a quick orientation."

"Did you meet the headmaster?"

"Headmaster? Is he really called the headmaster?"

"Headmaster Spadafora." I smiled.

"You really like saying "headmaster,' don't you?" She gave me the smirk again.

"Yeah, I guess I do."

"What's he like?"

"Man's man type. Tries a little too hard at the handshake squeeze, the puffed-out-chest lifestyle."

"Sounds like someone I know." She raised her eyebrows at me.

"Oh, fuck you. I'm a sensitive man of the 2010s. You should know that."

"I know when we sparred, and you punched me in the face,

you did it nicely."

"See...'course some of my opponents would claim the same thing."

She giggled. It was another one of the rare times when she acted even a tad girlish.

Just when I wasn't sure where that repartee was going to take us, we were interrupted. It was Halle.

"Duffy, oh, excuse me," She looked at TJ and then back at me. "I see the two of you met."

I got that strange, high-schoolish feeling that I had just been caught at something. Halle's facial expression changed, almost imperceptibly, when she saw the two of us talking.

"There's two students here," Halle said.

Chapter Twenty-Three

"Is it wrong to be gay?" Finn was a redheaded, round and pudgy kid. He had green eyes and had the look of perpetual worry. "I mean, there's the Bible and that stuff, but I don't get why gay people get made fun of and bullied and stuff."

"No, Finn, I don't think it is wrong to be gay," I said. I wanted my voice to sound sure and confident.

"How do people get to be gay?" He said.

"I think people are just born feeling a certain way. You know, like you have red hair and I have blue eyes. It's just how you're born."

He sniffed, wiped the bridge of his nose, and broke eye contact.

"How come people switch? I mean there's this kid in my neighborhood, and his mom divorced his dad. Now she's living with a woman."

I wasn't sure how this fit in with grief and crisis counseling. Still, there wasn't anything manipulative with his approach. The kid seemed curious and a little troubled. Maybe we'd get to the troubled part.

"It could be that she tried to live like a heterosexual woman because of the cultural pressure of society and found that she couldn't. Maybe it was a matter of getting honest with herself."

Finn scrunched up his forehead.

"Could she have just gotten sick of Ryan's dad and decided to, you know, try women?"

I got that feeling I get when I'm not sure of something and felt pressure to have a very clear answer. I'm pretty sure there was a politically correct answer I was supposed to come up with, but it didn't feel right. I went against the urge to lie.

"You know, Finn, I'm not sure how that works. I think a lot of people say that it isn't a choice, but, because I don't have those feelings, I have to honestly say that I don't know."

I felt uncertain, but I felt the uncertainty would be easier to live with than bullshitting the kid.

"I think sometimes people choose," Finn said. He didn't struggle with his words. "But even if someone did switch because they wanted to, I don't think they should get picked on."

"I agree. You know, Finn, you sound to me like you got your

shit together." Sometimes I purposely cursed with teens to send the message that I'm a regular guy and to get them to pay attention. It was cheap, and sometimes I felt funny doing it, but, at times, it seemed to work.

Finn smiled and giggled a little.

"Did you know the coach?" I said, moving to another place.

Finn got quiet.

"Yeah, I used to talk to him sometimes. He was pretty cool. You know, he was a tough football coach and everything, but he was a cool guy, too." Finn bowed his head and got quiet.

"It really sucks that someone killed him," I said.

Finn started to cry but put no words to his emotion. I let him cry.

He took a few moments and then had to sniff and use a tissue. I handed him a box.

"People suck." Finn had stopped crying and looked away.

"Yeah, a lot of times they do." I didn't have any problems with the congruence of that statement.

"This school is fucked up," Finn said. His mood shifted.

"How so?"

"There's weird shit going on. I mean weird shit." Finn shook his head.

"Weird?"

Finn didn't say anything for a while and thought.

"You want to tell me what's weird?" I was getting really curious, but I didn't want to pressure the kid into talking about something he didn't want to talk about.

"There's all sorts of rumors. Kids say the coach was gay. Kids say he was doin' guys on the football team. Kids say guys were getting into weird stuff," he said.

I thought for a moment about what to say. I checked my gut and reminded myself about authenticity. I also tried to evaluate what I needed to know to help this kid and what I needed to know because I was curious as hell.

"What do you think about the rumors?" I said. When in doubt, go with an open-ended question.

"I think it's bullshit—sorry."

"You can say 'bullshit' in here. I don't give a fuck," I said back and winked at him. "Why bullshit?"

Finn smiled at that.

"I mean, I don't care if the coach was gay or not. I think it's possible, and I think people make shit up because that's what they do about gay people."

I waited.

Finn's face tightened. Now he was more angry than anything else.

"That could be," I said.

He pursed his lips and nodded. He took a deep breath. He didn't say anything.

I waited.

"Is it okay if I go now?"

"Sure. Thanks for coming in. It was cool talking with you." I stood up and extended my hand. He shook it.

"Thanks, Duff," he said.

Chapter Twenty-Four

"What did your guy have to say?" TJ was waiting for me in my office. She had a cup of coffee in her hand.

"Confidentiality babe, confidentiality," I said.

"We're on the same team. It is crucial clinical information that we need to triage and strategize."

"Triage, huh? Not bad."

She smiled.

"Being serious human services workers, we'd never lapse into gossip, would we? It's all about helping," I said with an affected aristocratic accent.

"Indeed," TJ answered back in the same tone. "Dish it, dude."

"Kid started off asking about whether being gay was right or wrong. Said he didn't understand people being mean to gay people if they, themselves, weren't gay. He couldn't understand why someone would be mean just because someone else was different," I said.

"Kind of how I feel every goddamn morning when I open my eyes," TJ said.

"Yeah." We both let that sink in for a moment. "Then he went on to say something sort of... I don't know."

"What?"

"It was just strange. He said there was something weird going on at CA. I got the impression it related back to his questions on sexuality. Like maybe it had something to do with being gay, or at least about sex."

"Holy shit..." TJ said.

"My guy said something similar. Said something was going on, and there were a lot of rumors about sex at school and sex with the girls at Crawford because they're easy."

"Hey, watch it. I went to Crawford."

"Yeah, can you speak firsthand about that?" She lifted her eyebrows and smiled.

"Leave me and what I did with my first hand out of this," I said.

She laughed out loud, and it turned into the giggle that I liked so much. She covered her mouth with her hand, but it continued. For whatever reason, laughter brought down her toughness, her soldier training, and whatever hardness the world had brought. I loved the girlishness without the intent of seducing or manipulating. It was magnetic.

"Seriously, what did you make of it?" I said. As much as I wanted to linger in that space where she was, I knew if I tried to force it, it would dissolve.

"It felt honest. The kid seemed like someone who liked the coach and was really uncomfortable with something."

"His murder."

"Well, obviously, but, as strange as it may sound, it felt like something more." She had leaned back with her arms folded. She crossed her legs at her ankles and her argyle socks showed.

"I felt the same thing," I said.

"What could be going on?"

"First of all, it's high school. It could be anything or nothing. The kids I work with are constantly filled with drama. They also tend to exaggerate and fabricate."

"Are you about to break into a rap?" She said.

"They be exaggeratin', fabricatin', obfuscatin', all about fornicatin!" I did my best rap impression, which was awful.

"Ice Double D, rockin the house!" She did that dance move where she raised her hands over her head and pushed up while bopping. Her sweater rose up just a bit and showed her waistline and belly button. It was an image I'd keep for a while.

We laughed again for a few minutes.

We were still laughing a little bit when Ms. Halle stuck her head in.

"I didn't realize crisis counseling was such a side-splitter," she said with a half-smile. It was tough to tell if she was sending a message or trying to build rapport. "It's after four, and I don't think there are any kids left, so, if you folks want to call it a day, feel free." She winked and left.

Her visit broke our momentum, and we were quiet with each other, which felt just a tad awkward.

"Hey, you wanna get a beer at AJ's with me?" I asked, trying hard to make it seem natural.

"Uh," She hesitated and her eye contact wavered just a bit. "I can't Duff."

More awkward quiet.

"No sweat, maybe a rain check?"

There was just a second of awkward silence. A second too much.

Rain check? What real person said "Rain check?" Was I Robert fuckin' Wagner all of sudden?

"Sure," she said.

Chapter Twenty-Five

TJ grabbed her knapsack and headed out. I did my weak, nonchalant 'See ya later' routine while my insides flipped.

I didn't like feeling this way. It felt out of control, like a force other than from me was driving what I experienced. I felt nervous, depressed, and angry all at once and without a lot of justification for any of it. Combined with what was going on with Bobby, it just seemed like too many uncertainties in my life all at once. Bobby, the job, TJ—it all made me feel off-kilter.

The gym or the bar were my alternatives. Both would relieve stress, and both had their strengths and weaknesses. Another off day from the gym might be good. As I've gotten older, I've learned that overtraining comes with a price, and rest was essential. I'm sure drinking heavily also had a downside. In the present moment, the downside didn't seem all that negative, and, like many other moments like this in my life, I deduced that AJ's would be tonight's right choice.

"Duffy," I heard a woman's voice call to me as I was turning the lights in my office off. It was Halle.

"Yes, Ms. Halle?"

She smiled and took a step toward me.

"Please, Penny."

I did my best to smile back. The smart, black suit had just enough Lycra in the pants to hug her thighs and backside. The silk blouse and the single strand of pearls looked expensive.

"Do you have time for a cup of coffee?" She hesitated just for a second. "I'd like to get your perspective on something."

"Sure," I said and laid down my bag. I thought she had just told TJ and me she was leaving for the day.

"Oh, not here. Is it okay if we go across the street?" She smiled with a hint of anxiety.

"Sure," I said.

She grabbed her purse and keys, and we headed to the staff parking lot just out the door of the administrative offices.

"Okay if I drive?" She headed toward a midnight blue BMW.

Across the street seemed to imply walking distance, but something kept me from arguing. I didn't ask where we were going.

"I'd like to get away from school if that's okay with you," she said. It was the type of statement that I could tell didn't require a response. We were quiet in the BMW, and the radio played the adult contemporary station. Elton John was in the background, and, because we didn't speak, it was the only sound in the car other than the engine's hum. She drove about a mile and a half and pulled into the Spice Man's parking lot. The Spice Man was a trendy fern bar in town. I'm sure it served coffee, but it was a bar, and it wasn't across the street.

"Do you mind if we sit at the bar?" She said.

"Sure."

"Hey Penny," the bartender said. He had a diamond stud earring, a shaved head, and wore all black. "The Carinalli?"

She nodded.

Jake poured a generous glass of white wine in front of her.

"What can I get you?" Jake said to me, pleasantly.

The chances of a place like this having Schlitz was less than slim. I didn't want to hear the list of seventy-two beers they carried, so I just ordered Bud.

"We don't have Bud. We have Pualaner." He said it like Pualaner was a beer that a bourgeoisie like me could stomach.

My new friend, Penny, didn't mention anything about coffee.

"Phew, I'm glad to be out of that place!" she said. She crossed her legs, showing white stockings under her black suit. She let her foot swing playfully.

"Cheers." She tapped my beer glass.

Pualaner tasted heavy, and skunky, and like someone had purposely tried to make it bitter. I'm sure that was my unrefined taste.

Halle reached back and kind of absent-mindedly rubbed the back of her neck, which, intentionally or not, pushed her breasts out in my general direction. She tilted her head and looked up at me.

"You're a heavyweight, aren't you?"

"Yes, ma'am."

"I like the sound of that." She exhaled and brought her hand down from the back of her head and rested it just above my knee. She tapped her fingers lightly.

When it comes to women, I don't feel like I just fell off the turnip truck. I feel like the turnip truck missed my house and forgot to pick me up. However, I think I got what was going on here.

"You were looking for my perspective on something?" I said.

She smiled on one side of her face. Her bright, red lipstick contrasted with her very white and very straight teeth.

"There's something I'd like to show you out in the car."

Chapter Twenty-Six

On the way to the BMW, Halle grabbed my ass.

"A heavyweight." It wasn't a question. It wasn't even really a flirt. It was some sort of declaration.

I didn't have a smart retort.

"Get in," she said with a nod. She hit the remote button and unlocked the passenger door.

I felt something intense. She knew what she was doing, and it was having the desired reaction. That became physically obvious. The power and control thing viscerally stirred in me, but it wasn't entirely pleasurable.

"You had something to show me?" I said. My mouth was a bit dry, and I could hear the sound of my own voice.

"Hmm..." She snickered "You could say that." Her stare pierced, and the smile left her face. She held the look and undid my belt and the top of my jeans with her right hand. She slid her hand inside the elastic of my shorts.

"I see I've had an effect."

I had no ability to make any response.

"Now, here's what I wanted to show you." She hit the power recline on my seat until I went fully horizontal. She lay across the console, positioning herself so she could do exactly what she wanted. She seemed entirely comfortable.

She found a way to tease. She was deliberate in what she did, like a craftsman. The intensity level would go through the roof, and then she would allow it to cascade down. She'd wait and even softly chuckle, and then she'd incrementally escalate what she was doing again. It was like she knew my body and what I was experiencing better than I did.

There was no sense of time, but I rode it up and down. I wanted it to last forever, and I wanted it to end immediately. She knew it. She knew it all, and she relished it.

She stopped without warning.

"I have something else to show you," she said quietly and with an absence of girlish flirtation.

She kicked off the pumps and shimmied her suit pants off. She rose up and fiercely kissed me with an open mouth while letting her weight slightly sit back. And with that, I was fully inside her.

Just as before, she maintained total control. I felt her

breathing deepen. She moved with greater direction, and she rose up and down noticeably with more energy. But it was all within a measure of control.

She ripped at my shirt, and I heard the buttons pop. She used her hands on my chest for leverage and her nails dug deep into the flesh of my pectorals. She moved in tight concentric circles, and she did muscular things that I had never felt before. She escalated to panting, and her movements ground hard into me.

Her nails had drawn blood, and when I looked at her face, she was slick with sweat. She continued to increase what she was doing and then fell to my chest and shook with a spasm. She opened her mouth and bit down hard on my shoulder, which happened at the exact time everything else did for me.

I almost blacked out. I shook, and the sweat pressed between the two of us gave me a chill. We stayed still for as long as possible while our breathing returned to close to normal.

She pushed herself off of me. My blood was left on her chin. She didn't so much smile as she did smirk. Our mutual sweat had soaked through her silk blouse. She lifted herself off of me and flopped herself on the driver's seat. There was no hurry on her part to get her pants back on.

"Did you notice the extra attention I give myself?" she said, coyly glancing at the smooth area between her legs.

A nod was about all I could muster. I let out a deep breath and began to straighten the seat.

"I bet you never fucked your vice principal before."

I shook my head. I took a deep breath and silently counted to ten.

"Maybe I'll call you a crisis counselor," she said.

Chapter Twenty-Seven

She didn't feel compelled to make any small talk, and she dropped me back off at the school.

"Take care of those scratches," she said with a short smile. "You have counseling to do, and we need you." Her eyebrows went up, and she feigned a bit of a pout.

"See ya," was the best I could muster.

I'm sure there were times in my life when I wanted a drink more, but I didn't know when. It's funny; as a guy, you spend your whole life fantasizing about such interactions—the random meetup that's all about pleasure—but actually living it left me feeling, I don't know… uneven.

Physically, if it was even physical, I had that post-sex mellowness that relaxed me. What I had experienced was intense, and there's no question it made me feel alive. It just left me feeling uncertain about something.

The sun was heading down as I got to AJ's and the boys were there. They're never not.

"Of course, there's always Danny Thomas," TC said.

"The guy that owned Wendy's? He named it after his daughter," Jerry Number One said.

AJ slid the first Schlitz in front of me.

"The daughter was That Girl," Rocco said.

"What girl?" asked Jerry Number Two.

"Margo," TC said. "That's Danny's daughter."

"Marlo," Rocco said.

"Hey, AJ, didya hear that? Rocco's orderin' wine!" TC said. "Do you even carry Marlo?"

AJ exhaled hard, shook his head, and looked disgusted.

"Danny Thomas did something weird with hookers and glass coffee tables. I read about it on the internet," TC said, focusing the group on the original point. I let their conversation fade the best I could.

I didn't feel good. I felt like I had done something wrong. I was halfway through the Schlitz, and I was able to identify the feeling as guilt. Guilt? Really? I'm a grown, unattached man who had a sexual experience with an adult, as-far-as-I-knew unattached woman who very much seemed willing—actually, quite a bit more than willing—to share some physical pleasure with me.

I was supposed to be giving high fives out. I was supposed to be calling every guy I ever met to let them know about the wild afternoon I had. I was supposed to be thinking about how to make this no-strings-attached hookup go on and on.

"And then, they'd do it right above him on the table," TC said. The conversation came back into focus while I waited for a second beer.

"That's the most disgusting thing I've ever heard," Rocco said.

"You don't want that after eating at Wendy's," Jerry Number Two said.

She was hot. I mean, I've never met a more sexual woman. A woman more comfortable with what she was doing, and, frankly, a woman that was skilled. She knew every move, and every move she made was executed more than expressed. Was that my problem? Was I upset that there wasn't an emotional component to this?

Geez.

She knew what she wanted to do, and she was able to strategize and go for it. She clearly had a high sex drive and knew what she wanted. What's wrong with that? I mean, maybe she did this five days a week with anyone she was curious about.

"The coffee tables had to be at least eighteen inches high for him to fit," Rocco said.

I was down to the bottom of my second—or was it my third—but it wasn't even close to being enough. AJ placed the next one on the coaster.

She was in charge, no doubt. That was part of what got her off, and, frankly, her level of control was exciting. She was confident, and she knew what she wanted. She knew how to do it.

Was I somehow equating that because the woman was in charge and doing exactly what she wanted sexually that she was bad, evil, or a whore? I hoped I was more evolved than that. I knew I didn't consciously feel that way, but was there some sort of Puritan thing that lived inside me?

"Why the hell would Danny Thomas want hookers to do something like that?" I heard TC say in the background while I thought.

This afternoon did have a measure of excitement, no doubt, but it also had something else to it. It was hard to put my finger on it exactly, but it was at the bottom of what was making me squirrelly.

"Some men like to be degraded, or at least being degraded excites them sexually," Jerry Number Two's voice came into my ear.

It stopped my train of thou'

    "What did you just say

    "Hey Duff, welcome back. Yu.

little world there," he said.

    "What were you just saying about sex?"

    "That some men find being degraded a turn on. .

linked in with the excitement of things."

    I ordered a glass of bourbon.

Chapter Twenty-Eight

Saturday

Al got up at 3:45 a.m. and insisted on breakfast. Ahh, a relaxing Saturday morning at the Dombrowski estate. There's something about a polished steel ceiling and walls that just makes me feel at home.

I don't care what Cesar Milan says about being the alpha or adjusting my energy;let him try to sleep in front of an eighty-five lb. black, brown, and white barking machine and ignore it. He'd being calling Oprah for a Dr. Phil appointment.

That soupy and sickish rush to the head greeted me as I got out of bed. There was no doubt that last night's Schlitz and the Jim Beam bender exacted a toll. Al jumped up to my thighs and scratched me with his nails, bounced off, spun around, and brought the barking up a pitch.

"Asshole," I muttered under my breath.

I got the Elvis bowl out, threw in two scoops of kibble, and slid it under his snout. Let the scarfing begin.

The incessant barking was replaced with a crunch-slurp-snort symphony. I put on the coffee, went and got my Church Street Gym sweatshirt, and turned on the TV. *Pawn Stars* was on, and it was the one where the old man buys a tiny, electric, red car. I waited until I heard thirty seconds of coffee brewing before I got up and moved the pot and replaced it with my mug. I know the first cups would be too strong, and the last cups too weak, when I did this, but I didn't feel like delaying gratification.

Al heard Chumlee arguing with Big Hoss and lifted his head from the bowl. He double-checked that all kibble was accounted for and then joined me on the couch, flopping his head on my thigh.

Despite being robbed of four hours of sleep, there was something about the pace of a Saturday morning that I liked. I'd wind up taking in way too much coffee, prolonging the lounging that came with no particular place to go and no time to be there.

Not getting to see Bobby left me uneasy. I know there were hospital rules in place, and I wasn't family, but I had a connection with the kid. I was connected to him in regards to the murder, his beating, and whatever led up to both of those events. I just wanted to know that the kid was all right. I wanted to know why Russ gave him such a beating, and I wanted to know the truth.

On *Pawn Stars*, Rick Harrison got a guy with a triple barrel shotgun down from $2,000 to $650. He said people think something is worth a lot, but, when you break it down, things are only worth what someone else will pay. He had overhead and couldn't afford to pay retail.

Rick was right. Rick was always right.

Last night Jerry Number Two said, "Some men get turned on being degraded."

Halle didn't degrade me. She used me sexually; that's what casual sex is, right? Man, I can't complain about her focusing on my pleasure—the experience was intense. I just didn't know where to file what happened. A fling? The start of something? A notch on my belt?

I felt embarrassed to feel this when men are supposed to drag their knuckles, eat, drink, and fornicate without any thought. All the angst I was going through was for women—it was what they read in *Cosmopolitan* and what they whined to their friends about. Letting this sort of shit trouble me wasn't manly, or at least it wasn't what a cliché man felt.

Maybe I needed to focus less on clichés and more on what I was going through.

Halle was powerful and confident. There was something else to her that I wasn't used to. The women I've been with, even ones that weren't long-lasting relationships, had some measure of vulnerability. There was a tenderness and a sense of opening yourself up to someone that was completely absent with Halle. Sure, she wanted me to feel good; there was no doubt about that. Still, I don't know if that was about making me feel good or about showing me what she could do to me.

What the hell was wrong with me? Why couldn't I just get laid, tell a friend, yuck it up, and get drunk?

Rick Harrison and Big Hoss got the art expert to come in. They just let a guy know that his piece of art was fake. It was a reproduction—a very good one, but it didn't have any value because it was a copy of the real thing and not the real thing itself. The guy trying to sell it was devastated and almost in tears.

I think I drifted into a light sleep, which is why I watched *Pawn Stars* in the first place. It was interesting, but not too interesting. It was perfect for naps and early morning sleep sessions like this. There was never any shouting or loud music like Sports

Center or the news stations seemed to have. I guess the point is to keep the viewer's attention. My goal was to watch something that would let me drift away a bit. *Pawn Stars* did the job.

Around eight, the phone rang and Al grumbled off my thigh, spun a half circle, and went to sleep on his back with his paws in the air.

"Duff, you want to do some sparring today?" Smitty said. "Guy from Brooklyn, 14-0, has an upcoming bout with a lefty. Wants you."

"Sure," I said.

"They want eight rounds. The kid can hit."

"Eight's fine."

"He's big, goes about 250."

"What time?"

"Eleven, okay?"

I lay back down but didn't go back to sleep. Knowing that you have a sparring session will do that. I made myself stay on the couch and rest, but I never fell back to sleep. Around ten, I threw stuff in a bag and headed to the Y. I had time to warm up, get loose, and get in some work.

Fat Eddy was monitoring the towels when I walked by the health club on the way to the stairs.

"They feedin' you to that monster?"

"Mornin, Fat," I said. Calling him "Fat" wasn't insulting. Over the years, it had become his given name. "What are you talking about?"

"That kid from Brooklyn is b-i-g."

Apparently, the guy I was fighting was above average in size, or at least that's what Smitty and Fat tried to convey to me. I hadn't met him yet, and two people had already mentioned it. I headed on to the boxing room, picking up the rat-a-tat-tat and loud thumps of the bags and the smells of leather, sweat, and body odor. I turned the corner and noticed right away that the gym was a bit busier than usual.

Across the floor was who had to be today's opponent. They hadn't exaggerated. He had to be six foot six and he was ripped. He had on expensive gear, and he was with a cornerman who had handled two or three world champions.

That was registering when I looked over at the wall mirrors and saw TJ shadowboxing.

The bell sounded, ending the round. As I walked to the ring, a shoulder bumped into me not-so-accidently. It changed my focus, and, when I looked to see who it was, I got a weird feeling.

It was Russ. He was sending a message.

Today was going to be interesting.

Chapter Twenty-Nine

I ignored Russ. The kid was born on third base and acted like he had hit a triple, but I didn't care. He was a high school kid— actually, an immature twenty-year-old with a state championship on his mind—and he was full of testosterone. There was nothing else to do with him. He moved to the heavy bag, and he and Chico did a drill where they exchanged body shots.

Seeing TJ was a different story for me, or at least it felt like a different story. I couldn't ignore her.

The in-between round interval is set at a minute, so social interaction in a boxing gym is really limited, and is yet another reason I like boxing. TJ came over in my direction and stuck out her gloved hand.

"You sparring today?" She said.

I nodded without saying anything. In the gym, you don't talk a lot about sparring. In the gym, keeping your mouth shut is usually a good move.

"Who?" she asked.

I gave the most subtle nod to the big guy that I could while I started to wrap my hands. Her eyebrows went up, and the work bell sounded.

I finished my left hand and started on my right. The big guy was loosening up in front of the mirror. He had the kind of muscular definition that comes from genes and not from bodybuilding. Or maybe I should have said genes and hard work. Often, really big guys don't move well, but this guy did; at least he did in front of a mirror.

"Duff!" Smitty called without looking for me as he came out of his office. I stepped toward him while I finished the wrap. "Not sure if I like this boy. Very big and very strong."

"It's cool, Smitty," I said. I always got a little nervous before sparring, but honestly, that's what gave me the rush of doing it— both during the fighting and after it was all over. If it wasn't dangerous, there wasn't any thrill to it. Without putting a little on the line, it wasn't any different from racquetball.

"He can hit." That was Smitty's way of saying the guy had power and that I should beware. I've been with Smitty for fifteen years; he was economical with his words, but I knew what every one of them meant.

I took two rounds to loosen up, slowly increasing the

intensity of my shadowboxing to get the body ready. I introduced myself to Trevor, my opponent, who smiled and shook my hand, and I did the same with his cornerman. I got my gear on, and the gym did what a gym does when two pros get in the ring together—especially when one's from out of town and with a famous coach. Everyone sort of acted like their workouts just ended naturally at that moment. Everyone was too cool to admit they were stopping to watch the show.

At the bell, we went to work. Like most sparring, it started off slow, with both of us circling. I threw a jab that he caught with his left without moving, and he immediately countered with a straight right. It hit my glove, but the power of it knocked the glove into the side of my head with some steam.

Smitty was right. The boy could hit.

I doubled up my jab—he parried the first, but the second one landed, and I had a little bit on it. I hit him between the eyes, solidly. He smiled and pushed out his lower lip to sort of acknowledge his interest in it.

He threw another jab that I saw coming from far away and followed it with a right hand. I blocked both easily, but the force of them moved me back a couple of feet. I went to counter, but I was now out of range, and I held my hook instead of throwing it and missing.

We circled some more, teased each other with a few jabs, and the bell sounded. My heart rate was up, and the sweat was flowing now, but, by all accounts, it was an easy first.

"Move to your right, away from his power, and don't trade. Stay on the outside and box him," Smitty said. He squirted some water in my mouth and toweled my face off in the area that my headgear didn't cover. The strategy he gave me was standard for when your opponent hit harder than you did. I knew; it didn't need to be said, but reiteration was what Smitty did.

I looked down through the ropes and saw TJ watching me. She half smiled and nodded, which, again, is about the right amount of cheering during sparring. TJ got it. Russ was behind her, and he was doing his best to look uninterested while riveting his attention on the ring.

The bell sounded us back to work and, like the first round, we began to circle. He threw out a telegraphed jab, really more of a range finder, and left it out. He was taller than I was, and I couldn't capitalize on his failure to recoil it. I took Smitty's advice and circled to my right.

I doubled up my jab again, with the same result. He blocked the first, and the second landed flush on him. This time he didn't smile. Instead, he looked a bit annoyed and flashed a straight right toward my head. He went a little wild with it, and I saw it and got out of the way. It left him out of position, and I stepped in, then scored a quick jab-straight left combination on him. Both landed, and I circled.

It was what I did best, and it was what Smitty wanted. Move in and out, land fast, and get out again.

He touched his gloves together in front of his face to sharpen his focus and to vent some frustration. I may not have hurt him, but I schooled him a little bit with my last move, and, in the boxing world, that hurt a fighter a little more than getting punched in the face.

He tapped his gloves together again and set his stance. Then he lunged quickly toward me with a jab followed by a straight right. He was moving forward with all his weight, and, even though I blocked the jab, it pushed me back and rocked me. The right came through the split the jab wedged open, and it landed square, hard, and with all of this man's momentum.

It happened fast.

And that's all of it I remember.

Chapter Thirty

"Oh shit," Smitty said. "Duff, oh shit."

There was laughter—a mean laughter.

Smitty looked up to see.

"Shut the fuck up, boy. Get the fuck out of this gym!" Smitty never cursed in front of people.

"Don't get up, yet," the other trainer said.

The room tilted like it does when you're on an amusement ride. The same nausea went with it. I vomited in my mouth and tried not to spit in on the ring canvas, but it got caught up in my mouthpiece and made me gag. It wasn't a lot, but I vomited in the ring.

"Sorry, Smitty," I said.

"He said something," a woman in the ring said.

"Get the headgear off," Smitty said.

I felt the headgear get tighter as someone fingered the buckle and loop. Then it loosened, and they pulled it off over my face. The action pulled my head back and raked my face. Another wave of nausea came. The room tilted the other way, and it got murky grey right before I felt it come up my esophagus. It tasted like pukey coffee.

I went to go toward the spit bucket, and I felt a couple sets of shoulders push me down. I vomited down the front of my t-shirt. It had that awful smell.

"His eyes aren't right," the other trainer said.

"I'm fine," I said and went to get up.

Again, hands on my shoulder.

"Just sit, son," Smitty said.

"I'm fine."

"He's trying to say something," the other trainer said.

Smitty exhaled hard, and I felt it on my face. There was a smaller set of hands on my shoulder, gently rubbing.

"Just sit, son. Just sit."

"Sorry man, I just threw my shot," the big boxer said.

I reached up to touch gloves and Smitty pushed my hands down.

"Just sit, son. Somebody hand me the water bottle."

Smitty gave me a spritz of water.

"Rinse your mouth, son."

I did.

"Spit."

I turned my head to spit, and it landed mostly on the front of me. I noticed the taste of blood.

"Let me get your gloves off, Duff," Smitty said.

I felt him pull back the elastic and undo the Velcro. My hands were wrapped thick, so he had to pull hard to get the gloves wrested from my hand. The jerk sensation sent my head again, and I threw up in my mouth. This time I could swallow it down. It happened again when he did the second glove.

"You want to try and stand, son?"

I nodded and pushed myself up from the legs. I lurched to my left and Smitty caught me. He pushed me back down.

"Sit back down, son."

I saw TJ and realized she was the one rubbing my shoulders. I caught a quick look at her face, and she wasn't smiling. Her eyes were fixed on Smitty.

"Just sit, son. Just sit."

Chapter Thirty-One

Monday

I opened my eyes from what had to be the deepest sleep ever.

"Good morning, Mr. Van Winkle." It was TJ, and she was removing a warm towel from my forehead.

You know that kind of sleep you get every so often where you wake up, and you're not sure what's going on? This was like that, times ten.

"It's Monday morning, around six," TJ said. "You slept most of Sunday. We went to the emergency room, and you have a concussion. They gave you some medication and said to sleep." TJ delivered the news with as little emotion as possible.

I felt a stirring near my leg and realized it was Al. He stretched and did his purr thing. He went back to nuzzling my thigh.

"Your friend there hasn't left your side. He's ignored a full dish since I got here."

"Al skipped a meal?" I said. It was kind of like saying, "Aliens took over the White House."

I sat up and got a little feeling of wishy-washiness. My head had a dull ache, but nothing I couldn't handle. I've been through this before. I decided to stand, and, when I did, the nausea increased a little.

"When did you get here?" I asked.

"I went with you to the hospital."

"And then came back this morning?"

She hesitated.

"I've been here since," she said.

"Should I be embarrassed if you saw me in my boxer shorts at the emergency room?" I went to make some coffee and noticed TJ had already done so.

"You should probably be more concerned about how you got into those sweatpants you slept in." Her eyebrows went up, and she tilted her head.

"Oh," I said.

"Yeah."

I felt strange for about eleven different reasons, and my head didn't help matters.

"Did I get any phone calls while I was, well, out?" I asked to be saying something.

"Some guy named Boggsy called from Las Vegas. Said you and he were old friends. Wanted you to know that Angelique got a role in some big deal production. He also said to TCB." She said it like she wasn't sure what any of it meant. It made me smile.

It was quiet for a second or two. There was a question I needed to have answered.

"Did you see the shot?" I asked. I wasn't sure I really wanted to know.

"Yeah."

"What happened?"

She pursed her lips a little and thought.

"You squared up in front of him, and he threw kind of a lunging jab-cross. You blocked the jab, but the force of it spread your arms. The cross hit you flush."

I thought about what she said. "Squaring up" meant I was straight in front of him with my feet together, pointing at him. You're supposed to be one leg in front of the other and at a forty-five-degree angle. It minimizes the opponent's target area.

Getting my guard blown away just means I wasn't strong enough or braced sufficiently to stop his shot. As a fighter, there was less shame in that than having my feet fundamentally out of position. Actually, like most things in boxing, one was a function of the other. My hands came apart more easily because I didn't have my feet underneath me enough.

"Would I have made a ten count?" I asked. It was important for me to know if I would've got up before a real ref counted.

TJ hesitated and looked like she was thinking. It looked like the type of thinking you do when you're thinking about what to say, not the kind you do to try to retrieve information.

"I'm not sure," TJ said.

The phone rang, and I welcomed the liberation from the awkwardness.

"Duffy?" the male voice said.

"Yeah?"

"It's Spadafora. Can you get here early today?"

It took a second for me to recognize that it was the headmaster from CA. You know that feeling when suddenly you remember the rest of your life? Like you'd been taken away from it for a while, and now you were being brought back to it.

"Sure, what's up?"

"There might be something to that gay thing about the coach."

Chapter Thirty-Two

"I got a call from a man, sounded fortyish, said he was in a relationship with the coach," Spadafora said. He said 'relationship' with a thick dose of sarcasm. "He said he thought he needed to talk to me about a few things at the school."

"Like what?" I said. TJ came to the school with me but went straight to her office. She hadn't really developed a relationship with Spadafora.

"He didn't get into it. Said he didn't feel comfortable talking about it on the phone. Said it could have something to do with what happened."

"Do you have any idea what he is talking about?" I said.

"No. I don't have any idea at all."

"Did he tell you his name?"

"No, he wouldn't identify himself when asked. I guess there's no telling if he was even legit." Spadafora squinted like he was thinking the situation over.

"Why would someone fabricate a story about having a relationship with the coach?"

Spadafora put his hands behind his head and leaned back.

"I don't know. Maybe, to make it some sort of gay agenda thing."

I didn't respond to that. I tried to think how claiming to have had a relationship with someone who was murdered would somehow advance an agenda. I couldn't really come up with anything. Something else had me curious.

"Why did you tell me this?"

He sat up, unlocking his hands and moving them from behind his head to resting on the desk.

"I don't know. I thought it might help you with your counseling thing. Or, you know, if it comes up you could, you know, find some shit out."

I nodded and thought about that. We both knew the rule on confidentiality, but I didn't feel the need to remind him and just decided to ignore his request. We both sat there quietly for a little while. I decided to see if there were any kids who wanted to see me yet. When I stood up, I got a sickish throb that traveled from the back of my head to the front. It didn't last long.

"Good morning, Mr. Dombrowski," Halle said. She was

standing next to one of the secretaries who was holding some papers and pointing something out. She wore a black skirt, knee-high, black leather boots, and a white top with a burgundy jacket. Very Sarah Palin-ish.

"Good morning," I said. I felt like her look lingered and that there was a hint of a wry smile. I, however, didn't have a lot of confidence in my perception considering the events of Friday afternoon and Saturday morning.

She went back to addressing her clerical issue, and I turned toward my office. TJ was in the threshold.

Her eyebrows went up, and she tilted her head as she gave me enough space to get into my office.

"What was that about?" she said.

Immediately, I felt something in my stomach. Something sort of like guilt.

"What?" I said.

"That look she gave you," TJ said with a smile. She smiled, but it wasn't a cheery smile—at least, I didn't think it was a cheery smile. Like I said, I wasn't trusting my perception this morning. A concussion and a lifetime of male-female relationship insecurity will do that to you.

"She gave me a look?" I said.

"Duff, c'mon." She wrinkled her brow and made a face. "Don't pretend to be so naïve."

"What are you saying?"

"The woman looked at you like a piece of meat," TJ said. There was intensity to her.

"Why should she be different?" I tried to laugh it off.

"I'm not talking about a flirty thing. I'm talking about a possessive thing. It wasn't nice."

I looked at TJ, tilted my head, and let my eyebrows go up.

"You got this from a split-second look she gave me as a walked by? You are some sort of psychic when it comes to passion or something."

TJ stuck her jaw out and exhaled hard.

"Never mind," she said. "I don't expect you to understand. Something bothered her.

"TJ?"

She didn't answer and walked out of my office.

Chapter Thirty-Three

I sat there feeling uneasy. You ever have moments when just about everything feels off? It's like what you're used to somehow changed. I had it in spades.

First, there was this head thing. Part of it was physical and made me woozy and tired. That concerned me, and concentration was challenging. There was something else, and this is a little hard to explain, but did you ever spend too much time thinking about your thinking?

"Am I dizzy?"

"Am I a little nauseous?"

"Am I dopey?"

"Am I having problems focusing?"

"Am I having problems thinking?"

Those were all the getting-punched-too-hard-in-the-head feelings. I like to pretend that boxing's dangers don't concern me, but, somewhere in the back of my mind, they did. I know about Ali's Parkinson's, Joe Louis's mental illness, and Sugar Ray Robinson's Alzheimer's. I'd be a complete idiot if that stuff didn't catch my attention.

Then there was the just-had-weird-but-very-intense-sex-with-a-stranger confusion.

"Was that really pleasurable?"

"Was sex strictly for fun wrong?"

"Was she in control, and is that bad?"

"Did I do anything wrong because of TJ?"

That last one felt the most true, but how could it be? TJ and I had nothing going on, at least nothing except what happened in my head. I had no idea if she had feelings for me other than as a pal and a professional peer. Why should I feel guilt?

Maybe because I betrayed a dream.

Man, no one has to tell me why I drink.

There are times I hate being inside myself. Fighting took me away from that, and drinking helped it temporarily. Neither was recommended by the AMA, but ever since I was an adolescent—the age of these boys who come to me for guidance and consolation—it was what I had done.

I'm not sure what that meant about my "coping skills," my "adjustment," or my overall "mental health."

Fortunately, a knock came at the door, and I prayed it was a troubled kid who could steer this troubled semi-adult away from his own angst.

It was.

Aidan, the slight teen that had said the coach meant so much to him after the two had talked things over, was at the door.

"Do you have time to talk, Mr. Dombrowski?" he said. He was quiet and unsure.

"It's Duffy, Aidan." I smiled at him and stuck out my hand. He looked confused at first and then shook it. "C'mon in."

"Are you getting a lot of kids coming to see you?"

"I don't know if I'd say a lot. A few. Maybe a few more than a few."

He looked away. It was like he was working up to saying something.

"Is it normal to not like yourself? I mean, is it normal to question everything you feel and think?"

I thought about it for a second. I wondered if the kid had more insight than I did.

"Yeah, it is." I thought for a beat or two. "At least, I feel that way a lot."

He nodded. He went back to looking away.

"If I knew something about the coach, should I tell you? I mean, if I didn't think it had anything to do with anything, should I tell you?"

I gave that a second. That's all I needed.

"That's up to you, Aidan."

He looked down, then back at the wall.

"I saw the coach walking down Lark Street holding hands with a man once."

Chapter Thirty-Four

"So, when you saw him holding hands with another man, what was that like for you?" I said. I tried to keep it open-ended and allow for him to express what he wanted without me tipping my hand in terms of anything I might expect.

"What was it like for me? What do you mean?" Aidan looked confused.

"I mean, what did you feel like?"

He thought for a moment.

"I don't know. My stomach felt a little funny. I didn't know what to feel." He paused. "I wasn't, like, disgusted, you know."

"Uh-huh," I said, hoping he would continue talking.

"I don't get why people beat gay people up just for being gay. I didn't feel anything like that. You know, unless they were trying to force you to do something you didn't want to do."

I thought about that for a second.

"And forcing you to do something you didn't want to do would be reason to defend yourself in ANY type of circumstance," I said to affirm what he said and keep him talking.

"Maybe I felt a little sad when I saw them."

"Why sad?"

He itched under his nose and then exhaled.

"Just that what people said about him was true and that he had to be made fun of for it."

I let that hang there, not for any clinical reason, but because I couldn't think of anything to add. This kid had insight.

"The coach was a badass guy. I know lots of kids hated him because of his discipline, but, if he punished you, it wasn't just because he wanted to be a dick. It was because, you know, you did something against the rules," Aidan said.

"That was his job."

"So, if you got busted for something, instead of admitting you fucked up, you could just call him a fag or something like that. Like somehow if a guy's gay then you can, like, make your screw-up not count ,even if you're totally wrong."

I just nodded.

"That's fucked up," he said.

"Yeah."

Aidan waited a beat or two before he spoke again.

"Do you think I'm gay?" he said and looked right at me.

"I don't know." I shrugged.

"C'mon, I come in here and asking a bunch of gay questions. You must think I'm gay."

"Sure, it dawned on me," I did my best to get in touch with the truth. "When someone asks a bunch of questions about a topic, I naturally think about their interest. If you came in here and talked a lot about football, I guess I'd think a lot about whether you played, or you were a fan or something like that."

He pursed his lips and looked to the side and then down the front of his shirt.

"Aren't you supposed to say shit like 'It never dawned on me.' Or 'it's not important.' Or 'I see all people the same.'

"That would be bullshit," I said.

"Yeah."

We sat there without saying anything. It seemed like a long time.

"Are you going to ask me if I'm gay?" Aidan broke the silence.

"No," I said.

"Why not?"

I thought about it for a second.

"In this counseling shit, the goal is to stay focused on what the person who comes to see you sees as important. I don't think it's important to what we've been talking about."

"I've talked almost only about gay stuff..."

"No, you've talked about losing someone who meant something to you. You've talked about people being mean to others for shitty reasons. You've talked about being confused about how the world and the fucked up people in it work." I paused. "Aidan, that's not gay stuff. That's stuff that every fucking one of us worries about every fucking day."

He sat back in his chair. He looked like he was thinking.

"You know what else? It really isn't just in counseling that this is the stuff that is important. It's in life," I said.

He nodded.

"Yeah," he said.

Chapter Thirty-Five

TJ knocked at my door, and I called for her to come in.

"Who are all the guys in the fancy golf shirts?" she asked.

"Oh, the recruiters? Are they here again?" I said. "They're trying to get some of the CA stars to go to college down south for a great education and to play themselves some ball."

"Play themselves some ball?" TJ repeated.

"That was me doing Bear Bryant."

"Who?"

"Never mind. Let me tell you about my session." I told her about Aidan seeing the coach holding hands.

"Are you going to tell Spadafora?" TJ asked.

"No."

"Really?"

"It's not any of his business, nor is it any of his concern. It was said within the confidentiality. It also doesn't further any of his investigation, if that's what we'd call it."

TJ thought about that for a while.

"I talked to another kid who had more strange stuff to say." She was half sitting on the side of my desk with one foot on the floor and the other dangling. The dangling-leg thing made my stomach feel something.

"Strange? This is the second time we've heard stuff like this."

"Yeah, he insinuated again that some kids were getting into weird stuff at CA. Stuff that they wouldn't want people to know about. Stuff that they kept secret." She ran a hand through her spiky hair.

"Except, if this kid knew about it then it wasn't a well-kept secret, or he was part of it and was giving you a back-handed, half-assed confession," I said.

"This wasn't one of the 'in' kids. I think he's heard rumors, but not specifics."

I thought for a second. I decided to think out loud.

"What kinds of things do people, in this case, high school teenagers, keep secret?" I looked at TJ and raised my eyebrows.

She raised her eyebrows and exhaled.

"Well, anything that would get them in trouble," she said.

"Which would be?" I continued my Socrates act.

"Uh, breaking school rules, illegal things, shit that would get their parents mad..."

I sat up and put my elbows on the desk.

"Ahh, that shit always comes out, even when they pretend they don't want it to." TJ looked at me like she wanted more. "I'm thinking the stuff that people almost always freak out about are drugs, money, and sex."

"Sometimes all at once," TJ said. She didn't smile or laugh.

"Yes."

We were both quiet for a moment.

"There's a secret here at CA. There's a weird feeling to the place, a weird dynamic, and an old school sense of protecting the name. I don't like it here. I didn't when I went to Crawford and never liked the place as an adult."

TJ folded her arms.

"You sure this isn't some sort of deep-seated macho thing that's lingered since they beat you on homecoming?"

"Well, there's that," I laughed. "I think it goes beyond that."

TJ nodded and smiled out of one corner of her mouth. She had a way of smiling that lit her eyes.

"You do let macho stuff influence you, don't you?" she said. It caught me a little off guard.

"What do you mean?" I knew what she meant. I just needed time to respond.

She pursed her lips, tilted her chin down, and squinted in mock fashion.

"Oh, I don't know. Maybe it's the insistence on fighting, despite the threat of permanent brain injury. Maybe it's the little psychological wars you seem to engage in with every other male, or the way you, almost imperceptibly, size up and evaluate every other guy you come in contact with."

I smiled. Either I was more transparent than I realized, or TJ knew me better than I thought.

"Doesn't everyone see the competition in everything in life?" I said.

"No, Duffy, they don't."

"C'mon, everyone worth a damn."

"No, Duffy."

"This coming from Miss—oh, excuse me—Ms. MP Iraq veteran leading a group of men on some Humvee while taking on fire from all angles. If that isn't competition, what is?"

Her face went cold. She unfolded her arms and stood up. She

looked away.

I wasn't exactly sure how what I said was wrong, but I could tell by its effect that it was.

TJ left.

Chapter Thirty-Six

It was one of those moments that you replay over and over in your head. I didn't think I said anything wrong, but TJ's response wasn't at all what I expected. Was that on her or me?

Do you apologize for something that a person took the wrong way? The same person who spends all her time busting your chops?

I guess the answer is that if you hurt someone's feelings, even if you didn't mean anything by what you said, you should check in with them. Maybe it requires an apology, and maybe it doesn't, but if you want to keep a relationship with someone, it means you have to touch base.

I walked to TJ's office.

"Hey, sorry, I didn't—" TJ didn't let me finish.

"You didn't say anything wrong. Don't worry about it." She didn't look up.

"I—" Again, I got cut off.

"I appreciate it, Duff. We're cool." She hesitated. "It's my shit."

I stood in the doorway for a second, feeling like an idiot, while TJ pretended to do paperwork. I wanted more resolution. I wanted to know what her "shit" was. I wanted to really know that I was all right by her.

I also knew I wasn't going to get any of that. So, I headed back to my office. I didn't see TJ the rest of the day, and the afternoon dragged on. At a little after four, I grabbed my crap, stuffed it in a knapsack, and went to head out.

"Feel like coffee?" Halle had just appeared. She was leaning against my doorjamb with her boots crossed at the ankle—her right boot tilted on the toe and the four-inch heel parallel to the floor. She had just the hint of a smile. Actually, it was more of a smirk.

"Uh…" came out of my mouth.

"Relax, I was just kidding. I'll be here most of the night doing reports." She folded her arms, and the smirk turned more into a smile.

"I'm heading to the gym." I felt awkward.

"I hope we can have coffee again. Sometimes, I have to get out of here for a good, strong cup." The smile left her face.

"Yeah." Despite the Mae West line, I felt something inside. It was a mishmash of desire, excitement, nervousness, and a couple of other things it would take a bourbon, or two, to sort out.

It didn't feel good..

I stepped toward the doorway, and Halle didn't move. She waited until we were almost touching, then she turned just ahead of me and kind of leaned out of the doorway. I got a breeze of her cologne. It was what she wore in the BMW. That scent would stay with me forever.

I passed her and headed toward the exit. When I looked up, I saw TJ in her doorway. Our eyes met, and she turned away.

I headed down the stairs, and, as I did, I got a little bit of a woozy head rush. It wasn't bad, and, with the day I've had, I couldn't tell if it was the punch I took or the series of interpersonal interactions.

I was going to head over to the medical center, but, before I got involved in that, I needed to do something else. On days like today, when shit swam around my brain and things didn't seem to order themselves, working out helped sort them out. Maybe things got sorted, or maybe the muscle exertion and stress to the cardiovascular system relaxed me, so I got less anxious about figuring out the world. I didn't know what the answer was, but I knew I felt better after I sweated through my ratty, old t-shirt and hit things.

Actually, getting in the ring with another man was the best. Partly because of the workout, but more because it was a microcosm of facing my fears and pushing through them anyway. Going up against adversity was good for the soul, and it made it feel like I did something. In other words, it returned some of the power that life sucked away or maybe gave me the illusion that some of the power was being returned.

There was also a meditative aspect to fighting in that, while doing it, the mind had to be emptied. The kung fu jerk-offs sort of had it right with the "mind like water" and "empty mind" bullshit. Me—I just think it was a matter of not having time to think, because, if you did, it increased the chances of getting punched in the face.

That's probably as deep as I got.

The familiar sounds echoed off the stairwell as I headed into my meditative retreat known as the Crawford Y Boxing Club. It was dark and humid, and it smelled of BO and chlorine. I got there mid-round, and four or five guys were working various stations. Malik was back after a month in county lockup and was hitting the speed bag. Pig was laboring on the heavy bag while Carlos, a relatively new middleweight up from Brooklyn, moved in front of the mirror. There was another tall, lanky light heavyweight I had never seen before.

I started to wrap my hands when the bell ending the round sounded. Pig and I bumped fists, and Malik, Carlos, and I exchanged nods. The new guy didn't make eye contact and probably wouldn't until he spent enough time in the gym to pay his dues. Until then, he didn't carry the rank of social interaction.

Smitty emerged from his five by five foot office and stood in the doorway.

"Duff!" he called to me and motioned with his hand.

I headed over to his office.

"What's up, Smitty?" Usually calls to the office meant an upcoming fight or some paid sparring.

"Go on home," Smitty said.

"What?"

"Go on home."

"What are you talking about?" I said.

"Go on home."

"You worried about my head? It's fine. I ain't sparring today. Going to take it easy."

Smitty looked at me. He looked at the floor and then back up at me.

"Duff, it is time to quit," Smitty said.

Chapter Thirty-Seven

I laughed.

"I ain't playin'," Smitty said.

"I got lit up Saturday. It happens. I've had my bell rung before. It comes with doing this."

"You're getting hit more than I like. You're going down more, and there's some things I see I don't like."

His expression remained the same. I could tell that he wasn't enjoying this conversation, but he didn't hesitate, he didn't struggle with his words, and he didn't hedge.

"Alright, I'll take another week and just run, but I still think you're nuts," I said.

"No."

"What do you mean 'no'?"

He looked me straight in the eye.

"I mean you're done, Duffy. It's over."

My stomach felt sick. I looked into Smitty's eyes, and he looked at me hard. I turned away because I felt myself start to well up. I didn't want that in here.

I undid my wrap, threw it in the bag, and left without saying anything else.

It was hard to walk up the stairs. I suddenly felt unreal, like I was disconnected from myself. Sweat ran down the back of my neck along my spine. My vision narrowed. I was almost outside of my body.

"Watch it!" Something jarred into my shoulder.

It knocked me out of my trance.

"Punch-drunk fuck, watch where the fuck you're walking."

It was Russ.

"What did you call me?" I said.

"Punchy, you're fucking retarded from all the punches. Go drool on yourself." He went to turn around. I dropped my bag. I reached for his shoulder and turned him around.

"What?" he said.

I hit him with a right hook in the stomach. He didn't have a chance to tighten up, and it knocked the wind out of him. I threw a left hook into his kidney and a right just under his floating ribs. He went down hard on his knees.

I reached down and grabbed him by the throat, lifted him up, and slammed him into the wall. I headbutted his forehead and left my eyes in front of his.

"You, you fucking piece of shit, have no right—"

"Duffy—Jesus!" A forearm slammed on mine, and it broke the chokehold I had on Russ. "You're gonna fuckin' kill 'em!"

I felt a force push my body into the wall, and Pig came into focus.

"Duffy, Jesus Christ, Jesus fuckin Christ!"

"That fuckin' bitch cocksucker should die!" I yelled. I tried to push Pig off of me, but he was huge, and he smothered me.

Russ was coughing on his hands and knees. His whole diaphragm went up and down violently.

"Remember that you fuckin little bitch. Remember how you feel, and that I did it to you. And think of what comes out of your fuckin' mouth."

"Duffy, Jesus Christ, Jesus Christ." Pig pulled me out of the stairwell and through the push-door. He lowered his head and continued until I was in the locker room.

"Man, Duffy. Go home. See an exorcist or something. I love you man, known you for years, but I ain't never seen no shit like this from you." He was sweating, and his chest heaved.

I felt reality starting to creep into me. I felt scared. I felt panic, and I felt the beginnings of regret. Pig was still holding my shirt. He was breathing hard, and he looked scared, not of me, but scared of what was happening. His sunken eyes glared at me.

"Duff...Duff?" Pig said. He pushed against my chest to get my attention.

I looked down. I felt like I was going to cry.

"Sorry, Pig. I-I-I-"

Pig nodded at me, then raised his eyebrows. He didn't let them down until I nodded.

"I'm good. I'm alright," I said.

"You're leavin', right? You're not going in there and killing that fuckin' asshole kid, are you?"

"No."

"You promise?" Pig said.

"Yeah."

Pig backed up, keeping an eye on me as he walked backwards. I nodded at him and waved a hand, letting him know I wasn't going back into the gym. He kept looking at me.

I looked down and swallowed hard. I didn't want Pig to see me like this.

Chapter Thirty-Eight

"You gonna have another?" AJ said. It was dark outside. The Foursome was gone. It was just me and AJ.

"Yeah."

"Both?"

"Yeah."

AJ poured a Schlitz and refreshed the ice before pouring another Jim Beam. He placed them in front of me. I felt him linger.

"Something happen today, Duff?" AJ said.

AJ almost never got involved in conversations.

"Huh?"

"Not my business, but you seem...I don't know, not yourself."

Things moved a little slow. The drinking had taken the edge off the intensity, but my stomach felt sick.

"You know what I do, right?" I said.

"What you do?"

"Yeah."

AJ made a face.

"You're a fighter, and you're a counselor." He waited a second. "You're a dog guy. You're an Elvis fan. You like Schlitz and Beam. That covers it, doesn't it?"

I sipped the bourbon. After as many as I had, there was no harshness to it. It went down like Kool-Aid.

"Which one did you say first?" I said.

"Huh?"

"No, serious. When you said the things I do, which one did you mention first?"

AJ squinted and tightened his lips.

"I said you were a fighter." AJ had both hands on the bar. He looked like he was trying to understand me.

"How many fighters you know?"

"Personally? That's easy. One. You."

"Yeah." I sipped the beer. I felt something behind my eyes.

AJ shook his head. He took a breath and let it out slowly. The front door opened, and Kelley walked in. He took his seat to my left. I felt him look at me, and they lingered longer than they usually did. He and AJ made eye contact.

"Michael Kelley, crime fighter, good evening, officer," I said.

"What's up with you? Doing some sort of research for the

twelve-step programs?"

His hat rested on the bar, and he had untucked his shirt. He was definitely off duty.

"Anything new on the coach's murder?" I said. I didn't want to talk about the other stuff.

"They're now looking into the gay community. The bridge, the time of night, the rumors—it all seems to have some connection. Maybe some sort of hate crime, maybe something that's about to go serial, or a killer who used to target gay men and who took a break."

"Froggy tells me the coach wasn't a player," I said. The drinking loosened me up, and I wasn't going to hesitate to infringe upon our friendship for information.

"Froggy wearing the gold glam bike shorts and Hawaiian shirt when you spoke with him?"

"Yep."

"High top, pink Chuck Taylors?"

"Yep."

"Refer to the guy built like an inside linebacker he was with as 'Miss'?"

"Yep."

He sipped his beer.

"There's a source."

"Froggy's never lied to me. He said the coach hung around sometimes but didn't play in the reindeer games. Said he was known, but definitely not a player," I said. I drank some bourbon.

"Reindeer games? You getting some of your own bike shorts and taking a bridge walk soon?" Kelley said.

"I think the coach was in a committed relationship and went to the park for some other reason."

"Most of the people who make a bridge trip are in committed relationships, usually, to women," Kelley said. "No reason a gay guy couldn't step out on his partner for anonymous sex in the same way."

"True, but I don't think that was the coach's thing."

"They've identified a couple of high school kids who had started to hang out in the park recently. Trying to find out what their story is."

I thought of Bobby.

"You mean like, having sex in the park?" I said.

"Don't know. Maybe that, maybe looking to cause trouble for the guys in the park. Who knows, maybe they were just there getting high," Kelley said.

"When we were in high school, hanging out in Jefferson Park meant one thing, didn't it, Kell?"

"Yeah."

"It meant gay sex or 'rolling fags' for having gay sex, right?"

"Yeah."

Chapter Thirty-Nine

Kelley tried to convince me to take a cab, and, when I gave him shit, he left with my keys. That was Kelley. He didn't say anything, but he took them off the bar and left. No threats, no bitching, just action.

It was why he was a friend.

I had that multiple-hours-of-drinking drunk. It was the kind that was a steady intoxication—not like the buzz from the first four or like the craziness of eight. It was a long-haul drunk. I'm a little embarrassed to admit I knew quite well how it felt. I thought I knew how to manage it and, even through my drunken state, "knowing how to manage it" felt a little dysfunctional.

When I got like this, I walked. I wouldn't be sober in an hour, but it would lessen, and the motion would make me less miserable. If I went home, I might fall asleep for an hour, but then I'd wake up and stare at the ceiling for a long time with an unquenchable beer-thirst. I hated that.

No, walking would be better.

A mile or so from AJ's, I took the right on Lark Street. Even though it was after two, it still showed signs of life. This was Crawford's Greenwich Village, and the gay clubs stood side-by-side with the straight clubs. There was a head shop and a hip sex shop. "Hip" in the sense that it catered to couples, women, gays and had more of a boutique feel than an all guy, heavy breathing, hairy palms joint.

I thought about heading into a bar for another Beam, but, at this point, it wouldn't improve my drunk—it would just give me something to do. I couldn't get any drunker, and I was getting low on cash. I went past The Works—the city's oldest gay joint—and the house music blared out the front door. I looked at the signs on the front window for the upcoming Lights Festival featuring Gloria Gaynor and another poster for The Men's Health Clinic that recommended regular AIDS and STD screenings.

It dawned on me that, in some ways, the gay community had its shit together more than the straight community. You didn't see STD and AIDS warnings at straight clubs, and, Lord knows, you should.

I crossed the street and saw that Café California was busy. It was the place for twenty-somethings, mostly from money, who drove in from Vorheeses Park to try to affect a hipness. I went down a curb that I didn't see, and it jarred me. Right after that, I got a wave of wooziness that felt like the feeling I got when I was hit. I hated the feeling—not because of its discomfort, but because it reminded me of what had happened.

I did my best not to think—a skill I spent a great deal of time trying to master. It didn't work, and the effort, mixed with the bourbon floating through my digestive track, sickened me. I threw up in my mouth a little, which reminded me of the fact that that particular act had become an expression with the kids. I swallowed and knew that the next time I heard someone say it, it would have a different meaning.

Le Sexe Shoppe was straight ahead with its purple black lighting and window showcase. I moved toward it just to smirk at whatever was in the window. The nipple pincher things with small chains caught my eye and made me wince. A large, black, latex thing called "The Mandingodonger" made me think for a moment, and I felt bad for Ken Norton, the former champ who starred in *Mandingo*. Norton had an unbelievable body and got ripped off the three times he fought Ali. I thought it was embarrassing that he was in the slave movie and how he had become synonymous with the term "Mandingo." I'm guessing his estate wouldn't win any potential lawsuits over this product.

Simulated body parts designed to be filled with real body parts bewildered me. My self-esteem is pretty low to begin with, but if I were ever alone in my trailer and caught sight of myself humping a little mound of latex fashioned to look like Jenna Jameson's privates, I don't know if I'd ever not need psychiatric help. This was the stuff that they proudly displayed in the window. It made me wonder what was in the stockroom.

I was grateful when the jangle of the bells broke my train of thought when a couple came out of the front door. The street light backlit their silhouettes just enough that I could see that the woman, who, best I could tell, was put together pretty well, wore one of those spiked, chrome dog collars. Her shiny, patent leather pants reflected the streetlights.

My mind works funny. All I could think of was what the two went to the store for. It was after 3 a.m. now, and she was all decked out in horny wardrobe. What, precisely, did they need to pick up? Did a nipple clamp need WD-40? Were they out of latex disinfectant? Were they returning spoiled edible panties? I mean, what were they up and out for, and what possible consumer goods could they need at this hour?

They headed back in the direction I came from, toward The Works. I gave them a few strides and decided that following them was about the most interesting thing I could do. They started to hold hands, and then she reached around and grabbed the guy's ass. He yelped playfully and grabbed her, and they kissed deeply. The juxtaposition of the dog collar, latex outfit, and romance was a bit hard to process.

As they walked up the short hill to The Works, there was a certain familiarity to the gait or the stride of the woman. I was barely sober enough to be critical of my own perception, but I couldn't deny a sense of knowing. I concentrated on the man, and the same type of feeling began.

I kept a comfortable distance behind them, and, when they stopped to talk in front of The Works, they turned just slightly into the neon glow of the bar window's Stoli Lemon Vodka light. The light was an odd yellow-green, and the different colors made fine details difficult to make out. The half bottle of Jim Beam probably didn't sharpen my perceptive skills, either. Something told me to hang back—something reflexive.

The two stopped to speak briefly, and then they went into The Works.

I studied them.

It couldn't have been.

This was just some sort of drunken, Freudian delusion, right? No, no way.

I needed to start going to AA.

Because, if I saw what I thought I saw, I just watched Vice Principal Halle, dressed in fetish gear, go into a gay bar with a man I recognized.

That man was Russ.

Chapter Forty

Man, I wish I wasn't drunk.

This would've been hard enough to process without the buzz, but I didn't trust my perception with the alcohol. I mean, what I just saw was pretty unbelievable. I was drunk, but I've been this drunk before, and I don't remember hallucinations being part of the package.

That was them.

I know what I saw. At least, I think I knew what I saw.

Halle and Russ, out at night and going to a gay bar. What did that mean?

Yeah, I could've done without the booze.

So what do I do? Something told me not to go in and confront them—not that I had anything to confront them on. I'm sure there's a rule on dating students, but Russ was a senior and was of legal age. I also wasn't even an employee of CA, and it was none of my business. As for going into a gay bar, well, there was an underage thing, but I couldn't even tell if Russ was drinking. Of course, out at 3 a.m., accompanied by a woman with a dog collar, might suggest that underage drinking would be the least of what was going on.

My feelings were muddled. I did my best to sort them out, but it wasn't easy. There was definitely anxiety, but that was a friend that seldom left me alone. There was also a bit of revulsion, and I couldn't pinpoint where that came from. Part underage thing, part my hatred for Russ, and I'm sure the confused emotions over Halle figured in.

There might have been something else. Something else that I might not be able to admit except for the medication I had partaken in all evening.

Jealousy.

Yeah, deep inside me, in that place that I don't even like to admit to myself that I have, something stirred. It was something ugly.

Russ looked to have gone where I had gone. Fucking Russ appealed to Halle—what did that say about me? My self-esteem was in the sewer anyway, and this notion, through the Beam-haze, sickened me. It pissed me off.

Sure, I didn't have great feelings about what I did with Halle, but, at least, somewhere in there was that perverted, male feeling of conquest. If she did it with Russ, that made me no better than him and maybe not even as good. None of my thoughts or feelings were clear, but my confusion didn't diffuse the intensity of them.

I wanted to hit something.

Jesus Christ, I hated myself.

"Lookin' for a date, handsome?" The words broke my train of thought. I waited for my head to clear and my perception to focus. It was Froggy.

"Oh, Mr. Duffy, are you okay?" Froggy said with his Caribbean accent. He was alone.

"Hey, Froggy."

"You standin' out here decidin' whether or not to join our team?" His eyebrows went up.

"Not yet, Frog," I said.

"Uh-huh. You just standing on Lark Street, in front of The Works, at three in the morning? Uh-huh..."

I let it pass.

"Hey, Froggy, is it common for straight people to go to a gay club?"

"Depends on the club. Lotta women dance at The Works because they don't want to get hit on when they dance with their friends. Lots of fag hags."

"Fag hags?"

"You know, girlies who always have gay male friends."

"Oh...What about straight men?"

Froggy rolled his eyes.

"You'd have to define straight. Sometimes, the hags will bring a male friend to dance with, but that always seemed a little weird to even Froggy."

"Why weird?"

"Mr. Duffy, a straight man can dance any place—why would he come to a gay bar to strut his stuff?"

"I don't know..."

Froggy let out an exaggerated sigh.

"L-a-t-e-n-c-y, Mr. Duffy. Like you staring at the entrance at almost three in the morning," Froggy said.

I tried to think. It had been an hour and a half since my last drink, which didn't make me sober, but I was on the way down in terms of intoxication. Thinking was getting easier.

"You ever go in there Froggy?" I asked.

"Not often."

"Why?"

"Do you go in every straight club in Crawford? Sheesh, you act like we all one homogenous group of homos," Froggy said, making his own play on words. "I've been in there. I just don't like it much."

"How come?"

"Uptown fags. Snooty homos."

I wrapped my head around that. Something dawned on me.

"The coach ever go in there?" I said. "He was what I called a 2 a.m. poser."

Froggy smiled out of one side of his mouth.

"What does that mean?"

"He came out this time of night when fewer people were around. You know, getting his homo on, on the down low," Froggy said.

"Meaning, he wanted to hide it?"

"You think a prestigious school is the type of employer that invites diversity?"

I thought about that for a second.

"But if he was out at a gay bar, his sexuality wouldn't be a secret, right?"

"Not a secret, but if you're in The Works at 2:30 in the morning, you're in our club, or bein' a pretender, so you aren't likely to be talkin' about who you've seen. You know, if I'm ashamed of who I am, and I see you, am I really gonna get loud and out you?" Froggy was starting to look bored with all my questions.

"Still, he clearly wasn't 100% hiding his lifestyle, was he?"

"Lifestyle—I love that. It's like being gay is like playing golf or joining the Mormons," Foggy said.

"I didn't mean anything by that," I said.

Froggy gave me a perturbed smile.

"Oh, Mr. Duffy, you don't have to apologize. I know what you're all about."

"Yeah?"

"Um—huh," He said. He was playing a little coy.

"What am I all about?" I was dying to hear this.

"You about people. You got your ideas, but I can tell it don't matter because you care about people. You may wonder about park fags like me, but you don't ever let a curiosity turn into judgment or hate. You one of those that is about people first and the other shit second."

I thought about that for a long time. It made me feel really good.

"Thank you, Frog," I said.

"Now, don't go getting' all emotional on me. I have to save myself for Ms. Rhonda."

I smiled.

"She might just be the one, Mr. Duffy. Oh yes, she might be the one."

I smiled again.

"She's a lucky guy," I said.

Chapter Forty-One

Tuesday

I don't get hangovers often. I just don't. It probably has something to do with why I enjoy drinking as much as I do.

That doesn't mean I feel great the next morning. I don't sleep well, I feel dehydrated, and the food choices I make just before bed don't serve me well first thing in the a.m. I don't, however, get hangover-specific symptoms.

That rationalization didn't sit well, but the lack of sleep and overall shitty feeling convinced me not to fight it.

Besides, all my cognitive capabilities were focused on Halle, Russ, the S&M outfit Halle wore, The Works, and Lark Street at three in the morning. I needed to break down what I saw, what I thought I saw, and what it meant. The challenging part was washing this through the drunk filter while sober and exhausted. I wasn't exactly in the ideal state to be playing CSI.

Still, I knew it was them.

It had to be. I mean, if I mistook one person for someone while drunk, that would be conceivable, but two people closely connected to something together? That didn't seem likely. If I saw a good-looking, cougarish woman, and I had just done the deed with Halle, then it might make some sense that my mind might go to her. Yesterday, I went off on Russ in the stairwell, and it wouldn't be crazy to think he was in my unconscious either. That is, if you put stock in the unconscious.

Now, if I wanted to get all Freudian, I could make the case that they both play such symbolic roles in my life that it would make sense that I would hallucinate them together. I was, after all, in conflict and perhaps even competition with Russ, and dreaming of him with my conquest was consistent with psychoanalytic theory.

I guess.

Bullshit. It was them.

I never put much stock in Sigmund's ideas. Frankly, I thought they were mostly nonsense. Yet, in my whole life I seldom had more crap running around my head, soaked in bourbon, than last night. But I wasn't dreaming; I was awake. Awake, of course, with an overdose of the world's most popular sedative-hypnotic running through my veins.

If I supposed they were together, then it was clear that there was a sexual element to what was going on. They were leaving Le Sexe Shoppe. You didn't go in there for breath mints or a Snickers bar. They didn't, however, leave with any merchandise, or, at least, any visible merchandise. I'm not aware of the inventory, but I assumed there was something you could slip in a pocket or a purse.

It was also possible that Le Sexe Shoppe was a meetup place or a place to get information. That may be an assumption, but the idea that people into kink would use the store as a clearing house of info didn't seem like a gigantic jump.

And what to make of the trip to The Works...

A gay bar, not a subtle one, and the city's most famous one—it wasn't where you went for discretion. Why would a forty-something bring a guy half her age to a gay bar?

For the dancing?

Seems like a lot of trouble to get your groove on. Maybe to dance in a place where people weren't likely to question or talk? No, that just didn't fit.

And Halle's outfit?

At school, her stuff was tailored toward the suggestive side, but in a very designer-subtle way. She was more about Lauren and the idea of the little stretch material in some slacks without back pockets than she was patent leather fetish gear.

No, the getup wasn't a mistake. It wasn't likely that she wore it to unwind at the end of the day. These weren't her favorite, faded jeans and an old undergrad sweatshirt from her time on the crew. Latex pants and a dog collar were her expressions. She was making a statement.

And that statement?

Whew, you could do a psychology doctoral dissertation on that one. It could be stating something simple like "Look at me!" or "Look at me; I'm forty-five!" or "Look at me; I'm forty-five and I could rock your world!" Maybe, "Look at me; I'm forty-five and I have a boy toy!"

Russ as a boy toy...

The toughest kid in school. The most connected kid in school. The kid with the most powerful father in school. The captain of the football team.

Maybe Halle was telling us something else.

But what?

Here she was ushering an eighteen-year-old around at two in

the morning in an overtly sexual outfit and going to the city's most famous gay bar.

Was she embarrassing him?

What did I know about Halle?

She was provocative. She had an appetite for sex, and she liked to push Spadafora around.

So?

Then it dawned on me. The thing that took in the rest. The thing that defined her most elegantly. It was what got her excited in the bar with me and later in the front seat of her BMW. It was what got her off sexually.

It was what got her off, period.

Halle lived to be in control.

Chapter Forty-Two

I got to CA late. With the night I had, it was predictable, but still, being late never sat well with me. It set me up to feel off-kilter for the rest of the day. Who am I kidding; I hadn't been on-kilter for a long time.

I asked the secretary if there was any news on Bobby, and there wasn't. I told myself to be patient and let time work for him. It didn't do any good at all. I felt sick to my stomach.

That queeziness added to the deep emptiness that went with the possibility of losing fighting. I didn't know what to do, and it scared me. It felt weird, like something was taken away from me. The fact that it came from Smitty—the man I respected most in the world—made it worse. He was an unimpeachable source.

Despite the fact that it came from him, I wasn't ready to accept it. It made me sad, and it worried me that he felt so strongly; but honestly, there were other places to train and other trainers. Fighters switched gyms and cornermen all the time. Shit, Oscar De La Hoya did it almost every fight of his career.

The bigger issue was more central to who I was. Even through my drunken fugue state, AJ, of all people, crystallized it. People thought of me first as a fighter. Shit, I thought of myself as a fighter, and everything else was something else, something less important, something every other jerk could do.

I was a fighter.

I didn't care if you were an MBA, if you broke the sales record at Amway, or if you had more degrees than a thermometer.

I was a fighter.

I did something regularly that you were scared to do.

I did that thing all the time. I made a life out of doing what the rest spent all their time afraid of.

That's who I am.

In my mind, it made me different. In my mind, as arrogant as it sounds, it made me better.

There, I said it.

"Do you know you're talking to yourself?" TJ said. She was standing in the doorway. Today, she wore olive green, flat-front khakis and an off-white, V-neck sweater. No earrings, no makeup, and no lipstick. Sensible shoes, too.

"Was I?" I said, coming back to the world around me. "Was I

making any sense?"

"No more than the sense you make when you're talking to others." She winked.

I just nodded and looked down at the coffee.

"You all right?" She wasn't joking now.

"I had a cocktail or two last night," I said.

"It's not just that." She said it without any question in her voice.

"Smitty said something about me quitting."

I didn't say anything. She moved from the doorway. She sat on the corner of the desk.

"When I left the army, actually, when I left combat, I was lost. Some of it, I suppose, was the PTSD bullshit—whatever that is. But another big hunk of it was leaving something that no one else understood."

I didn't look up right away. I didn't know what to say. Then the silence got to me.

"I don't know what else to do," I said. I didn't want to say any more. It caught in my throat.

It was quiet a little while longer. I changed the subject.

"Did anyone update you about Bobby?"

It took TJ a second to adjust to the conversation shift.

"Uh, last I heard he was 'stable,' whatever that means," TJ said.

"The poor kid. Shit, his poor dad. How do you deal with this kind of nonsense?" I took a deep breath.

"What choice is there?" TJ said. "What does 'dealing' even mean? You get up after not sleeping, you feel sick to your stomach, and you go through the day."

"Or you drink or get high..." I said.

"Or gamble or have sex or shop or any of the other shit humans do to not feel." She put her hands in her pockets and slouched slightly.

"Whatever gets you through the night, I guess."

"That's how the John Lennon song goes." TJ grinned.

"And how is it that Russ gets out of jail immediately?" I said.

"I suppose, to the letter of the law, everything was done right. Probably not the spirit of the law, though," TJ paused. "There's all that, and daddy's considerable influence. There's also a state championship game coming up and a D1 scholarship hanging in the balance."

Halle poked her head in the office. She was wearing a burgundy suit with a black silk blouse. It fit just like the others.

"'Morning. How's our counseling team?" She said. There was a little too much perkiness to it. Just behind her was a smiling Anne Marie Redmond with a blue version of yesterday's monogrammed sweater.

"We're fine, you?" TJ responded for both of us.

"Oh, busier than a one-armed paper hanger," she said with a wink.

"I prefer 'Busier than a one-legged man in an ass-kicking contest,'" I said.

"You would," TJ said.

Halle moved on with Mrs. Redmond and TJ continued to sit on the corner of my desk.

"Remember we were talking about something weird going on here?" I asked.

"Yeah," TJ said.

I explained how I thought I saw Halle and Russ last night. She listened.

"Duff, alcohol can play tricks on perception, especially after an emotional day, but I can't imagine you were hallucinating." She thought for a second. "There's something about Halle... uh, I'm not sure how to put it... maybe predatory. Her interactions with you drip with it."

I felt something in my stomach. It might have been shame, but I knew, whatever it was, it was something I didn't want to admit to TJ. I felt like I just got caught.

I just made a face like I didn't get it.

"Oh, come on? You don't sense the flirting? Really, it's more suggestive than flirting."

"Flirting—what has she said that would make you say that?" I played dumb.

"It has a lot to do with body language, tone, and nonverbals. You know what I'm talking about. You're just not admitting it for some reason."

"Huh?" I said

TJ was dead on.

Chapter Forty-Three

"Never mind me. What do you make of her and Russ?" I tried to switch the direction of things, just slightly. "And the get ups?"

"The leather, the whole older-woman-with-a-young-stud-cougar thing?" TJ said.

"Yeah."

"That could be a bunch of things. It could be anything from harmless, or near harmless play, to something exploitative, dangerous, and illegal."

"Harmless?" The term threw me, especially coming from a self-aware woman like TJ.

"Stay with me a little and don't filter it through what you think is currently politically correct."

"Okay..."

"Some women get off on mere fantasy. Merely playing with the forbidden. In this case, Halle is acting inappropriate for her job, but, if all she's doing is hanging out with Russ, then she isn't doing anything illegal."

"Russ is almost twenty."

"Yes, so even if they had sex, there's no statutory legal thing going on. But, even more important, she could just like getting close to something forbidden."

She tilted her head and raised her eyebrows to ask me if I understood.

"Go ahead," I said.

"Or she could be flirting with him and getting a bit more physical because she gets off on turning on a young, strong, and virile man. Maybe she teases or promises him sex, but holds out to keep him close."

"There's a word for that," I said with a snicker.

"There are several. Don't give in to the urge to share them."

I took my minor scolding in stride.

"What else?'

She just sat and looked at me while she thought.

"Well, on the other end of the extreme could be a total domination and, in a sense, a corruption, of a young man," TJ said without humor.

"Oooh, this sounds dramatic."

"I'm not kidding, Duffy. Hey, Russ is well on his way to being an asshole for life, but right now, he's a kid. He's full of himself and his own bravado, but he's a developing young man."

"Pardon me if I don't get too emotional for him."

"I'm not asking you to. There are women who dominate young men in a predatory fashion. They control them through sex—through what a stupid young man may see as devotion, or even love, and they get in a kid's head in such a way that manipulation becomes easy."

"Manipulation to do what?"

"Anything the woman wants. Maybe just messing with the kid's emotions, maybe starving him for sex, and, figuratively or literally, bringing him to the edge without satisfaction. Maybe using him to do her dirty work." Her eyebrows went up.

"Dirty work?" I said.

"We've seen how she messes with Spadafora. That poor man doesn't know whether to shit or go blind when she's around. Maybe she's setting Russ up for something she's planning that we're not hip to. There has certainly been a shitstorm of negative attention surrounding this 'prestigious' school." She said 'prestigious' with sarcasm.

"And how is a woman so capable of doing these kinds of things?" I asked.

"C'mon, Duff? Still waiting for the turnip truck?" She got up off the side of my desk.

"Seriously."

"You doubt the power of sex? Or is it that you don't get how women can harness it and use it?"

"Geez, TJ, you're taking the fun out of things."

"Sex is fun. Sex is about love and devotion and all that Hallmark stuff. But more often than those things, it's about who's on top...figuratively. It's about who gets it, how they get it, who doesn't get any, and why. It's a drug, a commodity, and, in the right hands, it can be used."

She paused for a second.

"You think all this S&M stuff you hear about isn't connected to the power of sex? Men who run armies and control fortunes seek out chances to be humiliated and controlled and tie it to orgasmic pleasure. Why?"

"You got me." And she did. She really did.

"Because they've been conditioned to see sex that way. They've been brought along to experience it that way, and, when you combine orgasm with the conditions around it, you don't have to be Pavlov's dog to be set for life."

"Ring the bell," I said.

"And let the salivating begin."

Chapter Forty-Four

The topic was interesting, but my own rendezvous with Halle made me uncomfortable, to say the least—especially in TJ's presence. I felt like I needed to confess something, and that emotion was pretty strong. Logic told me to keep my mouth shut.

Halle reappeared in my doorway. Talk about logic and lack thereof.

She did the lean-thing that she liked to do.

"Hi," I said. "What's up?"

"I thought you might like to know that we just got some good news on Bobby. He is out of the coma and responding well."

"Thank God," I exhaled.

"Not quite out of the woods and some swelling needs to go down, but the mood is much more optimistic."

"Can he have visitors?" I asked.

"The family has requested that we wait a few more days." She adjusted her Sarah Palin glasses.

"And what will happen to Russ?" I asked.

She shrugged and made a face.

"That's not in our control. Apparently the police think 'Boys will be boys...'"

"Especially, if Russell Redmond's kid is the boy," I said. I didn't hide my disdain.

Halle just gave me a look. She didn't say anything and seemed to be doing her best to give me an expression that wouldn't say anything. It spoke volumes.

"Well, thank you for letting me know," I said, mostly to be saying something.

She continued to lean for just a moment, and I felt her eyes. Maybe it was TJ messing with my mind, but Halle's presence felt different. She hadn't moved, and she kept her eyes on me. She tilted her head, her eyebrows went up, and she half smiled. She moved out of her lean by lifting her back off the doorjamb and left. I felt something, and I didn't like it.

The phone on the desk rang, and TJ answered it. A commotion out in the main office distracted me.

"You need to get a handle on things here. My son is missing!" I recognized the voice but couldn't put a name or face to it.

I went to the door.

It was Russ's father—Mr. High-powered attorney. Chico was by his side.

Spadafora and Halle were standing in front of them.

"Rusty, let's go into my office and..." Spadafora was rattled, and it showed.

"I'm not going into your fucking office! I need answers, and I need them right now! Rusty's face was almost purple with rage.

I studied Halle. She showed none of Spadafora's panic. She remained confident and poised. Considering where I saw her, and who I saw her with, it was remarkable.

"Mr. Redmond, when did you see Russ last?" Halle said. Her tone was calm and somewhat reassuring. She was everything Spadafora wasn't.

"Saturday afternoon. We watched the Florida/FSU game on television." Redmond exhaled.

"Did he mention anything about his plans for the weekend? Friends, parties?" Halle said.

"I think he said something about going out with friends, or maybe there was a party. Frankly, I don't remember."

Halle nodded.

She was checking to see if Rusty knew about her and his son.

"If he hasn't shown up here, and he hasn't contacted you, then I'm wasting my time. I'm going to the chief and filing a missing person's report."

He turned and walked toward the door.

"Rusty, we'll do everything we can!" Spadafora said. Redmond ignored him and continued out the door without breaking his stride. "Fuck!" Spadafora yelled and punched the door with the palm of his hand. Halle folded her arms and shook her head.

I remained silent and watched from the doorway. When Halle made eye contact with us, it seemed to have a piercing edge. I went back in the office with TJ, sat down hard, and tried to think.

"Holy shit," TJ said. "What was that all about?"

"That was Russ's father. The kid is missing," I said.

"Oh my God..." TJ said." What are you going to do?"

"What do you mean?" I said.

TJ tilted her head, scrunched her face, and looked at me like I was insane.

"You're going to the police, aren't you?"

I didn't answer.

TJ waited.

"You ARE fuckin' punchy, aren't you?" she said. "You—"

"What did you just say?" When I stood up, the force slammed the chair into the wall. "What did you just say?"

Her face lost expression, and she looked panicked.

"Duffy, I'm sorry. I didn't mean—"

"Get the fuck out of here."

"Duffy..."

I pulled the chair from against the wall and sat at my desk and pretended to read *The Post*. Something wasn't right with my eyes, and my head did a little of the woozy thing.

After a long moment, I heard the office door close.

Chapter Forty-Five

"You had sex with the vice principal? Was that in the job description?" Kelley met me at the bar during his break.

"Look, I'm not proud of it, and I won't even try to explain to you how I was seduced," I said.

"Poor baby," Kelley said.

"I'm not saying it wasn't something I wanted to do, but it was, oh, fuck it...I feel silly explaining it."

"You ought to."

I blew out some air and decided to go on. Putting up with ball busting was part of being a guy and disclosing a sexual adventure couldn't not be commented on.

"The important thing is this. The other night I got bombed, remember?"

"Yeah," Kelley nodded.

"I walked it off after you took my keys, and I wandered down to Lark. I was standing by the Le Sexe Shoppe when Halle came out with Russ. She was all decked out in this funky, fetish gear, and she was with Russ, the missing kid."

"You were definitely bombed. I know that firsthand."

"I was drunk. I wasn't hallucinating. They walked to The Works and went in."

"And now the kid is missing?" Kelley said. "How old is the kid?"

"He's a senior. He's at least eighteen."

Kelley's eyebrows went up.

"What?" I said.

"He ain't a kid. He's an adult. He can go wherever he wants, whenever he wants," Kelley said.

"You know his old man?"

"Of course I do. I live in this city, remember?" Kelley scratched the back of his neck and looked at his watch. "There any sign of foul play in the kid's disappearance?"

"Not that I know of."

"So, for all we know, he could've gone to see the Statue of Liberty, bought a matching patent leather outfit in Greenwich Village to hang with the VP, or is in Central Park skipping school?"

"I guess."

Kelley shrugged his shoulders and held his arms to his sides with the palms up.

"Do I tell the principal that I saw the kid with Halle at three in the morning, and she was in a leather suit?" I said.

Kelley gave a half-laugh.

"That's not a legal matter, sir." He said it with a southern accent and tilted his hat over his forehead. "Duff, I got to run. Man, you lead an interesting life."

He headed to his patrol car and drove back toward the center of Crawford.

It sounded to me like I could keep my mouth shut and keep my dirty little secrets to myself. I could tell Spadafora that I saw the two of them together early Saturday night and leave it at that. I could write an anonymous note. I could call Redmond and let him know, and I could do that anonymously, too.

After that, I could just back off and let the wheels turn. Keep my name out of it. Keep my furtive interlude with Halle my own secret and still pass on what I knew. Legally, according to Kelley, I was in the clear. My reputation, such that it was, would take a blow if it was known that I boffed the vice principal.

Or would it? Maybe it would raise my status as a player.

Ick.

I didn't do anything wrong by having sex with her, did I? Why did I feel like it would be awful if it got out? Maybe it wouldn't be the best career move and my boss wouldn't be thrilled, but I didn't cross any ethical boundaries. Halle wasn't a client. I didn't coerce or manipulate her. We were both adults.

There was a football player missing, though.

She had something to do with it.

I knew it.

It was time to call it a night. I squared up with AJ and said my goodbye to Jerry Number Two, the only one of the Foursome left. Outside, the November air was a little warm and heavy for the time of the year. Before I put the key in the El Dorado's door, my cell rang. It was Kelley.

"You calling to apologize for being mean to me?" I said.

"Duff, I wanted to let you know about something before you heard it on the news."

I could tell by his tone he was 100% serious.

"Yeah?"

"There's been another murder. Another one at the bridge, another throat slashing."

"Yeah?"
"Duff, it was Froggy."

Chapter Forty-Six

Froggy was murdered shortly after he spoke to me in front of The Works and right after Russ and Halle went in. He was killed the same way the coach was and in the same place. He was left at the bridge to bleed out, and Ms. Rhonda found him when he didn't come home—wherever home was.

I'd known Froggy for ten years. He was an addict, on and off, but he never harmed another person. He tricked to get high, but he never robbed anyone or stole. He was a lovable man who was just a little bizarre—a nonconformist—but kind and endearing.

Someone wasted that life. My guess—it was because he was seen talking to me. Kelley was right, and I should mind my own fucking business more often. It's one thing if it wound up hurting me. It was another when the innocent got hurt. Or, in this case, got killed.

I knew one thing for certain.

This bullshit just got personal.

Any ambivalence I had was over, and I knew it was time to do what needed to be done. The first thing was to let the police know what I saw. I kept it simple.

The typed note read:

"Vice Principal Halle was with Russ Redmond at The Works Pub at 3:30 a.m. Saturday night/Sunday morning."

I had thought about it long and hard. I had rewritten it fifteen times, adding and leaving out detail. In the end, the hour I saw them and the place they were going to would tell enough of a story. There was no need to mention her outfit, Le Sexe Shoppe, or the type of bar The Works was. I left out the editorializing.

The process of leaving an anonymous note for the police didn't help me feel less like a coward. I pride myself on looking someone in the eye, even when it's a difficult situation—especially when it's a difficult situation. Whenever I took the easier way, I didn't like the price I had to pay by living with the feeling. The few moments of discomfort or awkwardness went down easier than the long time, alone, knowing I didn't have the guts to face up to something.

I hated the feeling of not facing something. It was almost pathological how much I hated it. In boxing, not getting in with someone because they might be better than you wasn't honorable. Avoiding fighting out of fear for one's own safety was bullshit. If you did that, you weren't a fighter. It didn't mean every man had to live by this, but, if you wanted to call yourself a fighter, you did. It was that simple.

It created a perpetual feeling of tension inside of me. Like it or not, it also set up this

never-ending competitive thing, too. It wasn't a competition of whether I measured up in skills with everyone I came in contact with. It was whether I measured up in doing what I said I would. It was kind of like courage, but not merely that. I guess it was about integrity.

If you said you were one thing, and you weren't that thing, then what were you?

You were a phony. You were a liar. You were bullshit.

It wasn't even about being that way to the world; it was about being that way on the inside. Having to live with yourself, knowing you were full of shit was hell to me. I mean, guys can create an image and be real good at putting that forward, but, if they knew on the inside that they were bullshit, how did they get through the day?

When it came to letting someone know about Halle, I measured the risk/reward equation, and the note made the most sense. It just didn't feel good.

There was something else that this bit of introspection underlined for me.

I wasn't ready to not be a fighter yet.

The notion of getting in the ring when I didn't want to drove me. It made me different, and it made me know I was different. Outside of the gym, it never left me. I knew I had something that other people didn't. I was in a fraternity that you couldn't just send your dues and application in to be part of. I feared not having the danger to fear. I feared not having a vehicle to practice acting against my fear.

Because, inside, I'm often scared as hell. I have been as long as I can remember, and I'm scared every time I get in the ring.

But since I was fourteen, I've gotten in the ring.

Scared as shit, but I got in that fuckin' ring.

And when I didn't feel like I fit in at school, I knew, at the end of the day, I could get in the ring even though I was scared. When I was too scared to ask a pretty girl out, I wasn't too scared to get in the ring. And when I had no idea what to do, I could get in the ring.

Even though I was really fucking scared.

It wasn't time for me to stop fighting. No way. Not now.
I needed to get in the ring.
God damn it; I needed it.

Chapter Forty-Seven

There's a gym in Albany, about thirty-five miles away. It wasn't the Crawford Y, and Smitty didn't run it, but, if I wanted to fight, those things had to be in my past. I loved both of them, but, if I wanted to fight, this was how it had to be. I was going to the gym, and then I was going to see Bobby.

Jimmy's Gym was in a warehouse section of town, in between a tile wholesaler and a plumbing supply operation. It had a big garage door in its center, and, when you went in, it had that smell that comes with big cement and steel places that had been seasoned with some sweat. Far as I could tell, nobody named "Jimmy" had ever worked there. The head trainer was a guy named Jake; he had fought as an amateur, but then got in some trouble for letting his hands go outside the gym. He liked to drink a bit, and they knew him at the county jail.

"Duff, what's up?" Jake said when he saw me. He was six foot two and about 250 now—probably forty to forty-five pounds heavier than when he fought. You'd figure his face would be marked up, but it wasn't; but his hairline was receding, and I could tell from his movement that he was feeling his forty plus years.

He was working the mitts with Roscoe Turner, a young guy who just turned pro as a heavyweight.

"Hey, Jake. Just looking to get some work," I said. "Work" was the gym term for sparring.

Jake wasn't going to win any citizenship awards, but he knew boxing, and he knew how to prepare fighters. Roscoe had won the Adirondack Golden Gloves last spring and was now 2—0 in his pro career.

"Where's Smitty?" Jake said.

"Uh, me and Smitty are done." It was the first time I said it, and I didn't like the sound of it.

"Hmm...never thought I'd hear that. Well, you know you're always welcome here."

It reminded me of when someone asks about your girlfriend, and you just broke up.

"Thanks, man. I appreciate it." Jake and I knew each other for years—not well, but it was always amicable.

"Roscoe was supposed to work with Edgar, but I just found out Edgar's in lockup. Him and his damn weed," Jake said. Edgar moved marijuana in the area, and everyone knew it.

"I'll work with Roscoe, if that's cool," I said. I felt a twinge in my gut. It was different than the usual feeling. This one was seasoned with Smitty's disapproval.

"Sure, get loose, and, when you're ready, glove up," Jake said.

I danced around for three minutes trying to get loose. I couldn't wait to get in with Roscoe, and I was also dreading it— exactly how it's felt every single time I've gotten in with someone who wanted to punch me in the face. Today, adding in the forbidden accentuated the emotion.

Roscoe was a good guy, but he had ten years on me, and, as a new pro, he knew it would get around how he did against an experienced guy like me. At this stage of his career, he was always proving himself. Ah shit, who was I kidding—after fifteen years, I never stopped feeling that way.

The timer rang, and we began to move in the introductory circles. He double jabbed, and I caught both with my gloves. I felt good—almost light. I wasn't sure, but I think my left-handed stance may have had Roscoe thinking a little too much. Some guys hated fighting southpaws.

He stepped in with a double jab again, this time with more on it, and he added a right hand at the end for power. He left it out a little too much and wasn't ready for my pivot to the right. I landed a solid punch, kind of a half hook-half uppercut, and it put him back on his heels. He went backwards and had to cover up.

I hit him with a three punch body combination and finished it with an uppercut that he didn't count on. It landed hard under the chin, and, I wasn't sure, but I think his knees buckled slightly. For the next minute and a half, he circled me with more of a blend of caution and confusion, and seemed reluctant to get off. The bell ending the round sounded, and Jake didn't waste any time.

"Jesus Christ, 'Coe,'" he said. "You need to get into this. You're not looking sharp."

I was pumped. I loved this, and I was loving doing it.

In the second and third round, Roscoe continued his cautiousness, and he had no answer for my left hand. Caution doesn't work very well in boxing because your offense is part of your defense. When you retreat into a strictly defensive mode, you wind up heading backwards, and, over time, you become a sitting duck. My left-handed movement just bewildered him. He stopped coming in after a while and was content to jab. He was disheartened, and, because this was just sparring and my first day there, I didn't take it to him. In time, he'd learn and adjust, so there was nothing to gloat about with Roscoe.

There was, however, plenty for me to be satisfied about.

Chapter Forty-Eight

The bell ending the fourth round sounded.

"That's it. Nice work, Duff," Jake said. "You sure know how to work that southpaw shit."

I touched gloves with Roscoe.

"Man, you got some power," I said to him after we did the brief, fighters' hug. He hadn't hit me with much, but it was etiquette to compliment another fighter after working together.

"Shit, man. I never touched you," Roscoe said. He shook his head.

I was bathed in sweat and felt loose. I was elated and felt like something was returned to me. It may sound weird, but I almost welled up. Fighting was intense, and it had an emotional tinge to it that hardly anyone ever acknowledged.

"Duff, what's up with Smitty?" Jake said.

I had my gloves off and was cooling down by walking around the gym, throwing light punches, and dancing a bit.

"Ah, kind of taking a break from the Y." I paused and chose my words carefully. "You know, you train somewhere for years and you can get stale."

Roscoe smiled. He just looked at me.

"What?"

"Nuthin'. You know, I've never poached another gym's fighters. That's not me. But if you were looking for a change, you know, if you were done up there, I'd love to have you fight for me."

I felt myself smile from ear to ear.

"Yeah?" I said.

"Fuck yeah. You kidding? You can fight, you know the game, and you're good people."

I was toweling the sweat from my face, and I went over and shook Jake's hand.

"Thanks, man, I appreciate it," I said. "I'd love to."

"Excellent. Would be great to have you around," he said. "Hey, I'm closing up, you want to celebrate with a beer?"

"Sure," I said.

Like a lot of city gyms, Jake's had no showers. I toweled off the best I could, threw on a clean t-shirt, and pulled a hooded sweatshirt on over it. My Yankees cap would cover the sweaty head, and I kept the short, white towel around my neck to wipe the sweat that would continue to come. Cooling down from sparring took a while.

We walked out of the gym, and Jake immediately lit up a Marlboro. It was a tough transition—the smoke didn't mesh well with my post-workout heart rate and breathing—but this was boxing, not a spinning class.

"Where we going?" I asked.

"Let's just go across the street. There's a strip joint called The Taco Stand. Beer's cold and the girls aren't hideous. Most of 'em, anyway."

I had no moral objection to strip clubs. I mean, as long as the women weren't coerced or forced to do something they didn't want to do, it was fine with me. From what I heard, the money was good, so I didn't see any problems.

I guess you could go a little deeper and start asking yourself questions about the self-esteem of women who danced topless and the other choices they had or how they were treated like cattle. Or even if they did it because of some sort of abuse thing that they now acted out on.

Maybe I did have some moral objections to it. The best bet was not to give it much thought and play the game in my head that all the women in this place would be self-aware, hip, powerful women who were freely and cheerfully using their sexuality to exploit men's fantasies.

I also liked the whole tooth fairy thing.

It was just twilight when we went in; the darkness and loud, metal music felt a little odd this early in the day.

"What's up, Duff?" the bouncer said when we came through the door. It was Squal, an old buddy from the gym.

"Squal, how you been?" I said, and we bumped fists.

Squal weighed about 280 and had the kind of physique that featured hard muscle covered with a little fat. Not the kind of fat that you looked down your nose at, but the kind that powerful guys layered over their muscle when they stopped training like they used to and got into their thirties. He played some college ball but got busted in a bar fight a few years back and now kind of drifted. I knew him a little from the gym, from stopping by AJ's, and because we went to Crawford together.

Some guys were behind us, so the interaction was cut short. The bar was half-full, and Jake and I took a corner spot, away from the speakers, with an obstructed view of the stage. I was kind of relieved that we weren't sitting center stage. That would've been weird.

Maybe Jake liked the place because it was across the street, and he could walk. Maybe he liked to look at the girls a little; I mean, who didn't? I was just glad he wasn't obsessed. I didn't need a creepy weirdo for my new cornerman.

The bartender was a very tan, very fit and short, early twenty-something with brown hair, severe eyebrows, and a diamond in her nose.

"Jakey!" she said and reached over to kiss him on the cheek. It was a brotherly thing. As she hunched herself up the bar, she practically spilled out of her top and displayed a pair of perfectly rounded and store-bought breasts. I'd be lying if I said I found them unattractive.

"Kayla, this is Duffy," Jake said like he was introducing a sister.

"Hi, Duffy," Kayla extended her delicate hand, and I felt the long nails of her French manicure in my palm. She had a cheerful smile and a high-pitched, girlish voice. The fact that I could see three-quarters of her breasts—and that the piece of fabric covering her privates was a triangle with a surface area less than three square inches—made the introduction just a tad on the awkward side, at least for me.

"Here's to a new team," Jake held his scotch on the rocks up. I toasted him with my bottle of Miller Lite.

"Duff, you know, there's a show coming up in Yonkers in three weeks—you want in?" Jake said.

Chapter Forty-Nine

The lame metal song—Cherry Pie, by I think, the band, Warrant—was fading out. The pale, redheaded Irish girl who was on stage gathered her shredded t-shirt and lingerie top that she had thrown off during her twelve-minute act. The DJ referred to her as "Whitey," and, under the lights, her almost translucent skin told us how she got that nickname.

"Three weeks, huh?" I said. "I got a little time to think about it?"

"A little," Jake said. "You know how nervous the matchmakers get."

Most fight fans don't realize that the heart and soul of boxing shows lie in the hands of the matchmaker. He or she is the one who finds the fighters and, when it's a low-budget show, the matchmaker is the one that finds fighters who are in shape, come to fight, and who are exciting to watch. When you're only paying a few hundred dollars, it's tough to find boxers who fit that criteria.

"Any idea who the opponent is?" I said. A new girl went on stage wearing a man's suit and dancing to Sinatra's "Summer Wind."

That was different.

"There's Al Nace. He's 11-9. There's also Don Trella who's 13-4. Nothing definite."

I nodded. The dancer was athletic as hell. She kept the fedora down over her eyes and wore Ray Bans. She almost assaulted the pole the way she spun around it. She slid down into a full, sideways split, laid her body flat on the stage, spread her arms wide like a cat, and then balled them into fists. She sneered at the audience.

This *was* different.

"Duff, Duff…" Jake brought me back.

"Oh, hey, sorry. She's good…"

"Tommie Gunn."

"Huh?"

"That's Tommie. Tommie Gunn, she's an ex-GI. Fucking rock hard and likes to prowl the stage like a damn panther."

Tommie Gunn pulled hard on the center of her tuxedo shirt, and the jacket, shirt, and tie combination came off dramatically. She was left with a skin-tight sports bra. She was small up top and much different than her co-workers. When she stalked the stage, you could see the definition run through her calves, to her thighs, and flex hard in her butt.

"Both of these guys would be tough, not setups, and you'd have to be focused and ready," Jake said.

"Yeah, okay. I gotta think about it," I said.

Tommie Gunn's top was off. Honestly, the lack of oversized silicone numbers looked good, and, when she did that kind of serpentine move with her upper body, you could see her six pack. She could do commercials for P90x. That is if P90x had some sort of late night, erotic component.

"Yeah, man, think about it. It'd be nice to have some heavies on the card."

I nodded, and I was truly interested in what Jake was offering, but I couldn't help but watch the dancer. Strippers usually bored the piss out of me, and, after the age of eighteen or so, I believe a man's taste really needed to evolve slightly.

Tommie Gunn seemed different, and I wanted to watch because she had me transfixed—also because I was equally as curious as to why she was having such an effect on me.

She was at the edge of the riser and spun around so that she had her back to the bar. She ever so slowly bent over, stretched way down, and placed her hands on the floor. It was erotic, but it was also athletic as hell. She had the legs of a stripper, but the kind of stripper who could kick your ass, too.

Tommie began to reverse the stretch, rising slowly and pausing when her torso was parallel to the floor. You had to work out to know what kind of core strength that required. She kept coming up, and, as she went to spin, the DJ hit the strobe light. Tommie broke into a series of aggressive spins, heading toward the pole. Her fedora fell off, and the strobe lit up the slight accent of sparkles Tommie had down her legs and up her arms. It was glitz, but, considering where we were, it wasn't overdone. When she ran a hand through her short, spiky hair, I smiled—at least, at first. Then it came to me.

I looked closer.

I studied her in disbelief.

The P90x body, the smart routine, the spiked hair, and the sparkle.

No, it couldn't be.

It was.

Tommie Gunn was TJ Dunn

Chapter Fifty

"Hey, Duffy, are you listening?" Jake said. "Jesus Christ, you never been to a strip bar before? If I knew a pair of titties was going to hypnotize you, I wouldn't have exposed ya to it."

"Huh? Oh shit, sorry, Jake," I said. " I didn't mean to be rude. She looked familiar, that's all."

"You're a drug counselor, right? Probably been in to see you for crack or something."

"I don't think so." I shook my head. I watched TJ gather her bra and suit from the stage. She put the bra and Fedora back on and handed the suit to the bouncer who went back stage. She approached the guys at the first table.

"Too bad. She'd be great to get on the couch," Jake said.

TJ moved into the audience and had her back to a forty-something guy who had his legs spread. She was shimmying her ass, and, from my angle, I couldn't tell if she was in contact with him. The guy was staring down at TJ's ass with a half-smile on his face. He was being served; TJ was dishing it, and the whole thing turned my stomach a bit.

"Hey, Jake, I gotta split," I said.

"You gonna finish your beer?" Jake nodded toward the half-full Miller Lite.

I chugged it and wiped my mouth with the back of my hand.

"Thanks man, it's gonna be great working with you," I said and extended my handed.

"Amen brother. See you soon," Jake said. He looked a little confused about my quick exit.

I headed for the door, and, just as I got there, I looked back.

TJ was up against a young guy with a wad of ones in his hand. She tossed her head back and giggled. She turned to the side while she laughed.

For a moment, our eyes met; at least, I thought they did.

Whether they did or not, I couldn't be certain.

But she stopped laughing immediately.

I couldn't hang around. It was just too weird, and I couldn't interact with TJ in that type of setting.

"Takin' off, Duff?" Squal said as I passed. "Canadian ballet ain't your thing?"

"Nah, Squal, it ain't for me," I said.

I headed back to Crawford and went straight to AJ's. My head was swimming, and I wasn't sure what I was feeling. AJ's was mostly about drinking, nonsense, and especially not feeling—and I needed a session. I didn't know where to put this stripper thing. Before an hour ago, I didn't think real strongly about topless dancing and right or wrong. I guess it makes a difference if someone you're infatuated with makes her living grinding her ass into strangers for a buck. It wasn't a crime against me. TJ and I had no claim on each other. I was attracted to her, and she might be attracted to me.

Logically, I got it. I always get shit logically.

The feeling part is something else. The ride didn't last long, but I don't remember passing anything. My mind was going 100 miles per hour.

"Yep, they buy more than anyone else," Jerry Number One was saying as I came in. I walked behind him and took my seat to his left.

"Cow eyeballs? You're serious," Rocco said. AJ slid a Schlitz in front of me and said the other word that comprised most of our historic conversations, "Bourbon?"

I nodded.

"I can't see why they would do that," TC said.

"Neither can the eyeball-less cows," Jerry Number One said.

"They buy the eyes separate from the cow?" Jerry Number Two said.

"What?" Rocco said.

"Do they buy the eyeballs separate from the cows, or do they just come with the cow? Because if they just come with the cow, then this definitely could be true." Jerry Number Two sipped his Cosmo in a self-congratulatory manner.

"Well, I would think they would be separate or we wouldn't be talking about it," Said Jerry Number One.

"Jerr, with your fucked-up logic, then they'd be the leading purchaser of cow penises and other parts, as well," Rocco said.

"I tend to doubt that they'd be buying cow penises," Jerry Number Two said.

"The Japanese do. They grind them up and sell them as afro-delinquents," TC said.

"Afrodesians, you idiot," Rocco said.

"Tusks. You're thinking of tusks," Jerry Number Two said.

"Whatever you wanna call them," Rocco said.

"What about a bull's?" TC said.

"What about 'em?" Rocco said, and he sounded annoyed.

"Their tusks. They got two of them, don't they?" TC asked.

Kelley came in and went unacknowledged by the Foursome. AJ cracked the Coors' Light and had it in place before Kell sat down. They nodded to each other.

"The topic is cow penises," I said matter-of-factly.

"Of course, it is," Kelley said.

"They've been milking it for a while."

"Jesus..." Kelley shook his head in disgust.

He turned toward the TV. Sportscenter was on; more accurately, it remained on.

Kelley stared at it blankly. A long moment of silent passed. Kelley wasn't the friend to talk to about my TJ angst. He just wasn't. I could pump him about the murder.

"Anything new?" I said.

Kelley exhaled.

"I'm guessing you're referring to the case."

I shrugged.

"Yeah, there is, as a matter of fact." Kelley took a sip. He didn't say anything.

"Well?"

"I suppose you'll find out, anyway." Kelley looked like the conversation pained him. I just looked at him.

"Your girlfriend, there, the vice principal..."

"Yeah?" I said.

"She's missing."

Chapter Fifty-One

"Missing? Halle?" I said. "The day after I see her walking Lark Street with Russ?"

"Uh-huh," Kelley said.

"And so is Russ."

"Uh-huh."

"You guys have any idea what's going on?" AJ slid a fresh Schlitz in front of me.

"The department got a call from a neighbor, said something strange was going on at Halle's house. The patrol guys got there, and it looked like she packed up and left in a hurry. When she didn't show up for a work meeting after school, and didn't return phone calls, the principal went by and saw the same thing, and he called it in, too." Kelley finished his beer and nodded at AJ. "Her leaving town isn't breaking any laws."

"Yeah, but—"

Kelley cut me off.

"The more pertinent issue is that two people are missing, both of whom are associated with an organization where an open, unsolved murder case is going on," Kelley said.

"Yeah—"

"And one's a forty-something teacher and the other is a high school senior," Kelley cut me off again.

"Why do you keep finishing my sentences for me?"

"Because I hate it when you start playing crime-stopper," Kelley said without anger and with only a hint of sarcasm. This wasn't the first situation where he told me to, in effect, mind my own business.

"Something weird is going on at CA," I said.

"Geez, you think?" Now Kelley's sarcasm thickened.

"I mean there's something sexually kinky going on. There has to be." I made eye contact with AJ and held my index and middle fingers three inches parallel to the bar. He slid a neat Jim Beam in front of me without hesitation.

"Oh, there has to be? Define weird and kinky?" Kelley said.

"I don't know. She's hanging out with a high school senior in the middle of the night, and they go into the city's most famous gay bar. That's gotta mean something."

"Pump the breaks a little, Sipowicz." Kelley lifted his right-hand palm up at me. "You told me this woman's a nympho and rocked your world in her car, right?"

"Yeah."

"Okay, so a forty-something woman likes sex. Maybe she even likes sex a lot. I mean, after all, she did you," Kelley said and rolled his eyes.

"Yeah, so?"

"So, she wants to do the young stud on the football team, too. She likes men who are muscular, strong, and younger than her."

I sipped, and the bourbon went down a little rough.

"But that's the sort of shit that ruins a career," I said.

"Yeah, but you're the semi-shrink; doesn't that all fit in with the forbidden excitement with chicks like this? I mean she was probably getting off, and it got out of hand or she thinks she's in love or some bullshit."

"Fucked up, though," I muttered.

"Fucked up compared to what? No infant is getting abused. No old person is being roughed up for her social security check. No one is dying of AIDS. It's just two horned-up individuals fucking."

"It's not that simple."

"Yeah? You sure? Today I busted a father for burning his three-year-old's hands with a Bic. You know why he did it?"

I shook my head.

"The three-year-old ate the last Chips Ahoy!"

I didn't say anything. It was quiet for a moment.

"So pardon me if I'm not fascinated with some cougar you boffed, boffing some high school linebacker."

The fourth sip of bourbon went down a little easier.

"What about the coach's murder?" I said, knowing I might piss Kelley off asking.

"Except that this couple you are fascinated with has disappeared—nothing new."

I wasn't going to go over my theories with Kelley. Not now, and not here, but I believed something weird was going on beyond their affair. I didn't know what, but there was something.

I knew there was.

Chapter Fifty-Two

I went home after the bourbon. I was spent in every way you could be exhausted—physically, from the work in the ring; psychologically, from trying to figure all of the bullshit out; and emotionally, from seeing TJ. I didn't know where any of it fit, what it meant, and where I stood on anything in my life. I can't ever remember a week like this, and, with it all, I didn't know which way was up.

As I started the car, it dawned on me that I forgot to visit Bobby. Shit, my own self-centeredness and naval gazing got in the way again. It was way too late now, and there was nothing to do except feel shitty about it.

I felt like I should've been doing something else, but I couldn't, for the life of me, figure out what it should be. I felt the muscles in my back and shoulders tightening from the day's sparring and maybe from all the other shit that brought me tension. The ring work felt like forever ago now, and the euphoria of having a new start in boxing had slipped away.

When I pulled into my driveway, I saw a motorcycle, and, when I looked up, there was a figure sitting on my stoop. The hard drive that was my mind spun, and it didn't take long for me to realize who it was.

"Hey, TJ," I said.

"Hi," she said. She was sitting slightly leaned over with her arms around herself.

"Arooooo... ruff, ruff....Aroooooo!" came from behind the front door.

"He been doing that since you been here?" I said.

"When I first sat down, he did, but he calmed a bit since then," she said. She half smiled, but I noticed her eyes were a bit moist.

"Arooooo....ruff, ruff....Aroooooo!" Same tone and cadence

"Look, if we don't go in, there will be no peace," I said.

I unlocked the door, and TJ followed me in. Al went nuts, jumping up and bouncing off me with his front paws, doing a three sixty, and then repeating the routine with TJ. Then he did it to me again.

"Take it easy, Al," I said in my regular exercise in futility. "Hang on while I get my Master dinner. It's a bit late."

TJ sat down on the couch while Al barked. He kept at it until he heard the scoop enter the dog food bag—then he went as silent as a yoga meditation class. I placed the bowl on the floor, and I waited for the stampede.

Nothing.

This didn't happen.

Ever.

Al not rushing to the food dish was like the sun not rising. I went out to the couch, and he was sitting next to TJ. She gently petted the top of his head while a single tear ran down her cheek. She didn't look up when I came into the room, but she spoke.

"In Iraq, I had 'Agnes'. She stayed with me at night, and we'd just sit and talk. Well, I'd talk." She looked up at me. "I don't cry in front of people, Duffy. Agnes would let me cry. Al is letting me now."

I just looked on. My instincts told me that I didn't need to say anything.

"When I got discharged after the accident, they came for Agnes, and she got reassigned." Tears rushed out of her eyes, but she denied them. She didn't sniff or wipe them away.

I didn't know what to say, so I kept my mouth shut. I felt scared for some reason.

"I planned on dropping by tonight to apologize," she said without making eye contact.

"Apologize?"

"I called you punch drunk, not thinking of your head injury and the stuff you're worried about. I know I hurt your feelings." She continued to look down.

I felt a heaviness in my stomach, and I felt something behind my eyes.

"That shit is on me. That's not your fault," I said.

"I..." She didn't finish. She lowered her head even more. Tears poured from her eyes.

I felt an emotional panic. I didn't know what to do or say. I didn't like the out-of-control feeling.

"I care for you, Duffy," she said, barely above a whisper. "And it scares the shit out of me."

My mouth went dry. They were words I had hoped for, but not under these circumstances. I didn't know what to do. I sat next to her and let my hand rest on her knee.

"When you saw me today, I was ashamed," she said.

"At the bar." I stayed away from the word "strip."

She nodded.

"You don't owe me anything," I said. "Especially a justification or explanation."

She sniffed and kept stroking Al's ears. Al was motionless and transfixed.

"I know I don't owe you anything. I dance for the money. It's easy; the money is unbelievable, and I distance myself from the shit." She didn't have to explain to me what the "shit" was.

"The shit?" I asked. I wasn't sure this was someplace I wanted to go.

She sniffed back some tears.

"When I got there, a woman owned the place. Her name was Belle. She was hardcore in the way she treated us, but, for her, it was all about money. I understood that. We all did."

TJ settled herself with another breath and started talking.

"Belle sold-out to this guy. He's a fucking pig. He expects stuff from the girls."

I didn't ask what stuff meant. I didn't have to.

"Most give in or do it because they think it will be to their advantage to get on his good side. Or they do it because they think so little of themselves."

I kept quiet. I was afraid not to. I wasn't sure I wanted to know.

"You know what pisses me off?" She looked up at me. "He's trying with me." She took a deep breath. "I don't say 'no.' I just avoid his conversation."

"What's so wrong with that?" I said. "I mean, if you want the job."

"What's wrong with that is that it makes it okay that he does it, at least on some level. And for the women who aren't in my place, it makes it okay that he does it to them."

It was a dynamic that I had never given any thought to. At that moment, it washed over me that there are things a man never really has to think about. I was a little embarrassed.

"So, I don't owe you anything," She took a breath. "But, I wasn't ready for you to see me like that." She inhaled deeply and squinted hard. Tears silently ran out of her eyes. "It's not about owing."

I put my hand gently on her knee.

"Dancing immediately felt different," she said.

I felt scared. I wasn't used to this, whatever "this" was. My chest felt warm and tight at the same time. My mouth was dry.

Al stayed by TJ's side and didn't eat.

"C'mere Al," I said and took him by the collar. He hesitated and planted his weight so I really had to tug at him. He relented, and I walked him over to his food. He first looked at the dish, looked back at me, then at the dish, and then back at me.

"Go ahead, boy, it's okay," I nodded at him, and he began to eat. I went back to the couch.

I could feel everything. I sat next to TJ, and, as gently as I could, I wiped the tears from her cheeks with the back of my hand. She closed her eyes.

I leaned forward and kissed her on the lips as lightly as I could. I let my hand gently cup the back of her head, and I let my lips stay on hers.

She kissed me back, and I felt her arms go around my shoulders. I let her weight push me down on the couch, and I felt her body lay across mine.

We never broke the kiss.

Chapter Fifty-Three

During it, we rolled onto the floor. Covered in sweat, my back itched from the old carpet, but I didn't dare move. TJ's head lay on my damp chest, her eyes closed, and her breathing almost still. I let my eyes stay closed, and I took a deep breath. I counted to ten to myself, and I let myself feel as much as I could without thinking.

We didn't say anything.

I resisted the urge to make a comment about her keeping her socks on, or about how, in my whole life, it never felt like this. Silence was called for, and even though I wasn't used to keeping my mouth shut, I had enough sense to let it happen.

She stirred just a bit and ran her left hand over my chest while she nuzzled in deeper. She softly kissed my chest. I let my hand move lightly up and down her back.

I heard the jingle and the slight movement in the floor. The moment was about to change—how, I wasn't sure. I never was.

"Whew! What! Ewww...." TJ jerked out of her post-coital meditative state. She rolled over on me—not to get closer to me, but to escape.

Her movement revealed Al, positioned exactly where TJ's ass had been. He was still sniffing.

"C'mon, Al, go." He lifted his head and looked at me, then tilted his head toward the ceiling and sniffed some more.

"His whiskers tickle," TJ said and snuggled into me. She wasn't mad; she was playful. "I didn't know what it was and it startled me."

"Uh-huh." It was all I could come up with.

"The lick kind of freaked me out," She started to giggle. "His tongue is scratchy and cold."

"Oh, yeah. Welcome to Duffy's love den." TJ got up and stood in front of me.

"I need a sweatshirt or something," she said.

Her body was amazing. It was completely built for function. Which, without being crass, I guess I had just found out.

"My gym hoodie is on the door. I've only worn it twice." I moved up to the couch.

She laughed a little, shook her head, and came back wearing my Everlast sweatshirt and her ankle socks. The hoodie covered what it needed to cover. I had lain back on the couch in my original position, and she lain back down with her head on my chest.

"You do this a lot?" she said without any warm-up. It came from nowhere.

"This?" I said.

"Yeah, *this.* "

"I've never done *this.*" I didn't say anything else and trusted she'd get my intent. She did.

She didn't look up.

"Why do I believe you?"

I shrugged.

"It has been a long time for me, Duff. A looong time."

I ran my hand lightly through her hair.

"I'm not sure what it means," she said.

I let it stay quiet. I didn't know exactly what it meant, but I had been with enough women to know that I didn't need to get 100% clarity on anything in this kind of moments.

"I know how wonderful I feel right now, though," she said.

I felt something illuminate in my chest.

She looked up at me, and I reached down to her waist and hoisted her up a bit. I held her face in both hands, and I kissed her hard. She kissed me back just as hard. My hands moved down her body and found the small of her back. I held her there for a moment and then moved my hands to her waist.

She sat up and pulled the sweatshirt off, and I felt something run through me fast when I got a look at her body, her tussled hair, and the intense look on her face. She leaned back down to kiss me hard, and I felt her whole body grind into mine.

It wasn't long before we were back on the floor.

Chapter Fifty-Four

Thursday

The next morning, there were some awkward, non-committal goodbyes that left me filled with uncertainty. I heard the high-pitched engine fade away from the Moody Blue, and, with it, I felt my own anxiety rev higher. I was used to uncertainty, but this was it on steroids. I was going to have to get over my discomfort, because I needed to work with TJ. Yes, in a couple of hours, we'd be back together, and I wondered what that was going to be like.

I refused to let myself compare this interaction with my BMW thing with Halle. They were worlds apart, not even the same thing, and it felt weird thinking of them in close proximity. There were some physical commonalities, sure, but it wasn't the same.

No, it was not.

I swallowed some coffee, got ready for work, and got in the car, trying not to think too much. I didn't understand how I worked emotionally and was pissed that I wasn't just ga-ga silly in joyous love after last night. My fuckin' mind just wouldn't allow it, and it affixed itself on to things that made me anxious. My thought process was like an obnoxious adolescent that just kept repeating bullshit about what was wrong with something or what could go wrong.

I was halfway to CA when I changed my mind and decided to see if I could visit Bobby. He was, after all, my client; now that he was conscious, I wanted to talk with him, even if it was a short time. Maybe they'd let me in, or maybe his dad would give permission for me to see him.

Mr. Simon was in the parking lot by the entrance smoking a cigarette when I pulled in.

"Hey, Mr. Simon, how's he doing?" I said.

"It's Ed, Duffy," He said, throwing the butt to the ground and grinding it out with a dusty work shoe. "He's a hell of a lot better. Out of the coma and making sense when he's talking."

"Thank God. You must've been scared as hell."

"I haven't slept in days." He exhaled hard.

I just nodded.

"What about the boy who did this? Redmond?" He looked right at me.

"I was at the school when they arrested him. His father came in and called the chief, and they undid the cuffs," I said. Ed Simon didn't seem like the kind of guy you bullshitted to, and certainly not in this kind of circumstance.

"Jesus...and he was out on bail in seconds."

"Yeah."

"And did I hear the kid disappeared?" He lit another cigarette.

"Yeah, that's what I heard," I said. I inhaled the second-hand smoke.

"Probably knew something was coming down, huh?"

I shrugged. It didn't seem like conjecturing would have any value.

We were quiet for a moment.

"I better go in." He discarded the second cigarette. "You wanna say hello?"

"Sure." I followed Ed into the hospital, to the elevators, and to Bobby's room.

The smell of the place sickened me. It seemed to seep into my pores. The nurses, aides, and orderlies that passed me by in the hallway added to my strange feelings. Their weird, pajama outfits— now in pastels—and their professional detachment made everything get under my skin. I understood it, but didn't like it.

Bobby wasn't hooked up to any breathing thing, but his head was half-shaved, and that heart thing that beeped and showed his pulse was right over his head.

"Hey, Duff," he said. It was weak, but not as bad as I expected.

"Bobby, how are you?" I said. It felt stupid, but I had to say something.

"Tired, a little sore, but I'm okay." He smiled.

"Thank God."

"My dad says you're the one who tackled Russ off me. And after that, you knocked him out with a body shot in front of everyone. That you made him cry."

I shrugged.

"Nice." Bobby held up his fist for a bump. It still had the IV thing taped to the back of it. There was an awkward moment when the three of us didn't say anything. Bobby broke the silence.

"Hey, Dad, can I talk to Duffy for a second? You know, alone?"

Ed's expression changed, and he looked at me and then at his son. He nodded and left the room. He didn't seem angry, but maybe a little surprised.

Chapter Fifty-Five

"Duff, can I trust you?" Bobby said.

"Depends," I said.

Bobby looked surprised at my answer.

"On what?" He said.

"On what you consider trust. It depends on what you tell me. It's not a black and white thing."

Bobby thought about that for a while.

"Alright, I don't care. I gotta get this off my chest," Bobby said.

I waited.

"Russ came up to me one time. It was outside the gym, after school. It was just me and him. He took me aside and started asking me weird shit."

"Weird?"

Bobby took a breath. He looked like he was getting tired.

"He asked me if I wanted to screw a cougar? He asked me if I wanted to be part of an orgy."

I listened. I tried to not show an expression.

"What did you tell him?" I said.

"I told him to fuck off and stop being an asshole."

"What did Russ do?"

"He said it was no bullshit. He said he could hook it up, and that it would rock my world. He really wanted me to say "yes."

"What did he say?"

Bobby looked away. He was struggling.

"He got crazy. I mean really, crazy pissed off. I mean, up until then, we were friends, but this set him off bad," Bobby took a breath and seemed instantly fatigued. "He mocked me for not being interested. Said I must be a virgin. That all I ever did was beat off."

I shook my head. "Russ is quite a guy, isn't he?"

"He's a douche. Every time I saw him after that, he'd call me 'the sixteen-year-old virgin." You know, like the movie. He started doing it in front of people—you know, girls and shit."

"What do you think this cougar and orgy thing was about?" I said.

"I don't know, but that's not all of it."

I waited. Bobby seemed to gather himself.

"Not long after that, kids started talking about Russ being gay, or, at least, that he had sex with a man or something. One kid said that Russ let a guy go down on him, and, because that's the way it happened, it didn't make him gay."

I ran a hand through my hair and thought about what Bobby was saying.

"What did you make of that?" I said.

"I don't know. Enough kids were saying it behind his back. Never to him. Everyone's afraid of Russ." Bobby paused. "I figured it had something to do with the coach."

"The coach?" I said.

"You know, the rumors about the coach. Russ is his captain; he's been his butt boy since we were freshman."

I gave my next question some thought.

"Bobby, why were you and Russ fighting?" I decided to use the term 'fighting' instead of asking Bobby why he was attacked or getting beaten.

"Russ called me 'the sixteen-year-old virgin' in front of some girls. I lost it. Duff, I really had had it. So, I asked him how he liked sucking the coach's dick."

"And he went off?"

"Yeah." Bobby took another breath. "Some of my buddies tried to defend me. His guys jumped in, and it became a huge mess."

"I guess that would set a guy like Russ off," I said

Bobby took a sip from the little, bent-straw, sippy cup.

"He get arrested yet?" Bobby asked.

I thought about what Bobby should know. I didn't want to hold out on him.

"Bobby, Russ is missing. No one has seen him for a few days."

"What?" Bobby was shocked.

"Yeah, Ms. Halle hasn't shown up for school, either."

Bobby looked confused.

"Ms. Halle? What does she have to do with this?"

I shrugged.

"There's some weird shit goin' on at CA. You got any clue what's happening?" Bobby said.

"No, Bobby, I truly don't." It was an honest answer.

We were both quiet for a moment. There was something I had to ask him.

"Bobby, why do you think the coach was involved with this stuff?"

He looked at me.

"C'mon Duff, it's pretty clear the guy was gay," Bobby said.

Chapter Fifty-Six

I called CA and told them something came up, and that I'd be late. There'd been enough talk about weird sex going on, and I had to find out about it. When it came to the seamy side of things in my hometown, there was one place to go to get intelligence.

The Caretaker.

Jefferson Hill, just south of my clinic, was Crawford's ghetto. Crawford was a medium to small city, but don't be fooled by size—everything that happens in Harlem or the south side of Chicago goes on in my town. Maybe in smaller numbers, but, I would guess, when it came to sleaze, we held our own on a per capita basis.

The Caretaker wasn't the mayor of the ghetto, and he didn't legislate things, in that he didn't make the rules or lay out discipline. He was more of Jefferson Hill's vice president of procurement. Drugs, gambling, and prostitution—he knew the how's, and the where's, and, most importantly, what it would all cost. Most often, he was a middleman—a smart position to be in because he seldom had anything illegal on him, and almost never could be nailed down for doing anything that was officially in the books.

A few years back, we did a little quid pro quo. I needed information on who might be dealing steroids, and he wanted them shut down. Don't get me wrong, The Caretaker didn't have a moral stance on performance-enhancing drugs or feel that Cooperstown was being sullied. The Caretaker had no moral stance on anything. He objected to the fact that his beak wasn't getting wet with any of the juice's proceeds. That wasn't acceptable to him.

His "office" was in the backroom of a place on Albany Street that sold DJ tapes, counterfeit Air Jordans, leather jackets, and whatever else came north up the Thruway from New York City. There was a twenty-something black guy wearing an Ecko warm-up suit and the whitest Nike's I'd ever seen. He gave me the slightest of nods.

I'd done this before. I knew the drill.

You had to ask to see The Caretaker.

"Can you tell him Duffy is here?" This wasn't a place for the verbose.

The brother moved from the counter and through the curtain with as much disdain as he could muster. If he expended any less energy, he would've been inert. In ninety seconds, he came back out.

He gave another, subtle head nod, signaling me to go to the back. The guy had nonchalance down to a science.

"Mr. Duffy, how good to see you," he said. He still had the skin condition that left his face whiter than mine. He still had the affected, almost British, accent, and today he was wearing a fedora and a black, pinstripe suit. He wore ankle boots that were buffed to an impossible shine. He sat in a high-backed, black, leather chair with gold accents. It was as real as a movie set with just about as much depth.

"I love the Al Capone getup," I said.

He sighed. He motioned me to sit down in the black club chair. A mahogany coffee table with a heavy silver ashtray separated us.

"The community has come to expect a certain something from me," he said. I had no doubt he understood the irony.

"I could use some information," I said.

"I believe that's how we met a few years ago." He crossed his leg at his knee like a European diplomat.

"This time, it's about sex. Kinky sex, S&M, dominance, orgies, older women, gay stuff...you know, not so much street stuff or even escort shit. Stuff that's a little out there, but, you know, uptown, " I said.

He gave me a wide smile without showing his teeth and brought his fingertips together in front of his face.

"You mean white people are doing it, don't you?" The Caretaker said, and he had a point. The guy was as inauthentic as anyone I ever met. Everything he did was contrived. He clearly had dreamed of being a Bond villain, but he was also very intelligent.

"Do you know..." He didn't let me finish.

"Of course, I know, Mr. Duffy. But alas..." He opened his hands, palms up, towards me.

I waited. I didn't get it.

Then it came to me.

"Oh, yeah. I almost forgot. What's in it for you?"

He gave me a satisfied smile, this time showing his flawlessly white teeth, and sat back.

"Geez, Care, I'm not sure in this one. The last time we did business, it just happened to work out for both of us. This isn't my world. I don't know what to offer."

"Oh, Mr. Duffy, you sell yourself short." He gave me a patronizing smile like a third-grade teacher would give a student struggling with the alphabet.

"Well…"

"You could help with a matter related to this. A simple matter." He stroked his chin like Vincent Price.

"Yeah?'

"If I give you a name of a, shall I say, business contact, who could help you with finding such a service—could you get me some information?"

"Information? I don't understand? You're the one who knows things around here."

He ran his hand around the brim of the fedora.

"You see, Mr. Duffy, there are many layers to what knowledge is. Things are rarely as simple as they appear. The contact information I give is only one layer of the organization structure. I'm curious about the project's funding."

"And you'd like me to find out who's bankrolling the thing?"

"Yes, that's precisely what I'd like."

I thought about that.

"How would I do that?"

He laughed.

"Mr. Duffy, we don't know each other well, but we know each other enough to know that you are definitely resourceful."

I smiled.

"Thank you, Care." We shared a laugh. "I'll do my best."

"You will." The Caretaker took a suddenly serious tone, and his face lost all expression. I knew what was expected, and, without anything being spoken, I knew there would be consequences if I didn't keep my end of the bargain.

He took out a pen and a business card and scribbled something before handing it to me.

"This contact will align you with all that you mentioned. The woman in charge, and I do use that word purposefully, coordinates and participates." He tilted his head and gave me a face to see if I understood. I nodded. "Now, I have to take my leave. I have an appointment," he said

"Thanks, Care. I'm going to take my leave, too," I said.

I looked at the card.

It read: "The Principal's Office. "

Chapter Fifty-Seven

When I got to CA, TJ was seeing a kid. I felt half-disappointed and half-relieved. I wasn't sure how the morning after thing was going to go, and it made me nervous. I was worried that she thought it was a disaster—that it shouldn't have been allowed to happen—and I was also worried that she thought it was the greatest thing ever, and that we should get married later that afternoon.

It pissed me off that I just couldn't be happy sometimes. I think the new-agers call it "living in the now." The AA guys say, "don't project" and "when you have one foot on yesterday and the other on tomorrow, you're pissing all over today." The Buddhist talk about Zen.

I just couldn't shake the idea that if things were going well, it was an illusion, or that God or the force of nature was waiting to bring things back to equilibrium by offering you a shit sandwich. I had a lifetime of events to back me up. Of course, so did everyone else and I cursed myself for doing so much internal whining.

Spadafora appeared in my doorway.

"You got a minute?"

We went to his headmaster's digs, and I took the wooden armchair with the riveted, leather upholstery across from his desk.

"Look, I'm going to tell you something in confidence. Can I trust you?" He looked at me real hard.

"Sure."

"Halle's missing." He stared straight at me.

"Missing?" I didn't want to say I already knew.

"She didn't show up and didn't call, which isn't like her. I drove to her place, and, through the window, it looked like her shit was all gone." He sat back in his chair and pursed his lips.

"Phew, you got your hands full, my friend," I said.

"You have any guesses what might be going on?" He sat up.

I felt that weird twist in my gut that I get right before I lie.

"No, how would I know?" I said.

"She seemed to like you." I might have been imagining it, but I thought he emphasized "like."

I shrugged.

"I'm going to tell you something, and again, I need you to keep it in confidence." He lifted his eyebrows, looking for my agreement.

I nodded.

"The police called me to tell me that they got an anonymous note saying Halle was seen at three in the morning with Russ, going into a known gay bar."

"What?" I said doing my best to be incredulous.

"Yeah." He waited. "Now, they're both gone."

"Holy shit," I said to be saying something.

"And everyone thinks the coach was gay…"

I let that hang.

Spadafora sat back in his chair and let out another long sigh.

"It doesn't mean that the two things have anything to do with each other, you know. The coach could've been gay, and Halle and Russ could've gone into a gay bar on their own," I said.

He rolled his eyes.

"Look Duffy, when you hear hoof beats, you think horses, not zebras."

I wasn't even sure what that meant, but, in the context, it must've meant that he believed they were related.

"There are a lot of gay people. Some are out, and some aren't," I said, trying hard not to sound preachy.

"Man, I liked things better when people hid that shit."

I didn't feel like lecturing, so I just let it go.

"Today is when the coach's *partner* is coming in to talk to me." He said "partner" with a mock, society accent.

"What do you think it's about?" I asked.

"I have no idea. You seem to be pretty comfortable with this sort of thing. You want to be a part of it?"

I thought about it for a second and agreed to.

"Sure," I said.

"Great, this ought to be a barrel of laughs."

His phone buzzed, and he answered it.

"I'll be out in a second," Spadafora said. "He's here."

Chapter Fifty-Eight

"He wouldn't tell me what it was. He was afraid to even tell me, but it was something...something..." Jeff, the coach's partner, said. He wore chinos, shined burgundy loafers, and a denim shirt. His light brown hair was thin but groomed, and he kept himself in shape.

"What was it?" Spadafora only marginally hid his impatience or nervousness.

"Students were in over their heads in something. Stan knew about it, but, for some reason, he felt powerless," Jeff said.

"But you don't have any idea what it was?" Spadafora asked. "How do you know that they were in over their heads?" He was showing less patience.

"I knew Stan very well, Headmaster." Jeff said. He didn't raise his voice, but he firmed it, and you could tell this was a man who didn't intimidate easily.

"Jeff, uh, what else did Stan talk about when he spoke of life at CA?" I decided to chime in. The little counseling training I had taught me to ask open-ended questions to get someone to start elaborating.

"He loved it and he hated it."

I didn't say anything, and Spadafora didn't reply either.

"He loved teaching and coaching. He lived to mentor, and that's what his life was about." He looked away and lightly rubbed his chin with his thumb and forefinger. "He really disliked the vice principal."

"Ms. Halle?" Spadafora said.

"Yes, I think that's her name."

"Well, there's something we had in common," Spadafora said. He waited a second. "I shouldn't speak of the vice principal like that, but I will admit we've had our differences."

I couldn't tell if Spadafora's choice of "something we had in common" was about the coach being gay.

"Do you think whatever the students were involved in had to do with the vice principal?" I asked.

"I have no proof or evidence, but the way Stan spoke of her made me think of that, yes," Jeff said.

Silence followed. Jeff sat still. He looked like he was containing a lot of emotion but chose to control it.

"Jeff, forgive this question if it is rude or uncomfortable. What was Stan doing in the park that night?" I asked. It seemed too direct, and I didn't like asking it.

He took a breath, looked away, then down. It seemed like he was struggling with it.

"Okay, I don't expect either of you to understand this. Obviously, Stan and I are gay." It looked like he painfully resented saying it. "Even though I, uh, we, were comfortable with our lives, it doesn't mean we were comfortable with talking about it or having others know about."

Spadafora and I waited.

"It also doesn't mean we were... I am, ashamed. Who we are is important to us. We are part of a community," He was struggling with using the singular and the plural. "Our community is important to us, even if we don't ride on a fuckin' float during the gay pride parade."

He made a tight face, looked away, and said another "fuck" under his breath.

Spadafora didn't say anything, and I sure as hell didn't know what to say.

"Stan worried about the gay men in the park. AIDS isn't gone, and these guys are playing roulette with their lives. I told him it was a waste of time, but he insisted on doing it a few times a week." It seemed to be getting easier for Jeff to talk. It was like he was into it, and it didn't matter at this point.

"Insisted on what?" Spadafora said.

"He'd go to the bridge and leave brochures about getting tested and being safe. Those assholes would laugh at him or hide, but he didn't care. It was important to him."

"That's why he was in the park?" Spadafora said. There was just a hint of disbelief in his tone.

"Yeah—and because I know you want to ask—no, he wasn't going there for sex, ever. I know because I went with him a few times, and the idea of it repulsed him." His eye welled up, but I believed he willed them not to tear.

It got quiet.

"Did anyone at CA know about Stan doing this?" I asked. I had a suspicion.

Jeff let out a joyless laugh. He shook his head.

"Yeah, that bitch vice principal. She saw us there one of the nights I went along and made sure she gave us a big, sarcastic hello. We were holding hands and walking. Ever since then, Stan said she would make snide comments to him." He let out a long exhale.

"Comments?" I asked.

"She said shit like 'Wouldn't it be interesting if all the parents knew where you spent your time at night?' and 'You have an interesting group of friends.'"

"She was letting him know she could out him," I said.

"What are you talking about?" Spadafora was frustrated.

"That's exactly what she was doing," Jeff said. "She was—very clearly. Letting him know she had something over him. Stan was proud, but realistic and knew CA couldn't handle his sexuality."

The three of us were quiet. Finally, Jeff broke the silence.

"What that woman was doing in Jefferson Park by the bridge at 2 a.m., I'll never know," he said.

I had to ask something, and I wasn't sure how to do it. I broke another silence and just said it the best way I could.

"Jeff, if Stan knew the vice principal could out him, could she blackmail him? Like, if the coach knew something might he keep it in, even if it was heinous, because he didn't want to be outed?"

Jeff looked down. I saw his jawline tremble. He balled up his right hand into a fist and punched his left hand.

"He loved working with kids. He was a goddamn leader, and his life with me, or anyone else, had no impact on that. He had no reason to hide who he was except this bullshit macho fucking hypocritical place." He punctuated what he said by punching his hand and gritting his teeth. "You're god damn right she could blackmail him! That's how much he loved the students." Jeff said.

Chapter Fifty-Nine

"I've got this sick feeling about Halle," Spadafora said. He ran a hand through his hair.

"Yeah, you got any idea what she was involved in?"

"No. All we know is she didn't like the coach or had something on the coach or something. Shit, every school I've ever been in was a mini Peyton Place." He paused.

"This is a little more than that, wouldn't you say?"

"Of course, Duffy, don't be a jerk about it. We also know that maybe she was seen in an inappropriate way with Russ—that she, herself, liked Jefferson Park at night, and that she's now unaccounted for."

"And so is Russ," I added.

Spadafora didn't say anything. He just blew out some air. I sat there in silence for a moment or two, and, when it seemed like there wasn't going to be any conversation, I got up to leave.

"The state championship game is Sunday. This should be our shining moment..." He was just speaking out loud. He wasn't talking to me. I paused for a second and looked at him before I turned and headed out.

I was at the door when Spadafora spoke.

"Hey, Duff?"

I turned and looked at him.

"Thanks." He said it almost with a nod of resignation.

I headed back to my office, and, after this diversion, I felt the familiar TJ uneasiness in my stomach. I took my own deep breath and tried to assure myself that it was going to be fine. I really sucked at convincing myself of shit when I felt insecure, but I couldn't not do it. I made myself go to her office.

She wasn't there.

I turned to the woman behind the office counter—the one who I thought was Halle's secretary.

"TJ leave?" I tried to sound nonchalant, and I was aware of the timber of my own voice.

"Yep, 'bout an hour ago," the secretary said without so much as looking up.

My stomach soured, and I headed to my workstation. I felt a flash of pins and needles all over my body for a quick second before they subsided. That was followed with my usual dread and nervousness.

It really would be easier to not get attracted to someone. I don't know if it was a stretch, but sometimes I thought that all this kinky shit that people got involved with was a way to avoid the feeling I had in my gut. If you focused on the gymnastics and the friction and the physical pleasure that sex brought, you probably didn't have this feeling that often. Or maybe it was just suppressed, and that's why the kinksters never have enough. Eventually, they have to sit with themselves and their longing to have someone that means something. At that point, it's probably time for them to get out of the swing, the latex outfit, or the nipple clamps.

Without getting all romance-novelish, that world seemed miles away from whatever TJ and I had last night. Or at least it did to me. The fact that TJ didn't come to work the following morning, where she'd see me, left me with a lonely and, honestly, scared feeling.

I heard a familiar baritone voice at the counter ask for Spadafora. I leaned forward to see and saw that it was Rusty Redmond. Chico was next to him.

"Hi, Rusty. I'm so sorry—" Spadafora didn't get to finish.

"This is Michael Inchico, one of our firm's investigators. Please give him your time and attention."

"Of course," Spadafora said. Apparently, Chico had a title—at least one other than limb breaker.

"I don't care what else is on your schedule, please clear it," Redmond said. "And what is this about the vice principal and my son?"

That seemed to catch Spadafora off guard.

"I don't know, Rusty. I honestly don't know," Spadafora almost stammered. He certainly didn't anticipate the question.

Rusty nodded to Chico and turned away, barely making eye contact. His coat dramatically waved with his spin out the door.

The guy was efficient, if not terribly emotional. His son was missing, and he got his guy on it, told the principal to be on his best behavior, and then he went to work—a checklist kind of man that got things done.

A cold bastard would be another way of putting it.

Chapter Sixty

I had never called for professional sex services before, and, even though I was doing it to gather information, I still felt a wave of something like guilt, poor hygiene, and anxiety. When I thought about it and was really honest with myself, there was also something else—something I didn't want to acknowledge or admit to even myself. I didn't like that it was there, and I didn't even understand it.

It excited me a little.

"Hello," a woman's voice said when I called. "This is the Principal's Office." There was nothing remarkable about it.

"I'm, uh, interested in, uh, joining," I didn't want to sound like I was new to this or at all uncomfortable. I did my best to use the same tone of voice I used when I ordered from Domino's.

There was a pause.

"Were your referred?" she said. Businesslike.

"Yes, The Caretaker," I said.

"When were you interested in an appointment?"

My mouth was a little dry. It was weird, but I felt, I don't know, maybe a little intimidated.

"As soon as possible," I said.

"You could come tonight at 9 p.m. The donation is $300."

"Okay." Three hundred dollars? I already felt dominated and slapped around.

"And be prepared."

"Prepared?" I asked.

"To be subservient. To do what you're told. That's what you want from the principal, isn't it?"

"Uh, yeah," was the best I could come up with.

She gave me the address and hung up.

I swallowed hard. I had no idea what I was about to get into. I wasn't sure if this was a good idea or not, but something told me that the answer to everything at CA had to do with this operation: the coach's murder, the disappearance of Russ and Halle, and whatever the hell else.

The rest of the school day dragged by, and, at 4 p.m., I got out of there as fast as I could. My appointment was in Albany, which was a bit of a ride, but I still had a few hours to kill. I had a feeling it was going to be a late night, or at least it had the potential to be, so I needed to get Al out of the house for some exercise.

He was happy to see me and did his bounce off my body followed by the spin-and-repeat move. I grabbed the leash, and he jumped up and headbutted me. I did my best to ignore the crack to the skull and concentrated on getting the leash on him.

We headed down 9R and, when Al slowed, sniffed, and circled, I got my bag ready. He wasn't quite there yet and moved to another spot to repeat his three-step process. Al could do this for twenty minutes on a "walk," and I've learned, over the years, that there wasn't really anything to do about it. I used to curse and yell at him, and I tried the Cesar Milan thing—trying to be as confident as possible while I led him out of his OCD shit routine. It didn't matter; every time I tried to be the self-assured pack leader, I'd wind up yelling four-letter words and, ultimately, pleading and whining with Al to please move his bowels.

I thought about subservience. I was the human, and Al was the dog—but who was really in charge?

That led me back to tonight's appointment. I had no idea what I was in for. I guess the unknown, sexual part of it was a little exciting, but, if there was an actual submissive part, that idea didn't thrill me. For that matter, wanting to dominate someone didn't set me on fire either. I was hoping they'd give me a menu like a Chinese restaurant, and I could pick from column A and column B and leave the ickiest stuff out.

I didn't get the turn on of S&M. There had to be something to it because so many people were into it, and, hell, a good portion of the porn industry revolved around it. Maybe tonight, I'd find out a bit more about it.

Gravity helped Al along, and I bagged it. A few hundred feet down 9R was a storm drain, and I continued my personal game of dog shit hockey. I threw the bag from about twenty feet out, skidding it just so it would slide the last five feet and into the eighteen-inch sewer opening. Tonight I was dead on, and I pumped my fist when I heard it splash. One of my little, daily victories.

During my end zone celebration, I remembered Jack Daniels. I owed her a call, and, while I gathered up Al's leash in my left hand, I hit her programmed number with my right index finger. She picked up on the first ring.

"Daniels." She gave me the same semi-annoyed, semi-bored greeting that Kelley always gave me.

"What is it with you law enforcement types?" I said. "It's like you all need a Dale Carnegie course."

"Duffy!" she answered. "And what is it with you counseling types? You didn't get enough hugs from Daddy, so you look to every interaction as a chance to make up for that?"

"Touché," I said.

"How's Bobby?" Her tone changed.

"That's why I'm calling. Good news—he's awake, alert, and they think he's out of a trouble."

"Good to hear it. You want to tell me about what the hell's going on in that hayseed town of yours."

I thought about it, and getting Jack's input might make a lot of sense.

"You got some time?" I said. "This hayseed town's issues aren't simple."

"It's either this or I go to Neiman Marcus and overpay for a handbag."

"Alright then, get comfortable. This ain't a short story," I said.

"I'll grab a beer."

"Bobby told me that he got approached by a teammate, Russ—the captain of the football team—about having sex with a cougar. Bobby thought the guy was making it up, but then he turned serious. They were close friends, and when Bobby refused, the guy got pissed."

"We're talking cougar as in older woman, right? Not the predatory cat. Because that could leave a mark."

"Older woman. My town isn't *that* hayseed."

"I'm not so sure about that. But continue."

"After that, Russ started teasing Bobby about turning down the orgy thing. Kept calling him "the sixteen-year-old virgin" in front of the team and the pretty girls in school. You know, to humiliate him." I was trying to parcel out the story the best I could so it made sense.

"Okay, gotcha so far." I heard her sip some beer.

"Then Bobby got busted for smoking pot just when the team won the sectionals and were going to the state championship. That's when you called me. But after a few visits, Bobby got all pissed and told me he wanted to kill the coach. That night, as I told you, the coach winds up dead, remember?"

"Yup."

"Now, it gets a little weird and sordid—"

"Oh, *now*, it does?" Jack said. "Up until this point, I thought it was an episode of *Andy Griffith*."

"The coach's murder took place in the city park known for anonymous gay activity. There have always been rumors about the coach being gay. Since then, I've met the coach's partner, and they seem like very upstanding men. The partner was emphatic about their commitment and that the reason the coach went into the park regularly was to pass out information about the Gay Men's Health Center, so the guys wouldn't infect each other."

"You believe him," Jack said. I was glad she was following me.

"Yeah, Jack, it's just a feeling, but I definitely did," I said.

"Trust that. Go on."

"Now, what I know, think, and feel gets murky. Several of the students I counseled referenced 'weird' things going on at school. Some mentioned 'weird sex.' One hinted at gay sex. In fact, that was Bobby. He heard a rumor about the coach and Russ, and the day he took the beating, he asked Russ how he liked sucking the coach's dick."

"Geez, Duff, don't feel like you've got to soft-pedal it because I'm a woman," she said.

"Uh, um sorry Jack, I—"

"I'm just fucking with you." She paused just a second. "So, Bobby asked the football captain if he was doing unnatural acts to the coach in front of a bunch of girls—that'll get you a beating in high school."

"Yeah. I asked Bobby why he thought it was the coach that Russ was having sex with, and Bobby said, because he thought the coach was gay, it made sense." I felt like I was going way too fast, but saying it out loud helped me organize my thoughts.

"Well, not such a crazy leap for a sixteen-year-old, I guess," Jack said. She took another sip. Listening to her drink was making me thirsty.

"Then there's the vice principal. I saw her and Russ walking through our club section at two in the morning. She was dressed in vinyl fetish gear, and they headed into a gay bar." I deliberately paused.

"The vice principal and the captain of the football team, at two in the morning, cruising a gay club?" She waited a beat. "Okay, forget the hayseed stuff altogether."

"The coach's partner said that the coach hated the vice principal. That he saw her in the park in the early hours of the morning, and that she made a comment about how interesting it would be if the folks at the school knew," I said. "He said the coach had a sense that she was up to something evil, and he couldn't put up with it." My head was starting to swim a little.

"She was letting him know she could out him," Jack said.

"Exactly," I said.

"So, you got some unconfirmed info about some sort of orgy stuff going on, maybe gay orgy stuff, with high school kids. You got the kid recruiting others, and the vice principal going to a gay bar in the middle of the night, all duded up in kinky gear." She paused. "That sum it up?"

"Pretty much."

"Well, I agree there's some funky stuff going on, and it points to the VP. However, I'm not sure anyone's breaking the law, unless there are minors involved." She exhaled and took another sip of beer.

"Yeah, that's what Kelley tells me, except people keep showing up dead. One of the gay guys I know was murdered just after he spoke to me the night I saw the pair go into the gay bar."

"Whoa... Duff, that's an important part of the story. Unless it's a crazy coincidence, they killed that guy for talking to you. That and the coach is dead after his partner insinuated that he might know something about the VP..." Jack seemed to stop to think. "Why are you in the middle of this again?"

I didn't have a good answer to that, and Jack wasn't the type to bullshit.

"Yeah...that's what I thought. Duffy, back off. Tell the cops what you know and think, and let them do something if there's anything to be done."

"I went to see a street connection I know and asked about where kinky shit went down. I got an appointment tonight," I blurted out.

Silence. I could sense her impatience with me.

I waited.

Finally, Jack came back.

"Are you out of your fucking mind?" She was angry.

"There's something else, Jack," I don't know why I felt like I had to say what I was about to say. "I had sex with the vice principal."

"What!" I heard spit out her beer. "That's a Goose Island Bourbon County Stout I just choked on. Ten bucks a bottle." I heard her take a breath. "Okay...Duff, I don't know what kind of Oedipal, Freudian shit's going on here, but you are in—bad choice of words— are involved way, way too much to even see clearly. That and the minor fact that you have no law enforcement status at all."

"I need to find out. I need to settle a few things..." I said.

"Yeah, Duff, you do. But you should probably be doing it in a shrink's office. Was it her fetish outfit? Got a vinyl kink? I know a guy named McGlade who can set you up with one of those suits with a zipper for the mouth."

I paused and tried to think, but there was no point. I knew I was going to do what I was going to do.

"Thanks for listening, Jack. I gotta go feed Al."

She laughed without humor. "Lotta good talking to me did." She had waited before she said her next words. "Duffy, be careful."

"Thanks for caring, Jack."

"That's what friends are for. And if you get plugged, you won't be able to pay me that fifty you owe me on the Jets game."

"I thought we bet twenty."

"It was fifty. And I'll bet another fifty you're next on the killer's list."

Chapter Sixty-One

I get told to mind my own business a lot. I don't pay attention to it all the time, especially when someone I know is being victimized. I didn't know the coach, but it seems like he was a good man. I knew Bobby, I knew his father, and I felt somewhat of a responsibility to Jack because I said I'd look after them.

I definitely knew Froggy. His life was taken, and he never hurt anyone. Someone in this killed that innocent man—a man I cared for. That was an account that needed to be balanced.

My cell phone buzzed. It was a text from TJ.

"Duff?"

I wrote back a simple *"Hi?"*

"Sorry I wasn't around today"

I wrote back:

"No worries."

I hated that expression and didn't know why I used it. It might not have been as bad as "rain check," but it was close.

Al was in his post-meal, zen state. He sighed, spun around, grunted, and lay down.

My phone buzzed again.

"Last night can't happen again, Duff. I'm sorry."

It was like a straight right hand to the gut when you didn't have your abs tight.

I froze.

I just stared at the message.

I felt sweat start around my chest, and I felt warm and cold all over. My mouth went dry. I wasn't sure how to respond, especially with a text.

"Why?" was the best I came up with.

I waited.

Nothing.

I looked at the time on my phone. I waited a minute. I waited another minute.

Nothing.

At minute six, I took a deep breath and put my phone away. I decided to leave and go do what I had to do. I couldn't stay here. I had to get moving. Outside, it was a little tough to breathe. My mind wouldn't focus on one thing, and the knot in my stomach grew tighter. I felt slightly off-balance as I walked to my car. I heard Al give his half bay/ half groan and he scratched the door from the inside. He was concerned. He knew when she got to me.

I didn't send another text. I couldn't. I was frozen, and I had a sinking feeling that I knew this was coming. It always was; why shouldn't it happen again? She disappeared on me last year without any explanation, and that was before anything like last night. I was a fucking idiot for getting involved, and this is what I deserved.

Al bayed again and scratched the door some more. He kicked it up a notch, and experience told me he wouldn't stop for a while. I hated to leave him upset, but, if I went back and told him things were all right, he'd pick up that I was lying, and it would get worse.

He knew. He's been through this before with me.

I drove to Albany trying not to think. Elvis was there to keep me company, just like he had with every broken heart I've experienced since I was fourteen-years-old. When the eight-track clicked on *Indescribably Blue*, I had to swallow hard. After a short time, I didn't fight it, and I felt the warmth of tears cover my cheeks.

TJ meant something to me. More than something, too. More than sex. More than companionship. I don't know what that's called, but she was different.

Except now she wasn't. She was exactly the same as every other woman in my life.

I was still ninety minutes early for my appointment, and I decided to go to my new gym. The gym, like Elvis, was always there for me when I felt like this. I wasn't even going to work out. I was going just to be in a place that felt like home. Yeah, it was a new gym, but it was the closest thing I had. There was always something to talk about or plan, and it consistently gave me purpose.

I decided to let Jake know I'd take whatever fight he had for me in Yonkers. Fuck it—I could throw myself into training and push everything else out. It's what I had always done.

There was only one fighter there, and I didn't recognize him. He was with Jakey's assistant trainer, Eduardo. He looked like a welterweight, and he and Eduardo were on the other side of the ring working the rope ladder foot drills. The fighter bounded from side to side of the ladder while Eduardo yelled at him to go faster.

Jake came out of the bathroom still fixing his belt and seemed a little startled when he looked up and saw me.

"Geez, you surprised me," he said, shaking his head.

"I wanted to stop in and let you know I'm in for Yonkers. Doesn't matter who; I want to do it," I said it with a smile on my face.

"Uh, yeah, Duff..."

None of the previous enthusiasm was there. Jakey didn't look at me, and he started to fidget with his hands a bit.

"What's the matter?" I asked.

"Duff, I talked to Smitty. I had to bring some USA Boxing shit to him." He still wasn't looking at me.

I knew what was coming. I just didn't want to hear it.

"I'm sorry, Duff. I..."

I stood there for a moment. It wasn't for effect. It was because my legs wouldn't move.

"It just isn't safe, Duff. I'm sorry."

I heard his voice trail off as I turned and went through the door.

Chapter Sixty-Two

It was time for my appointment. I felt crazy in about ten different ways, so going to see a dominatrix at this moment just added to the out-of-touch feeling. With everything that had built up inside of me, I was ready to look Halle square in the eye and confront her. It was bizarre, but it needed it to be done, and I needed to be the one to do it.

My interaction with Jake was another punch in the gut I wasn't ready for. I thought I had found my answer, my outlet, even if it was just a band-aid for what I was feeling. God, I felt like a fool in so many ways. It was a feeling I was accustomed to, but the things in life that kept that feeling a little distanced were slipping through my fingers.

For the rest of the night, I had to put it out of my mind.

It headed back to Crawford and the dominatrix's office—is office what you call it where a dominatrix or madam does her thing?—and it was just off of Lark Street. It was a non-descript, four-story, walk-up brownstone that looked like all the other gentrified homes on the street except it had a small parking lot just to side of it. The single car in the lot was a late-model Mercedes. Apparently, judging from the choice of auto, slapping men with issues around wasn't that crazy as a vocational choice after all.

The door was on the side of the building, and a professionally-lettered sign in the bottom, right pane read, "Ring the bell and come in." The door opened to a ten by ten foot waiting room with an old, leather sofa, matching club chair, and a coffee table on top of a red and black Asian rug. A small, but ornate, dimly-lit chandelier was the room's only lighting. There was a door in the middle of the facing wall, and, when I heard the knob turn, I felt a bolt of anxiety.

"Please come in," the voice in the shadows said. Pretty polite for being so supposedly dominant.

I entered a dark library like the kind you see in old movies depicting rich and refined people. There were two, high-back, wing chairs with a subtle pattern. In the chair facing me was a woman sitting with her legs crossed.

It wasn't Halle.

She had black pumps, seamed stockings, a very tight, but not short, red dress, and a white blouse with two buttons opened. She

185

was busty, had jet-black hair worn with bangs and black horned-rimmed glasses. The heels were at least four inches, and she definitely had an hourglass shape, but she looked more like a fifties version of a pin-up than what I conceptualized as a dominatrix.

"Welcome," she said without smiling.

"How you doin'" I said. It sounded—I don't know—a little too familiar, but I hadn't read the etiquette manual on conversational kinky sex and S&M.

She gave me a perfunctory smile—the kind a busy receptionist might flash you.

"How can I help you?" she said. Her hands were folded neatly on her lap.

"Uh, I heard there's some kinky stuff here. The Caretaker said you could hook me up with whatever I wanted," I said, doing my best to sound sincere.

"Ah, Dush," she said and smiled.

"Excuse me?" I said.

"Oh, I'm sorry. I know 'The Caretaker' as Dush. Dush Pathmanandam
is his given name."

"You're kidding me?" I knew we were off-topic, but I couldn't resist.

"Strangely enough, he was raised in England. He's quite the financial expert, you know?" She paused. "We've digressed, and I have other clients to see at the bottom of the hour."

"I'm sorry."

"What did you come here for?" she said. It wasn't angry or impatient. It was more like when the guy at Home Depot spots you wandering around and asks if he can help you find something.

"What is available?" I said.

She chuckled, but without humor.

"Pretty much anything on the spectrum you could be interested in. You could be dominated; you could be teased; we could role-play any of a number of fantasies; there is latex, PVC...it would really be easier if you could let me know."

I swallowed hard.

"I'm interested in group action," I said. It felt weird, and my voice seemed detached.

"What kind of group? We have couples, swing groups, and several other alternatives." Her expression never changed, and she could've been describing Home Depot products.

"Uh, I'd like to experience, you know, uh…" I wasn't being coy; I really didn't know how to speak this language.

"You want to experience other men, don't you?" she said and smiled. "That's very popular and so difficult for many men to request."

"Uh, yeah." I said. "I want there to be women, too. But, I want the men to be, you know, fit, athletic, and, uh, not old?"

She nodded.

"Of course," she said.

"That is available, and, because you are a friend of Dush's, we can expedite that."

"I want to get started," I said. I felt like a creep.

She opened up the small, ornate jewelry box on the table next to her and took out a business card. She wrote something on the back and handed it to me.

"36 Dove St.," was all it said. "Teacher's Pets," was hand-printed on the reverse.

"Teacher's Pets?" I asked.

"It's the safe word to get you in," she said.

"When is this?" I asked.

She uncrossed her legs, placed them together, and leaned forward. She smiled, lifted her eyebrows, and looked at her watch.

"They've already started, but it's right around the corner. If you hustle, you can join in."

Chapter Sixty-Three

Dove is five blocks from "The Principal's Office" and I decided to walk. I'm not sure how you're supposed to feel about going to an orgy, but I'll tell you; I didn't feel good. Nor did I feel excited, stimulated, or desirous. In fact, it was about the least sexual I've ever felt. It feels weird to say it, but I felt revulsion.

The block was filled with two-hundred-year-old brownstones, BMWs, and yuppies. When I was a kid, it was close to a ghetto, but it had a resurgence in the 80's, and now the rents and property values were out of sight. The fact that there was a kinky sex prostitution business in the middle of all of it seemed bizarre.

Or maybe it didn't.

Maybe yuppies were at least as perverse as everyone else.

Maybe more so.

The address was a brownstone that looked like all the others on the street. It had one of those historical markers that said, "1803" on it and some understated flower boxes in the first-floor windows. There was a sign identical to the one at The Principal's Office inviting me to enter on my own. I swallowed hard and braced myself for what I might see.

Again, there was a sitting room appointed with antiques and a closed door leading out. A fortyish woman, a little overweight, with glasses sat behind an oak desk. She was reading a Nicholas Sparks book and put it down when she saw me. She frowned almost imperceptibly and said, "Can I help you?"

I handed over the card.

She gave me a pleasureless smile and made a check mark on the notepad in front of her.

"Three-hundred dollars, please," she said without smiling.

I handed her my wad of cash and thought to myself that this was an expensive hobby.

"Right through that door, and we ask that you please use protection. Condoms are available in bowls throughout the lounge." She said it in that perfunctory tone that an airline attendant uses when they go over what to do in the event of a crash.

I swallowed and went through the door, bracing myself. I entered an oval-shaped room with a self-service bar near the entrance where two men and two women were chatting and having cocktails. They were fully-dressed, but they were paired off and had their arms around their dates' waists. The women were older, maybe mid-forties, and the guys were twenty-somethings. They talked loud, drank fast, and seemed to force a lot of laughter.

"Drink?" the woman facing me said, smiling and tilting her head. Her date, if that indeed was the right word, didn't make eye contact with me. She was slender, but not particularly attractive, with dyed, blond hair and way too much cologne. I think I recognized it as "Obsession." It stunk, and I had a little bit of an allergic reaction in my throat.

The other couple turned around, and again the guy didn't look at me. The woman had long, brown hair and was curvier than her friend—maybe carrying forty pounds too much. She had a silky blouse with a loud pattern that showed a fair amount of cleavage. She wore a gold chain with a series of diamonds forming a star pattern in the center, right above the opening.

"It's your first time, isn't it?" the blond said. "Let me get him a drink." she said without asking and talked about me like I had left the room.

"What would you like?" she said, just a little too perky.

"Bourbon," I said.

"You're big. You work out," the brunette said and smiled at me. It was forced and overly coy.

"You probably don't know how this works, do you?" She lifted her eyebrows and nodded at me. "Through the French doors is where the party is. Out here is for drinks and chatting. Clothes are suggested out here and not allowed in there. We're all regulars and aren't in as much of a hurry. Though, we'll definitely join in."

The blond handed me the bourbon, and, as she did, she ran her other hand across my back.

"They've already started," the blond said. "We're waiting for the boys to be through."

"Huh?" I said.

"There's no rush. Some of the girls get all worked up when it's a varsity night. More will be coming when the first half is over." The two women giggled.

"Varsity night?" I asked.

They looked at each other and smiled. The blond answered.

"The high school football team, or at least some of them, get treated to a room full of cougars." She stopped abruptly. "Oh, they're all seniors and of age—so it's cool."

"Yeah—nothing to worry about. And the boys have gotten so

much calmer and accomplished," the brunette said, and the two of them giggled. They clinked their glasses of white wine.

"The first night was over fast, if you know what I mean!" the blond said, and the two laughed even harder. Their dates were now talking to each other, having removed themselves, for whatever reason, from the conversation.

"Those first nights, they just looked on in awe." The blond shook her head.

"Yeah, and now, hell, they're into everything," the brunette said. "They'd even be into you." The two women high fived.

"Huh?" I said.

"I think Penny has the boys strung out on cougars. I think she has them doing whatever she wants just so they can get some of us experienced women," the blond giggled.

"You know those boys are as hetero as it gets. Penny just wants to please the other clientele," the brunette said. The two shared knowing glances and clinked glasses.

I might as well have been on Mars.

"All that is mostly first-half action. We'll wait to play in the second half when we can be the starting team," the brunette said.

They laughed and clinked glasses again. It seemed to me that they were just trying too hard at making this such a great experience.

"Can I have another bourbon?" I said.

The blond ran her hand across my shoulders.

"Let me get it for you." She gave me a long look while she reached for the bottle of Beam on the bar. "After this, wanna play? I don't think I want to wait for the second half, since you showed up," she said and smiled at me.

"Sure," I said and reached for the drink.

"I'd love to see the shoulders." She tried a cutesy, girlish laugh that sounded silly.

I turned and looked at the French doors. The windows were frosted, but you could hear stray voices and some other sounds coming from behind them.

I felt a hand on my shoulder; it slid down to the small of my back, and then went lower and grabbed my ass.

"Go in with me," a breathy whisper tickled my ear. The Obsession was awful.

She took my hand, looked up at me, and smiled. She stopped, grabbed my face, and gave me a kiss, pushing her tongue into my mouth.

"I can't wait to go to work on you," she said.

What the hell had I gotten myself into, I thought.

She reached for the knob of the French door, again looking up at me as provocatively as she could—even rolling her tongue over her lips.

"I'm going to rock your world," she said and did her best seductress look.

She turned the knob. I took a deep breath.

That was when the gunfire rang out. A series of shots, in short succession, followed by screams, commotion, and the bang of a door slamming.

Chapter Sixty-Four

The blond screamed and hugged on to me. She kept screaming and dug her nails into my flesh. Her two male friends, clearly shook up, looked at each other and, without saying anything, bolted for the door. The brunette scurried out behind them.

"Get the hell off me!" I yelled and peeled her arms off my upper body. She continued to be hysterical—both crying and screaming. She looked up at me from a self-protective crouch and pathetically cried.

I went to the French doors and threw them open.

I've never seen anything like the scene in front of me.

The room was candlelit, and it was tough to make out specifics. There were eight naked bodies in front of me. All were covered in blood.

They were motionless. It looked like two women and six men. I moved closer and almost wished I hadn't. Their eyes freaked me out. They were open, staring off into space, oblivious to the scene. The first body I approached was a woman's. She had a single wound in her forehead, her gaze was frozen at the ceiling and her mouth was slack. I noticed she had a sleeve tattoo of flowers that covered her right arm.

It was the stripper from The Taco.

I looked at the two male bodies next to her. It took a few seconds to register, and then it did in a horrible way. I recognized the older of the two men as Chuck, the college recruiter. The younger man with him was the appointment I had who mock-pretended to be gay. Next to them, I thought I recognized a couple of the other recruiters and maybe some members of the team, but I couldn't be sure. All of them had head wounds.

The bodies were on top of three king-size mattresses, and they all had blood-stained, satin sheets. They were in positions suggesting what they were doing the instant before they came to their end. I felt myself vomit a bit into my mouth, but I forced it back down.

I did my best to shake off the trauma and concentrate. I moved closer to the bodies to the left side of the room. The two corpses at this end were pressed together and covered in oil. Half of the one woman's head was gone, and there was a bloody hole in the center of the man's back that was still oozing blood. I forced myself to look at the frozen masks of the faces, and it wasn't easy to do. The blood and oil made a disturbing mixture on the bodies, and I fought off the nausea.

There was no need to check any pulses.

I moved so I was positioned directly over them. Witnessing the nakedness of the women in this state felt like I was violating something, and I steadied my stomach the best I could. I scanned her body from head to toe. She was thin but conditioned, and her slightly bent thighs told me she worked out. My eyes traveled between her legs, and I noticed that she was closely trimmed.

I caught my breath.

I looked at what was left of her face, and through the blood in the tangle of her hair the best I could.

I directed my gaze to the man and looked at the frozen eyes, the jaw line, and the expressionless mouth. He was young, and I recognized him from the football team, too.

I stopped breathing for a second, and I noticed that my hand was over my chest. I tried to process what I saw as best I could. It was impossible. I couldn't do it.

I looked back at the first body—the one that looked familiar. It registered.

It was too much.

Just too much to take in all at once.

I left the room, stopped at the bar, and drank the bourbon right from the bottle while I got my cell phone out. I hit Kelley's number, and he picked up right away.

"I found Halle," I said. "She's dead."

Chapter Sixty-Five

It took about seven minutes for the first five cop cars to arrive with uniformed police officers. It was about twelve minutes before four detectives came, and about sixteen minutes before the photographers and the crime scene guys showed up. In twenty-two minutes, there was a coroner present, and in twenty-four minutes, the TV trucks and newspaper reporters were trying to get past the yellow tape that was out front.

"What were you doing here?" a detective asked me. Kelley was close by, and he was listening. The detective was thirty-something and a big guy who lifted weights. He introduced himself, but he had an Italian name that I had already forgotten.

I did my best to explain why I was at an orgy.

"Why would you do that?" he asked me.

"I didn't think anyone would believe it so I thought I would gather some information to present to the police," I said.

He tapped his pen into his notebook just like they do on TV. Kelley stepped closer.

"Tony, he's a friend of mine. He's telling the truth about his motives," Kelley said.

The detective looked at Kelley and then at me and then back to Kelley. He shook his head.

He glanced over at the scene. Yellow tape closed off the threshold into the room. There were four professionals in the room with gloves, masks, and booties. They were looking without touching, and they were talking to each other.

"What made you think something like this was going on?" the detective asked me.

"I've been working at the school, and I heard a few things, saw some others, and just had a gut reaction to all of it," I said. I didn't mention my conversation with Kelley from earlier in the evening.

"A gut reaction?"

I shrugged.

"You're a counselor." He didn't really ask it as a question.

I nodded.

"Students were telling you about this shit?"

"I can't say what students told me, but they alluded to weird stuff going on. I got the sense that it was sexual stuff. I also saw the vice principal with Russ, one of football player, late at night one time, going into a gay bar."

He tilted his head and looked at me.

"The woman was the vice principal? The dead one? Jesus Christ."

I told him about the night I saw them on Lark Street.

"I heard something about that. You were the anonymous guy?" he said.

"Yeah."

"Why anonymous?"

I thought about it for a second and decided to not keep any secrets.

"I had sex with her once myself. I was afraid of how it would look," I said it as steady as I could.

His eyebrows went up.

I felt dirty.

"Do you know the others?" the detective asked.

"Besides Halle, I recognized one kid for sure. He's a football player. The guy with him was one of the recruiters who has been visiting CA. The other woman is a stripper from The Taco. I can't say for sure, but I think the others are football players and recruiters."

"How could you tell?"

"I was in a room with the college guy a couple of times. Plus, he had that paw print tattoo," I said. "I've seen the woman dance."

"Detective, several of the bodies have a paw tattoo," one of the uniform cops said.

He did the tap on the notebook thing again. His eyebrows went up, and he took another deep breath and shook his head. "Gonna fuck up the state championship," he said, mostly to himself.

Chapter Sixty-Six

Two more detectives interviewed me. None of them were pleasant, and none of them offered me any respect. I guess when you do that all day for a living, it gets inside you, and if I had to be around crime scenes like this, I think I might not be pleasant either. Still, I didn't do anything wrong, but they sure made it seem like I did.

They told me not to leave town. They each wrote down my cell, home, and office number and asked me where I planned to be. I told them the truth as honestly as I could. The reality was, I wasn't sure about anything, least of which was my state of mind. Anything after that, I just couldn't guarantee at all. They said I was free to go, and I can't remember ever wanting to leave a room more than this one.

I took a deep breath when I got outside. It was dark, and I tried to breathe in as much as I could, like it would somehow cleanse me.

It didn't.

I walked, and my legs began to feel weird, like they weren't exactly part of me. My head was swimming, and things didn't feel connected. The visuals of what I saw came in and out of my consciousness, and I tried to push them out. It made them come back in with anger, and my stomach soured. I stopped and took a deep breath, trying to focus on nothing but the air and my lungs. I did my best to count to ten and let my muscles relax as much as they could.

I vomited, bracing myself against the side of a tree next to the curb. Not much came up, but I wretched again; it was so hard the contractions tightened my abs in pain. My mind got cloudier, and it went back to some other shit I was a part of a few years ago. I saw pools of blood drained from corpses; I saw decapitated heads; and I saw a Mexican boy with a bullet hole in his forehead.

Then I was throwing punches—endless punches—at a bald, tattooed biker trapped in a corner. Each shot sprayed me with his blood, and I kept hitting his lifeless body. I saw a metallic throwing star in an eyeball, and another in a throat, in front of me. Shony, the young, black girl whose mom was murdered in prison, was in front of me. A man was raping her. I was reaching to stop it but she was just out of reach, and something kept me from advancing.

I wretched again. I slid down the tree to my knees. Things were grey in my mind, and there were no more images. It was murky and filled with hate, like the images became their evil essence. I knew this stuff from my past didn't ever leave me, but it never came to the surface like this. Not this completely, and I had no defense for it.

God, how I wanted to hit something.

I pushed myself to my feet. I tried to swallow away the taste in my mouth, but it went nowhere. My balance was uneasy, but I made myself walk. I fought to not think, to not feel any of what just happened or what it brought back. I let my mind go grey and attempted to put a distance between me and my thoughts. I made an effort not to force the thoughts out, but to let them pass through without giving them meaning. It was a balancing act, and not an easy one. I did my best to ignore my own thoughts and just focused on the motor activity of walking up the hill.

One foot in front of the other.

Over and over.

Not thinking. Not feeling.

One foot in front of the other.

I don't know how long I walked like that. I guessed it was an hour, but it could've been a lot longer. I doubt it was shorter. Somehow, I got back to the Cadillac. I started it and made the drive to AJ's.

I just didn't know where else to go.

Chapter Sixty-Seven

Things cleared around my third bourbon.

AJ and the Foursome knew when to leave me alone. They've seen me like this before. It didn't happen often, but they've been witness to it.

I was exhausted, but the worst of whatever it was had cleared. I didn't have a name for it, but I knew it was what exhausted me.

"You're back," AJ said.

I looked up at him. His eyebrows were up, and his forehead was wrinkled. He didn't need to say anything else.

"Another?"

I nodded.

I looked to my right. Only Jerry Number Two was left.

"Hey, Duff," he said gently.

I nodded and tried to give him a half-smile.

It was quiet.

"We saw the news…" Jerry said. "That sounded like some crazy shit."

I took a sip of bourbon. The feel of the bar was eerie.

"What time is it?" I asked.

"A little after one," AJ answered.

I sat and tried to think, but it didn't come easy. AJ and Jerry knew what happened. That meant that everyone knew.

"What did the news say?" I asked.

Jerry looked at AJ. AJ gave Jerry a slight nod.

"That, uh, a massacre occurred at a sex club with members of the CA football team, the vice principal, and some college recruiters. They all were dead. They insinuated the boys were involved in prostitution." Jerry's voice was weak. "Kelley was in one of the camera shots, and you were behind him."

I looked at Jerry.

"They didn't mention anything about either of you," AJ said.

I nodded. It felt like a strange point, but one that, as I thought about it, made more sense. I had been embarrassed in the papers before, and the guys knew about it.

"Did they say anything about who did it?" I said.

"They have no idea," Jerry said.

"They're locking down the school indefinitely, canceling the

Super Bowl. All other local schools are on high alert, whatever that is," AJ said.

"I remember when we had bomb scares and thought that was a big deal," Jerry said.

"What kind of sick fuck does something like this?" AJ said. "Of course, how do a bunch of high school jocks get involved in gay prostitution?" He was talking rhetorically.

I let myself drift away from the conversation. It was tough to focus on anything. I was tired—exhausted, really, of playing Sherlock Holmes, but it was pretty clear I was right, and Halle was running some sort of prostitution thing using the football players, and it had gotten to the point that she was pimping them out to the recruiters.

My God.

But who killed her and the whole room full of sex players?

And where was Russ?

Did Russ leave in disgust after he found out about this? Did he fly into a jealous rage? Or was it something or someone else? I didn't have the clarity, nor the energy, to process it all.

Thank God the bourbon didn't talk back to me. At least, tonight it didn't. There were other nights, many other nights, when I had long conversations with my rocks glass. Mr. Beam didn't talk back, or, he, didn't very often, but his listening skills were unparalleled. No, tonight, after the first one, it just was brown liquid with an acrid taste that went down hard. It held no answers and didn't give me any company.

Seeing a room full of dead people short-circuited my entire being. It didn't just throw me off emotionally and psychologically, but it did something to me physically that I don't think could be entirely explained away by what they call psychosomatic. I think there's something evolution has built into us that reacts when we see death. The fact that it was in the midst of sexual acts did something to augment all of this—something about the essence of life and death or feeling life and experiencing death.

Ah, fuck me.

I was never going to be the same.

I'm not even sure what the "same" was. I don't know when I stopped being it, but I knew now there was no chance of going back to what most people feel on a day-to-day basis. Tough to get worked up over paperwork, getting fired, or staying out of the way of Claudia. How could I care?

I did care about something.

I cared about TJ.

She might want to walk away. She may not want to deal with me or avoid how she felt. She may not be ready with where she was in life or whatever. Too bad—she was going to have to be.

I left money on the bar and got up.

"Hey, Duff, where you goin'?" AJ said, breaking his all-time conversation record. "Of all nights, man, stick around. On the house."

"On the house? There's another sign of the apocalypse, right there," I said.

I headed out.

"Duff? You all right?" Jerry Number Two said. "Take it easy, will ya."

I turned and did my best to smile. Jerry and AJ were looking at me, and I felt their eyes follow me out the door.

Elvis sang "Long Black Limousine," "That's Someone You Never Forget," and "It's Midnight," on the way to Albany. I cued up "Stranger in My Own Hometown," and "Hurt" after those. They came close, but they weren't exactly right.

The Taco's lot was full. When I pulled in, a group of a half a dozen twenty-somethings, loud and drunk, were heading toward the entrance. It was almost three in the morning, and I guessed this is where you went when you struck out all night—go hang out with women who are paid to be sexual and look interested in your pathetic sexuality.

Squal was at the door. I gave the guys in front of me a little space to get in ahead of me so I wouldn't have to interact with them.

"What's up, Duff? You all right?" he said. I already knew I looked like the walking dead, and it didn't concern me or make me feel like I had to apologize for it.

I just offered my fist for a bump, and Squal went back to being a badass.

"She's just about to go on," he said when I headed in. I looked back at him and nodded. A dancer named Whitey was finishing up, and, by the looks of things, Whitey had lost her enthusiasm for her profession. I didn't blame her.

The announcer called Tommie Gunn to the stage and blasted the song "Kiss Me Deadly." Lita Ford sang, "I went to a party last Saturday night. I didn't get laid; I got in a fight," and TJ swung around the pole.

She had spotlights in her eyes, and I stood in the dark. I didn't trust my senses, or how they related to my emotions, but TJ seemed distant. Her outfit tonight was distressed camo with a sports bra top and matching camo boyshorts. She didn't wear heels and instead did her spins, jumps, and splits in combat boots tied halfway up with pink laces.

Lita Ford's voice sang, "I know I like dancing with you," as TJ skipped across the stage in a *Flashdance* reminiscent strut. Her abs flexed when she turned and pointed at the crowd. I looked at her eyes and they weren't focused. They went into the crowd without connecting.

"Kiss Me Deadly," transitioned into "Girls, Girls, Girls" and she finished her set with "Enter Sandman." My throat was dry, and my plan to talk to her all at once seemed misguided. I didn't know what to say, and, in this context, I didn't know how to say it. I stood there in my spot, frozen among the drunk and dysfunctional readying their one-dollar bills.

She feigned enthusiasm and shimmied her body with half-hearted smiles and cheek kisses. I was two guys away when she saw me. She dropped her hands, her smile left her face, and she looked right at me. My chest felt tight, my mouth went dry, and, as much as I didn't want to, I felt something in my eyes.

I tilted my head, motioning her to go outside, and I turned and walked to the door. I didn't look to see if she followed.

I couldn't.

So I just kept walking.

Chapter Sixty-Eight

"Duffy, wait," I heard TJ say. I was terrified that she wouldn't follow me and terrified that she might. I turned and looked at her.

She was in her stage outfit. The Lycra camo boyshorts, the sports bra, and especially the dash of glitter just seemed absurd when it came to real-life human interaction. The conversation I wanted to have was hard enough, but relating to someone, even TJ, while they were dressed like a stripper made the awkwardness even more pronounced.

I looked at her, and I didn't say anything—not because I waited for an explanation or an apology and not because I wanted to make it hard on her in any way. I was frozen, and I had no idea what to say.

"I'm sorry. You deserved better," she said. She looked panicked and uncomfortable. I got that sick feeling that I've gotten a million times in my life when a woman I cared about was about to give me the "It's not you; it's me." speech. I exhaled hard because this wasn't what I came here for.

TJ wiped the sweat from her forehead with the back of her wrist. She stood up straight and faced me, but somehow it looked like she wanted to crawl out of her skin and avoid all of this.

"What happened? I mean, what happened? Did I read everything wrong that night? Was I an idiot?" I said, and it all began to come out at once. I could feel something shift inside me, and I knew I was on the brink of losing it.

TJ looked at her feet. The pink laces loosely holding the combat boots looked ridiculous in the context. She didn't say anything and sniffed. I realized she was crying; I wanted to hold her, but something told me not to. I could feel my heartbeat, and it pounded in my head and throughout my entire body.

"I'm engaged." She looked up briefly and then away. "I mean, I was engaged."

I tried to process what I heard. I didn't say anything. I couldn't. I stared at her and felt cold sweat run down my back. My mouth went dry.

"He left. Military, covert military bullshit. I mean, I'm not engaged...I don't even know..." TJ was the one talking fast now. There was a desperation to what she was saying. "I don't expect you to understand, fuck, I don't even understand. I don't even know if he's alive."

I just looked at her.

She looked down. She began to talk again. It was quieter and without the desperation. She sounded defeated, like she went to a place she tried so hard to avoid.

"It was all okay for a long time. I did this shit. I did the hotline. I worked out. I kept my distance from feeling. I tried not to care. I did my best not to think. I have no idea about where I was in life, but I was able to keep it at bay. At least..." Her tears came, and I could see her face wince. She was in pain, and it was the type of pain that comes from acknowledging a hurt that you've put away for a long time.

My stomach turned over. My hands were damp.

"At least, what TJ?" I said. I stepped close to her and lightly held her upper arms. She was cold, and she shivered.

I heard her swallow.

"At least until I met you," she said and then pulled away. I could hear her crying, now, without any control.

I went after her, but a voice from behind me took us out of our private world.

"TJ, the rules are that if you leave the club, you're only to go out the back. The girls aren't supposed to be out front," the deep voice said.

I turned to see who it was. It was Chico, Rusty's thug. He gave me a quick, surprised look but then recovered and looked away at TJ.

"Go on, now. Back inside," he said to TJ. "You know Kaneesha never showed and you have to take her spot in the rotation." He then headed around the side of the building by the parking lot. TJ went in the entrance. I stood frozen where I had been. I didn't have any idea what to do or feel.

TJ poked her head back out.

"Duffy, I can't talk now. This whole thing with us, it just can't—"

I cut her off.

"Do you know who that was?" My concentration had shifted.

"His name is Chico. He manages the place."

"What's the owner's name?" I said.

"Don't know his name. He's never here."

"What about Chico?" I asked.

"Mostly he keeps a low profile backstage, except to be a pig to the girls. I think he pimps some of the girls on the side."

She had no idea of the connection.

"TJ, Chico is the bodyguard that travels with Russ's father. You didn't know that?"

"I was always in my office when he came in to CA."

"Is Rusty here tonight?"

"I don't know who Rusty is, but the owner never comes here."

My mind was racing.

"You don't know what happened tonight, do you?"

"Huh?"

I explained the murders.

Her jaw went slack.

Not everything fit neatly, but now I knew Chico managed a strip joint. It struck me as a weird sideline for a guy who worked for a prestigious law firm. Sure, he had a sordid past, but it would be a hard thing to keep from his boss, Redmond. What the hell was going on?

Before I could finish my thoughts, a black BMW came out of the parking lot and took a left. Chico was driving.

Chapter Sixty-Nine

I ran to my car and did my best to catch up with him. Fortunately, the Central Avenue traffic lights kept him from putting much distance between us. He was headed toward Crawford and I stayed back four or five car lengths to minimize the chance of being spotted.

He continued up Central, and, even though the late night traffic helped conceal me, I still dropped back another block. It was a straightaway, so from a distance, I could keep an eye on him. I watched him make a right onto Lark.

I made the turn on Lark, and, just as I did, I saw the BMW make the turn on Chestnut. Now, it started to make sense. I knew, or at least I thought I knew, where they were going. I decided to park and catch up to them on foot.

Parking isn't easy on Lark, and having a fifteen foot, 70's ride doesn't make it any easier. I pulled it into the Planned Parenthood lot and parked underneath a sign that expressly warned me not to. It was six blocks from where I was heading, and, if I trotted, I'd be there in a couple of minutes.

Lark was busy with hipsters, even at this hour, and trotting in street clothes brought some looks, but I didn't care. I took a right, passed the dirty bookstore that I saw Halle come out of with Russ, and went left on Chestnut. I took the quick turn down the driveway and stopped running. I walked in far enough to see.

I was at The Principal's Office, and, just as I guessed, the BMW was parked by the front door. A light shined through the shade on the second-floor window and things started to fit together very clearly. I moved to the edge of the driveway, out of the light, and waited. I wasn't at all sure what I was waiting for, or what I was going to do, but I knew if I stayed put, eventually something would happen. Someone would come out, or someone would show up, or something important would go on. It would have to because too much hung in the balance.

It turned out that I didn't have to wait too long.

Another car pulled into the driveway. The red BMW's engine shut off and the driver waited a moment or two before getting out. When the driver emerged I immediately had a sense of familiarity, but it took a long moment for it to sink in. When she rang the bell and anxiously tapped her dress boot, it came to me.

Anne Marie Redmond.

I heard the buzzer and the click, and she entered. I moved closer, into the small parking area, and did my best to listen. I heard doors open and close and muffled voices in a normal conversational tone. The conversation went on for a few more moments and then it stopped.

It went silent.

The door opened, and Chico came out first. Rusty was next, and Anne Marie was behind him. None of them spoke. Chico opened the black BMW's back seat for Anne Marie and joined Redmond in the front. Chico backed out the car at a normal speed, like nothing special was going on.

I didn't know what to do, so I did the first thing that came to mind.

I stood in the driveway and blocked their exit.

Chapter Seventy

"Excuse me, buddy, would you mind—" Chico stopped and looked at me before he got angry. "It's you. What the fuck do you want?"

I just looked at him.

"C'mon. Chico, let's go!" Redmond yelled from the front seat without looking. Anne Marie turned, and, when she saw me, she made a face that showed half confusion and half annoyance. Redmond yelled again, "Chico!"

When nothing happened, he got out of the car to see for himself.

"What the fuck is—" He looked at me and blew out a bunch of air.

I stood and stared at him.

"I guess the Super Bowl is off," I said.

"Boss, what do you want me to do?" Chico said, moving his glare away from me.

I didn't let the conversation go on. Things started to make sense to me, and, all at once. Anne Marie emerged from the back seat.

"This was your thing, wasn't it?" I said to Rusty.

"What are you talking about?" Rusty said.

"C'mon Rusty, the strip joint. Pimping the dancers out. The recruiters? My God, the recruiters," I said. Rusty just looked at me. I could tell it was registering.

"Shut him up, Chico," he said, averting my eye contact.

"Halle seduced the kids, right? Turned them on like you knew she could and hooked up her cougar friends." I looked him right in the eye.

"Chico, shut him up!" Redmond said.

"You didn't count on Halle and Russ falling in love or at least getting together and joining forces, did you? That's what happened, right? You had to kill Halle before she talked. She had you blackmailed."

"Shut the fuck up!" Redmond was starting to lose his composure.

"You bankrolled it. You fuckin' found the sickest fuckin' recruiters who would trade football scholarships for boy-sex. You make my fuckin' skin crawl."

Chico's gun did that clickety-clack sound. I looked, and he

had it out and down by his side.

"What about the coach? He knew, didn't he? That's why you killed him. Halle was going to out him, and that kept him quiet until he found out just how depraved it was, and, when you couldn't keep him quiet any more, and he didn't care about being outed—you killed him."

"What you want me to do, boss?" Chico repeated. He wasn't sure what to do next.

"And where's Russ? Did you kill your own boy?" I said.

"Chico..." Redmond said through gritted teeth.

"I can't, we're on the street, boss..."

"But why Froggy? Because he was talking to me, right? You thought he was worth taking out, and no one would miss him," I said.

"That's enough!" Anne Marie yelled. Everyone went silent, and the men looked directly at her. I heard another set of clickety-clacks. The angelic face was gone and replaced with a mean, angry glare. She had a large handgun pointed at me, and she looked very comfortable with it in her hand.

"Take him, Chico," she ordered. "Get him, and put him in the back seat."

Chico stepped toward me, the gun at his side, and I braced myself. When he got close enough, I thought about how I would blast him with a left hand. If I timed it right, it would catch him before he could fire and I then I could take him. As he came closer, he raised the gun and pointed it at my face. In that moment, my plan fell apart. My left wasn't as fast as his trigger finger.

"Tape him. I will keep the gun on him," Anne Marie said.

"Eyes straight ahead," I heard her say. "Move and you're dead. It's that simple. Hands behind you."

I did what she said, and I felt the duct tape go around my wrists. My arms not only couldn't move; they were locked behind me in a position that made me ache. When Chico was done, he put duct tape across my mouth, grabbed me by the back of the head, and moved me toward the back seat.

"Wait!" Anne Marie ordered.

She stepped toward me with the gun in her hand. She walked confidently, with a smirk on her face. She looked at me with disdain and hatred. She slowly lifted the gun and then jabbed it hard into my temple. It made me wince, and I could feel the blood ooze from it breaking the skin.

"It wasn't them." She glanced back toward her husband and

Chico. "You're too fucking smart for your own good, but you didn't get this right." She gave me a half-smile. "Sure, Chico does what I tell him and took care of the coach and your faggot friend." She paused and looked at the men. "But I did Halle myself. I don't take well to betrayal." She smiled out of the corner of her mouth before giving another order.

"Get him in the car," she barked at Chico. "Let's get to the park and get this over with."

Chapter Seventy-One

As Chico drove, Anne Marie and Redmond remained silent. They drove deep into the park and pulled over in a dark area about thirty yards from the Peace Bridge. They cut the lights in a non-parking, grassy area off the road that ran the perimeter of the park. The heritage street lamps throughout the park sprayed light in five foot circles around their poles, but the rest of the area was as dark as the countryside in the middle of the night.

Chico opened the back door and pulled me out. It sent an ache up through my upper back and twisted my rotator cuff in an awkward way that sent pain up my neck and into the back of my head. I looked at Redmond, who was now holding a gun.

"I'll say this once. If you try to run, I will shoot you in the back of the head," Rusty said without any hint of emotion or drama. A sick feeling went through me.

Sick and hopeless.

My hands were taped behind me, and a gun was pointed at the back of my head. An MMA fighter walked by my side, and a sociopath with a pistol walked ten feet behind me. His darling wife looked on from fifteen feet away. If I ran, I'd be shot. I could try to kick but, without great kicking skills and no ability to balance with my arms, that strategy gave me no realistic chance. They walked me a few hundred yards in the dark, and I saw the Peace Bridge appear in the dim lights up ahead. The bridge covered the man-made pond that narrowed to about fifteen feet in that area. The ornate cast iron and wooden structure divided the pond in half and was the central focus of the entire park.

"Stop here," Redmond said from behind me. He walked around so that he stood with Chico in front of us.

"How do you want to do this?" Chico said. Except for the sound of distant traffic and the occasional bullfrog or bird, we were in silence.

"Like the others," Anne Marie answered. "Make it consistent. But let's not fuck around; the police are bound to be staking this location out." Chico's face remained expressionless.

"Give it to him," Anne Marie said to Rusty. He moved in front of us, reached behind his back, and pulled out something. It was dark, and, in the night, I couldn't make out what it was. At least, at first I didn't. When he handed it to Chico and pulled off the cover, I knew.

It was a machete of about eighteen inches in length.

"Keep the serial killer thing going," Anne Marie said, like she was ordering a monogrammed sweater.

I felt sick to my stomach, and I could feel the back of my shirt soaked in sweat. I tried to think, and I tried to focus, and I came up with nothing. My senses sharpened, and I saw the dim park lighting, and I heard traffic in the distance. I saw the two men in front of me, the pond, and the steep hill on the other side. I had no idea what to do.

"This will be less painful for all of us if you don't struggle," Chico said.

I surveyed my senses again. The darkness, the pond, the hill, the distant traffic. The traffic sounds grew; the engines got louder. I distinctly heard a high-pitched engine sound. It was moving toward us.

Redmond steadied the gun on both of us while Chico moved behind me.

"Move up to the top of the bank," Chico said. Both sides of the pond were lined with five foot banks.

My chest heaved, and I swallowed hard. I heard the engine grow louder.

"Let's get out of here. Do it now," Anne Marie said and looked directly at Chico.

The conversation stopped. Time stood still, and I felt like my chest was going to explode. My senses seemed to sharpen.

The engine noises got closer—much closer and louder. They were near. And through the sounds, I heard the high-pitched engine rev. It came closer.

"Move!" Chico commanded, motioning toward the bank.

I hesitated. I listened for the sound. I began to realize what it was.

It was a motorcycle engine, and it was coming fast. I looked just over Chico's head and saw the Suzuki speeding down the steep hill that ran along the pond and down to the bank. It had to be going ninety; it was barely in control and now the engine sound got everyone's attention. It didn't slow as it approached the bank, in fact, it accelerated and it accelerated hard. The engine revved, and the god damn thing went airborne—the driver pulling the front wheel high as it easily cleared the fifteen foot stretch of the pond. It was all in an instant, but it froze time and it froze all of us who watched on.

The bike crashed into Anne Marie, and she hit the ground—her head making a sickening thud. The bike bucked, then skidded violently through the center of the three of us, and the force scattered and knocked all of us down.

Chapter Seventy-Two

TJ rolled off the bike in a crashing summersault. She stayed down for just seconds, then got up, staggered, and ran to me. She pulled out her utility knife and cut through the duct tape on my hands.

Anne Marie's head was in three pieces, and she had taken her last breath.

Redmond was up and lunged for his gun. TJ was closer to it; she pivoted away from me and charged him at a full sprint. When she jumped and threw a side kick, she blasted it into his ribs and took him off his feet.

I had no time to admire her work because Chico came at me. The machete had flown out of his hands and was too far away, on the bank of the pond, in the bridge's shadow. Now, it was man against man, and he was trying to get the jump. He came at me low and hard, like an MMA fighter would, and I was ready.

I shifted my weight back and timed his lunge. As he came forward, so did my body weight, and I rotated my hips into everything I had. I drove a left uppercut, and it split his hands and landed hard on his chin, right where it was supposed to. It drove him back, and it staggered him. I turned the fist around, shifted my weight again, and shuffled in—this time with an overhand left that caught the cheekbone under his left eye. His knees buckled hard, partly from the force but more because I could tell he was still wobbly from the uppercut.

I came around with a right, trying to finish him off with a hook to the other side of his head, but he got a left forearm up and blocked it. He caught my arm, turned it, locked it, and drove a right hand toward my face. I slipped most of it, but some of it landed hard on my ear and that sent a piercing pain to the center of my head. He took that opportunity to headbutt my forehead, and I saw stars and flashing light and felt myself get nauseous.

The force of the shot freed us, and I backed up. He rushed me, but I was able to get my feet underneath me in time. He came in a little sloppy, and I hit him with a three-punch combination: a right jab to his eye, a left to his nose, and a right to his throat. The left broke his nose, and the shot to the throat made him choke a bit. He reflexively grabbed at his neck, and I threw a hook into his liver and another into his left side before returning another left into his liver. I saw him wince, and he dropped to a knee.

He was on one knee when I came hard with an overhand left that landed just behind his right ear. He went face first into the dirt and went silent.

I was in the zone. This is what I did. This is how I lived. It felt right.

The feeling didn't last for long. I looked up at TJ and Redmond. TJ could fight, but it didn't matter what belt you were when you were up against someone 100 pounds heavier, who was a foot taller, and who played college tight end.

She was on her feet, and they circled each other. TJ threw a series of kicks that kept Redmond at bay, but didn't connect. I ran toward them and let out a scream. TJ threw a roundhouse; Redmond stepped in and took it, pivoting and catching most of it on his back. He winced, but TJ went down. She scurried back up and was ready for more. Redmond went in the other direction, dove to the ground, rolled up to his feet, and came up with his gun pointed right at TJ.

He was heaving from all the exertion, but I could see his eyes were clear. Neither TJ nor I were close enough to rush him without one of us taking a bullet. We were frozen.

"Hands in the air!" Redmond said. He wiped a trickle of blood that came out of his nose, looking down at it briefly. His chest heaved, and, when he looked up, his expression was filled with rageful hate. His eyes went quickly back and forth from TJ and me, and then he spoke.

"Get ready to die."

Chapter Seventy-Three

"Move!" he shouted at me, motioning me closer to TJ. His was facing away from the bridge and the street light backlit him.

"If we both rush him, he'll only get one, maybe two shots off," TJ said.

"I—"

Redmond fired the gun. Dirt skidded past me.

"Keep talking," Redmond said. "See what happens."

He held the gun on both of us.

"Move." He motioned us to the bank. "Nothing's changed here. You put up a good fight. You knocked out a good man, Duffy, I'll give you that. And you, you're a tough little cunt."

He looked at his wife's body.

"And you saved me the trouble of doing that myself."

He sort of half smiled. He was regaining his arrogance. We had moved up to the bank of the pond.

"The shots will be inconsistent with the knife wounds, but that's okay. There's no way it points to us." He smiled.

"You're fucking scum," I said.

"Yeah, well." He laughed a little bit.

I looked at TJ. Her lips were tight, and I could tell she was thinking. Still, we had a gun on us from ten feet. The man was out of range, he knew how to use the gun, and he had nothing to lose.

"Maybe I'll get a little of this tight, little bitch. Wanted to since Chico told me about her routine at the club. Why waste it?" He half smiled and raised his eyebrows. "It'd be fun for you to watch, wouldn't it, Duffy? It'd be the last thing you'd ever see."

I felt like I was going to be sick, and I stepped toward Redmond.

He turned the gun toward me, and I heard the sound of him readying it.

"No Duffy!" TJ said.

I froze.

"Listen to your little whore." He smiled again. "C'mere, bitch. I got something for you." He held the gun steady in his right hand while he began to undo his belt buckle with the other. He took a step backwards, toward the bank and out of the street lamp's glow. "I've wanted this since seeing you on stage."

TJ moved reluctantly toward him. She gave me a short, but

desperate, glance. She stood directly in front of Redmond. I could hear my own breathing.

"Get on your knees," he said, pointing the gun inches from her forehead.

In the darkness, a figure darted from underneath the bridge and, in one sweeping lunge, I saw the street lamp catch the shine of steel for an instant. It was dark, and it was fast.

Redmond let out no more than half a grunt as the machete sliced through his neck, all the way to his spine. His body went down—his mouth still moving, but with no sound coming out. Blood silently poured out of him, and I knew that the sight of his mouth silently moving would stay with me forever. The rest of him was gone—his body limp, lifeless, and forever in a position to do no more harm.

TJ shrieked and instinctively backed up toward me. The figure walked out into the street lamp's light.

Standing over the body, with the machete at his side, was Ms. Rhonda. He wasn't dressed as a female; instead, he wore cargo pants, a plain, black t-shirt, and Adidas cross trainers. His biceps bulged against the short sleeves, and his dark expression gave him a look of serious danger.

He stood and looked down at Redmond, seemingly oblivious to our presence. There was little light, but, against his black cheek, I could see the shine of tears. He didn't bother to wipe them.

Chico moaned and began to stir. It broke Rhonda's concentration. He looked up, and I saw him adjust the grip on the machete.

"Rhonda," I called to him softly and tentatively.

He turned in my direction and looked first at me and then at TJ.

"Ronnie," he said in a deep but quiet voice. He continued to grip the machete.

"The police will come soon." I spoke deliberately, and I tried to keep emotion out of it. "He will go away forever."

Ronnie looked at me. He looked at Chico, who stirred some more.

"Justice..." he said in a whisper.

I didn't know what that meant. I didn't know Rhonda, and I certainly didn't know Ronnie. I didn't know what to say.

Ronnie moved slowly toward Chico. He stood over him, straddling his body for a moment. He reached down, grabbed Chico's hair, and pulled his head and most of his upper body up. Chico came to and tried to shake his head to clear the cobwebs. Ronnie's strength kept it motionless.

In one quick motion, he sliced the machete across Chico's neck.

Chapter Seventy-Four

"Thank you, Mr. Duffy, for doing what you did," Ronnie said. "Froggy respected you, and he knew you respected him. I will always be grateful." He paused. "I thought I was done living under bridges but..."

He didn't finish. His speech was flat, his eyes empty. Blood spilled out of Chico and spread in a growing circle around him. Ronnie bent over, gathered part of Chico's shirt, and wiped the handle of the machete.

"I need to go. Tell the police it was me. I've lived my life underground. I've slept under that bridge for years, until I met Froggy. It was the life I chose. I can go back to being invisible. It won't be hard for me to go and to go unfound." He turned and began to trot over the Peace Bridge and out of the park.

I looked at TJ. The start of the line of the sunrise could be seen in the distance. We didn't say anything. Everything seemed to wash over us but also pass by us in a cloud of the surreal. Our eyes stayed together.

A long, long moment later I said, "In a few minutes, I'll call 911. Ronnie could use the time."

TJ just nodded.

I had my phone in my hand when the red BMW pulled up next to its black twin, just out of the streetlight's glow. Instinctively, I looked down at the bodies. Anne Marie, Rusty, and Chico were accounted for. When I saw Russ walk into the light, I noticed right away that he was carrying a handgun, and immediately I remembered neither TJ nor I retrieved any of the weapons that were just held on us.

"Don't move!" Russ said. He walked directly toward me, the gun still at his side. TJ and I exchanged glances, but it was clear that we were once again caught. Russ took in the harsh reality splayed out in front of him. His mother, father, and mentor were dead and in a pool of blood. He turned and looked at me without saying anything.

Finally, he spoke through restrained tears.

"I fucked up again. Because of me, they're all gone. It's my fault," Russ said. Silent tears ran down his face. I looked at TJ, and she looked back at me. The gun stayed at Russ's side. He hadn't even threatened me yet. This wasn't the arrogant linebacker. This was the never-good-enough pawn his parents raised.

"Oh my God, I fucked up again..." Russ began to cry, his tears choking him.

I decided to speak.

"Russ, you're not the fuck-up. THEY were the fuck-ups. For Christ sake, they pimped you out."

He held his head in his left hand and cried hard.

"I loved her. My mother shot her. She cared about me. My mother killed her. Oh God!"

He was talking about Halle.

"She made me feel like I could do something besides play ball. She believed I wasn't a fuck-up."

"Russ, listen to me..."

He was crying so hard now that he held both hands to his face. He wiped his eyes with the back of his right hand while it still held the gun.

"Fuck it!" Russ said and lifted the gun to his temple.

I dove at him, throwing an overhand karate chop at his right arm and trying to slam my body against his at the same time. The gun went off, and our bodies went down together awkwardly. The thud of the hard ground hurt my ribs. TJ scooped up the gun, and I held on to Russ.

His blood ran across my face, mixing with my own, but I held him as tight as I could. I could feel his diaphragm quiver, and I could feel him crying in my arms. I looked at his head; it was bleeding from a gash over his ear, but I could tell it was just a glancing blow. It bled a lot, and it was all over my face and in my eyes.

"You're not your family. It's not your fault. You're not your family," I kept saying over and over to him. He didn't break from me, and he continued to cry hard while I felt his body shake involuntarily.

I continued to hold Russ in my arms while TJ called 911. The sun was three-quarters up, and as I held him, I noticed that all of the pools of blood had melded together. It seemed like seconds later that we heard the sirens in the distance. TJ and I remained silent and just looked at the bodies in front of us.

I watched the sun clear the horizon. The red lights flashed across me, and the sound of the sirens made hearing anything else difficult as the five cars pulled up. Instinctively, we both put our hands in the air and turned to the police. In the process, I let go of Russ.

Kelley was the first one to approach us. The sun was fully up, and it made him squint.

"He's unarmed and will need some hospital-type help," I said. One of the uniforms with Kelley cuffed Russ and put him in a patrol car without incident.

Kelley looked at both of us and down at the bodies.

"You both okay?" he said. There was a real concern in his voice, no sarcasm, and no judgment. That was Kelley. It might come later, but, right now, he was a friend first. He glanced at the bodies.

"Dead, right?" he said.

We both nodded.

"Jesus..." Kelley said. "What a fuckin' mess."

TJ and I didn't say anything. Kelley looked the bodies and back at us.

"You?"

I shook my head.

"Ms. Rhonda," I said. "He's gone." I nodded in the general direction of Rhonda's exit.

"We'll never find him," Kelley said, mostly to himself.

Ambulances, detectives, and coroners came. TJ and I stood around and answered questions, but after awhile they had us stand off to the side with Kelley watching us. After a few minutes, Kelley took a call and stepped a few feet away. All the activity was winding down. TJ and I hadn't spoken in a while.

I broke the silence.

"It's ten, right?" I said.

"Ten?" TJ said.

"Dead. These three were responsible for ten deaths," I counted in my head first and then out loud. "The coach, Froggy, Halle, and the seven others at the orgy."

"Jesus..." TJ said.

We got quiet again. I swallowed. My Adam's apple felt big, my breathing felt like I couldn't get enough air in, and I could hear my heart beat.

"Where does this go?" I asked.

I looked right at TJ for the first time in a few moments. She looked me in the eye.

"What do you mean?" she said. Her voice was hushed.

"You know," I said.

I watched her. Her eyes moved between the two bodies, down at her feet, and then straight up across the pond. She let out some air.

"I don't know where it goes." She turned toward me. "But it doesn't go away."

"Yeah," I said. We both knew she was right.

"This one's going to be with us for a while," she said.

We stood silent for another long moment.

"TJ?" I waited.

"Yeah?" she said, looking at the police cars.

"I almost forgot. Thanks for the whole Evel Knievel rescue thing."

She chuckled just a little.

"How did you know where I was?" I asked.

"I followed you out of the parking lot. I wanted to finish our conversation and got more than I bargained for."

"I'll say," I said.

"I lost you when you parked the Caddie, and you went on foot. I went up and down the side streets and was three blocks behind when I saw them put you in the back seat," she said.

"Well, uh, this is a bit of an understatement but, uh, thanks," I said. I turned and looked at her. She looked right back at me.

Chapter Seventy-Five

Six weeks later...

Two weeks ago, I went back to work. After the shit hit the paper, and the police were done with their endless questions, interrogations, and call backs, Claudia had me evaluated by the county shrink. She recommended a month off and gave me the disability papers. I didn't fight it.

They haven't found Rhonda yet, and, according to Kelley's off-the-record conversations, they had no leads. They didn't even know Rhonda's, Ronald's, or Ronnie's real name. The activity in the park has gone away, so there isn't even the community of men to ask. I'm sure eventually it will reemerge, or it has already moved on to a llesser-known location.

Russ spent some time at a private psychiatric hospital and has since withdrawn from Crawford Academy and moved away. I squared up with The Caretaker with the info he wanted as payback.

Al and I bonded for a month. We took a lot of naps, went for regular walks, and hung out at AJ's enough during the light hours that some might say that the Foursome had grown into a sixsome. I started to get worried when the conversations started to make sense to me and when I felt the need to argue my point with the crew.

Working seemed to bring a degree of normalcy back to my life.

A degree.

I welcomed the structure, but I felt like folks kept a close eye on me and were just a little apprehensive about my mental state. Trina, who was still involved with her boyfriend, brought me chocolate chip cookies on my first day back and gave me a tentative hug that I wished lasted a little longer than it did.

It was Saturday morning, and I was waiting for a phone call. Al was half on the couch, and half on the coffee table, I was on my third cup of coffee, and we watched *Pawn Stars*. It was the one where Rick buys a book that he thinks has Isaac Newton's handwriting in it. The creepy handwriting expert comes in and tells him it isn't Newton's writing and that the book isn't the treasure he thought it was. Rick is bummed, but goes right back to business looking for his next deal.

"Not everything turns out to be a treasure, but that doesn't make it worthless. You never know, the next thing just might be," Rick said.

The phone rang just as the old man was about to insult Chumlee.

"May I speak to Duffy, please?" the man's voice said. It wasn't the call I was waiting for.

"I'm Duffy."

"Uh, this is Jim, uh, the coach's partner." I could hear the awkward hesitation in his voice. "I hope you don't mind me calling you, especially at home and on a Saturday."

"Of course not. What can I do for you?"

He paused for a moment.

"I wanted to say thank you for all you did." His voice wavered a bit. "When everyone assumed something, you didn't. The benefit of the doubt means so much."

I waited for him to finish.

"Thank you for saying that. I really don't think it should be any other way," I said.

He didn't say anything. I heard him sniff.

"So, that woman, the vice principal—she was getting the students involved?" he asked.

"Yeah, that's what it appears. With the lawyer financing it and getting the recruiters involved."

"My God..." he said. He hesitated and then spoke.

"Do you think Stan knew?" I could sense his desperation.

"I can't say for sure, but I think once he knew the extent of what was going on, he let her know it had to stop. She probably then threatened to out him, and I think Stan made up his mind to go public with the sex ring, even if it meant him getting outed." That was my best guess.

"And that cost him his life..." Jim said.

I didn't say anything to that.

"Well, again, thank you for what you did. I'll never forget it," he said.

After that, we hung up I checked my phone again to see if the call I was waiting for had come in while I was talking to Jim. It hadn't.

I had someplace else to go that I had been putting off. The gym was often slow late on Saturday mornings, and I risked the chance of getting Smitty when he could talk. I said hello to Fat Eddie, on my way, who returned the greeting without any commentary on where I'd been. That was unusual and made me wonder if it was out that I was all through.

There wasn't any of the usual rhythms as I headed down the stairwell, and when I came through the door, there was just Raheen, who was shadowboxing in front of the mirror. He gave me a nod. Smitty was in the office.

"Can I sit down?" I said. Smitty nodded at the chair.

"I heard about that mess," Smitty said. "You awright?"

I nodded.

My stomach felt funny, and the general feeling of nervousness I've had for the last month went up a notch. I just came out and said what I had to say.

"If I get all the tests, will you let me train?"

Smitty leaned back in his chair and looked at me. He didn't speak for a long time.

"Son, why do you want to keep doing this? There's no title on the line. There's no prize at the end of this. You've gotten out of this what you're going to get."

I exhaled hard.

"Smitty, I want to keep getting out of it what I've been getting out if it." I knew he understood.

He looked at me for a long time. He sniffed and then sighed. He closed his eyes just for a moment and folded his arms. He looked me in the eye.

"I want to talk to the doctor when you get the results," he said.

I nodded and agreed. I left his office and headed up the stairs. Pig was coming down the stairs at the same time.

"My God, it's good to see you," Pig said. "Welcome back." We shook hands and I kept going.

I felt tears run down my face and I felt a whole lot lighter.

Chapter Seventy-Six

My cell rang at the top of the stairs.

"Can you get there by four?" It was Shelly. "There's going to be forms for her to complete and other bullshit to fill out." It was already 2:45.

"So, it's going to happen? It's definitely going to happen?" I had trouble containing my excitement.

"We don't react well to 'no's' in our organization," Shelley said. She wasn't playing, and I've known her long enough to know she was telling the truth.

"I'll be there," I said.

Sometimes I get ideas that seem great right up until their execution is about to start. This was one of those times.

TJ and I had spoken on the phone twice a week since the shit happened. We went out for coffee once a week. These were limits that we imposed on, well, "us." Whatever "us" was. I found out a bit more about her engagement, the man she was involved with, and a little bit about the complicated covert stuff he was involved with.

The second time we had coffee, TJ started to refer to him as her "ex" fiancé. I didn't ask for clarification, but, since then, every time she's mentioned him she did so without using his name and by using the "ex" term. She had done this six times in our sixteen conversations—not that I was counting.

She was also done as a dancer.

"I'm in a real jam," I said when I called her. "I need a ride to the airport. Now. There's a fight thing."

"A fight thing?" She sounded caught off guard. "I was going to—"

"I wouldn't be asking if I didn't need it," I said, cutting her off.

I told her to drive her bike to my place, and we'd take the Cadillac. That was going to be a necessity that I didn't explain. Al and I waited on the stoop for her to show up, and she was there in twenty minutes.

"Al is coming?" TJ looked confused.

I threw her the keys.

"He insists on seeing me off whenever I go any place. You can keep him for a few days, can't you?" I said.

"Uh..."

"C'mon, my flight leaves in a half hour." I hefted Al into the back seat.

We listened to an Elvis movie compilation on the way there while I dodged questions about my "boxing thing." "There's a Brand New Day," the closing number from *Roustabout*, played, while we parked. *Roustabout*'s the movie where Elvis comes back at the end to save the circus.

"C'mon, we gotta hustle," I said and ran slightly ahead of her with Al. I saw Shelley's van parked illegally near the entrance and smiled at her style.

We entered the baggage area at 4:02 p.m.

"Duff, this is baggage. What airline are you on?" TJ said.

I ignored her and scanned the carousel area. I saw the long, blond hair and the familiar face and called to Shelley. Duke, her deaf basset, was there wearing a bogus service dog getup that Shelley used to get him into airports and other places.

They ran over to us. Duke and Al got reacquainted while I introduced the two women. The dogs did the sniff thing, followed by the hop-around-each-other-in-a-circle thing.

"Excuse me, Shelley, I don't mean to be rude but, Duff, you're going to miss your flight," TJ said

Shelley giggled.

I laughed a little.

Duke let out one of his long, scary moos that he did instead of barking. Travelers stared at us.

"You didn't tell her, huh?" Shelley said. She shook her head.

TJ looked at me.

"Excuse me guys. You two fight and watch the dogs. I'll be right back," Shelley said.

"What the hell's going on, Duff? I had shit to do, and you had me drop everything and dragged me out here for some sort of joke. You know, I don't think it's—"

"Barrrrrooooooo!" A loud, deep, throaty, baritone bay shook TJ and interrupted her. It didn't come from Al or Duke, but they began to bark up a storm in response.

"Rooooooooo!" it came louder. It literally vibrated the floor. There was a scratchy sound on the tile, airport floor.

TJ's face lost all expression, and she spun around in the direction of the commotion.

Shelley was walking with a uniformed soldier. In between the two of them walked a very large bloodhound.

"Oh my God..." TJ had both her hands on her chest. "Oh my

God…"

The soldier let go of the leash as Agnes pulled away.

"Barrroooooooo!"

TJ dropped to her knees as the 140 lb. hound jumped on her and knocked her on her back on the airport floor. Agnes's tail went crazy, and she licked TJ face relentlessly.

Al and Duke went nuts. Shelley applauded, and the rest of the airport got an idea what was happening and they joined in and formed a huge circle around the two soldiers and their reunion. TJ and Agnes were oblivious.

"Lieutenant Dunn," the young soldier who accompanied Agnes said. TJ got to her feet while Agnes continued to jump up and down and bump into her. "Mr. Dombrowski contacted ABC Basset rescue, and Shelley Gordon here, and made a formal request. Mrs. Gordon contacted several senators and, if I may say off the record, sir, this woman never took no for an answer."

TJ had a confused look on her face. The soldier addressed TJ.

"Lieutenant, I am happy to report to you that canine officer, Agnes, has been given a full and honorable discharge. She is being released to you, Ma'am."

TJ didn't hide the tears. The airport erupted in applause, and Shelley and TJ spontaneously hugged each other while the hound cacophony echoed through the building. They broke their hug and TJ continued to cry. She looked at me and punched me hard in the shoulder.

"You son of a bitch," she said, breaking into a huge smile. "You did this."

I couldn't control my own tears.

"I got friends in high places," I nodded at Shelley.

TJ threw her arms around me and hugged me tighter than I ever have been hugged before. I didn't want it to end, and I could tell TJ didn't either. Agnes jumped on TJ and pushed her even closer to me.

"God, I love you," she said into my ear. It went completely through me and lit my entire being.

"I love you, too," I said and held her as close to me as I possibly could.

I couldn't believe it. I just couldn't believe it, and I felt my heart race.

I held on to TJ. There was no sign of it ending.

The hounds were deafening, my chest felt warm, and it felt like I was floating.

I took the deepest breath I could and let it out, and, when I did, I counted as slowly as I could to ten.

THE END

ABOUT THE AUTHOR

Tom Schreck is the author of five novels, including *Getting Dunn* and *The Vegas Knockout*. He has worked as the director of an inner-city drug clinic and today juggles several jobs: communications director for a program for people with disabilities, adjunct psychology professor, freelance writer, and world championship boxing official. He lives in Albany, New York, with his wife, three hounds and three cats.

Visit him at www.tomschreck.com

Made in the USA
Middletown, DE
25 November 2014